SONAYA NIGHTS
BOOK TWO

"Tomas Marcantonio has written an entertaining noir that sits comfortably between 'In the Miso Soup' by Roy Murakami and 'The Plotters' by Un-SunKim. Dark black shadows splashed with blade runner neon nuances provide the perfect backdrop to a world alien to even the most adventurous tourist. Easy to read with clever turns of phrase, This Ragged, Wastrel Thing could be the start of a bold series."
— **Sebastian Collier** —

"This witty, futuristic, dystopian noir has some fucking pair of legs! It hits the ground running and doesn't let up until the very last page. It's all drugs and guns and soju and sake; grungy bars and rooftop parties, metalhead biker chicks and corrupt politicians; revenge and deception and dark city underbelly. Sonaya is an absolutely brilliant and fascinating character all on its own, and our protagonist Dag is one of the most strangely likeable leads I've read in ages. Go and get yer mitts on this one!"
— **The Next Best Book Blog** —

STORGY

BOOKS

STORGY® BOOKS Ltd.
London, United Kingdom, 2022

First Published in Great Britain in 2022
by STORGY® Books

Copyright TOMAS MARCANTONIO© 2022

The characters and events portrayed in this book are fictitious.
Any similarity to real persons, living or dead, is coincidental and
not intended by the author.

Published by STORGY® BOOKS Ltd
London, United Kingdom, 2022

10 9 8 7 6 5 4 3 2 1

Edited & Typeset by Tomek Dzido

Paperback ISBN: 978-1-7397350-4-3
EBook ISBN: 978-1-7397350-5-0

Cover Design by Tomek Dzido

Also available from STORGY Books:

Exit Earth
Shallow Creek
Hopeful Monsters
You Are Not Alone
This Ragged, Wastrel Thing
Annihilation Radiation
Parade
Pain Sluts
Talking To Ghosts At Parties

FLAMINGO MIST

TOMAS MARCANTONIO

"Nothing stays damaged for long.
Everything fixable.
Except people."

Embers of War, Gareth L. Powell

Typhoons strike Sonaya like a fist to the face. They're calling this one Little Sister, hot on the heels of her brutal brother who only crossed from Kyushu two weeks back. He gave the harbour a free makeover and buried the strip under sand, and Little Sister seems to share his destructive desires. She's spent the past few hours stirring the East Sea into a rusty sundae and now she's spitting mucus all over the coastline.

The radio tells us to stay inside and ride it out, but I haven't had much company recently and another typhoon sounds like the kind of friend I need. Typhoons don't harp on about the past or ask you to be something you're not; they simply destroy and depart, leaving carnage and chaos. And a chance for fresh starts.

As soon as I leave the boarding house I'm met with a nice wet kiss. The Little Sister touches her briny lips to the broken bridge of my nose, slides her calcium tongue along the cavern that was once an ear; now a defenceless wormhole leading to a muddled sack of membranes.

The first slap of Little Sister's wet hand washes a week of hangovers away. I wish she'd wash the tribal tattoos off my neck and jaw, too. They're from a different time, a different me, when

1

I had half the city on my tail. There's no one trailing me now, but that doesn't mean I'm free. Something's still got a hold of me, somewhere deep within, clawing at my conscience; an unseen predator fused from guilt and shame.

Concrete blocks grow out of the mist. The alley ahead is a narrow gallery of cracked stone, broken ladders hanging lame from fire escapes, aglow with the flickering neon signs of singing rooms. The usually raucous rooms are quiet tonight, save for the howling complaints of the wind as it rattles their battered windows. There's no one around except me, and that's exactly how I like it.

I bury my hands in the pockets of my baggy cargos and introduce my chin to the nape of my neck as I enter the maze and turn right into a winding passage ahead. Loose wires swing between buildings like they're trying to rip themselves clear of the walls, whipping the iron bars of the windows with threatening cracks.

A solitary red light penetrates the darkness above. I stop in my tracks and stare it down. A drone: a mechanical mosquito with a blinking camera between its splayed legs. A few miles away in a cosy office a uniformed sheep is watching me on a big screen. We study each other long and good, me and this hunk of hovering metal. He can look all night; I've done nothing wrong and I'm free to roam this city all I want. Moments later the drone veers off towards the coast, and I'm alone again with nothing but a drizzle on my lips that tastes like fish piss.

I delve deeper into the Rivers, the untamed labyrinth that holds the city together. I don't have a destination in mind; anywhere without a familiar face will do. The closer I get to the heart, the more I'm smothered by revolving beams of kaleidoscopic light. Giant concrete blocks sprout from the ground, concealing the sky and showering me in a prism of colours. Bars, restaurants, massage parlours; their clashing fluorescence casts a psychotic glow over the alleys that sulk and slither between them.

Nakata's bar is near, Ganzo's too, but I don't need a shoulder to cry on tonight. Just for one evening, I wanna escape my stinking attic and drink whisky from a glass I don't have to clean with my own blood-stained hands.

I approach Ryusui—the Busy Stream—the central vein of the sprawling web that spreads out from the city centre. An izakaya sits on the ground floor, and through its smeared windows I glimpse wooden beams and patrons with equally wooden expressions. The second floor is a snooker hall with a lurid green signboard above two smashed windows. The third is a bar; a leather-faced man leans out of the open window, tilts his bottle and watches beer dribble down onto the street below. As I pass beneath him he stops and stares at me like a cow glaring at fake grass. Then he points his chin to the sky and chugs.

I make for the unmarked door beside the izakaya. There's no signage except for a minimalist chalk sketch of a whisky bottle. Perfect. I push the door open and follow the winding staircase into a small dark room with a long bar and endless empty stools. The only sign of life is the old barman behind the counter with a cloth that looks like it's been in his hand for twenty years. His lined face is punctured by surprised little eyes and a thin white moustache that curls up neatly at the ends. Polished beer pumps line the bar and a variety of dusty liquor bottles sit in a gold-encrusted glass case behind him. He must have twenty different kinds of whisky. I'm about to ask for a recommendation when a red light flashes behind the bar and a buzzer blasts from somewhere unseen. I'm not surprised; this isn't the only bar in the Rivers with a tagging sensor.

'Sorry old boy,' the man says. His voice adds ten years to him, and it's ten years he doesn't need.

'I'm just here for a drink,' I say. 'No trouble.'

He drags the cloth absently over the bartop before slinging it over his shoulder. His beady little eyes calculate the cost of my clothing. It doesn't take long.

'What were you tagged for?'

I don't know what to tell him. So I tell him everything.

'Twelve years ago, I killed the only person who ever loved me. It wasn't my intention, but I guess that doesn't make much difference. I did my time in The Heights, and after I got out I stabbed her husband. He tried to frame me for murder, one I had nothing to do with.'

'He died?'

'He did, but it was an undercover detective that killed him, not me.'

He glances at the void that used to be my left ear.

'You're Daganae Kawasaki,' he says.

'I can change the name if you want.'

'It wouldn't do you any good, old boy. I'm sorry, I've a reputation here. A tagged man is a risk I can't afford. Forgive me.'

I stare at the empty stools while he nervously twists the ends of his moustache, like I might pull out a gun and shoot down his best bottles of Scotch. I leer at him and turn on my heels and head back up the stairs. It's not the first time and it won't be the last; this damn contraption on my ankle is giving me more grief than I expected.

I re-emerge into the drizzle as the wind picks up. An empty beer can somersaults down the street and crashes into a wall, twitching like an animal that's been shot in the sternum. As I turn into one of the bigger tributaries off the Busy Stream, a motorcycle hurtles around the corner and almost takes my nose off. I fall back against the wall as the bike speeds off in a blur, quickly followed by half a dozen more. The riders look identical: black helmets that shimmer in the rain, skin-tight leathers clinging to their bodies. Even their bikes are carbon copies of each other. The only thing that isn't black is the flower that's embossed on the side of every helmet and fender—purple stars with yellow stigmas. I'm no good with flowers, but I know for damn sure they're not roses.

4

After the sixth bike speeds past there's a brief moment of stillness and I listen to the wind. She sounds mighty fine when she's angry. I'm about to resume my brooding walk when another bike swings around the corner. The ride's the same as the others but the rider is different; feminine curves squeezed into bright violet leathers. I expect it to disappear around the corner with the others, but it pulls up at the end of the street and the rider rests one foot on the shining asphalt. I can tell by the way the helmet tilts to the left that she's staring at me through her wing mirror. It's a spectacular sight, the rider and her bike, illuminated beneath a mercury-vapour street lamp.

She turns her head to get a better look, so I detach myself from the wall and give her a full silhouette to enjoy. She maintains her position for a good minute more before revving her engine and disappearing.

I haven't seen a motorcycle helmet in twelve years and now I've seen seven at once. Either the government's introduced a new law I didn't hear about or there's a new Rivers gang marking out their turf. Either way, it doesn't bother me. Gangs have been pissing against lampposts in the Rivers for decades, warring for squalid spoils right under the government's nose. As long as no one gets between me and my drink, the flowered punks can fight over garden plots as much as they want.

By the time I'm treading the cobbles of Ryusui, Little Sister's put her belly into it and the typhoon is in full swing. The wind attacks with a swift right hook and follows up with a heavy shower that drenches me from head to toe. Rain descends in fat diagonal lines that hit the cracked cobbles and splinter off to soak my ankles. It's a shame the tag's waterproof. Suddenly the street is alive with posses of people huddled under broken-limbed umbrellas. Cyclists splash through polluted puddles while glistening rats scurry for shelter. I try to duck into a bar but the owner shakes his head and slides the steel shutters down. He bows his head and darts off into the grainy darkness.

Little Sister's ruining my night.

○

I return to the boarding house soaked like a sponge, my shaggy hair in drenched disarray. I fish for my key and clock the motorbike parked up front. I know the bike well—a fire-red Ducati with retro stickers plastered over the fuel tank—and I can't say that I'm pleased or shocked to see it.

As I enter the lobby my old landlady is dozing in an armchair stitched together from leftover curtains. She brushes greasy grey bangs from her eyes and greets me with a disgruntled growl as I shake myself off in the lobby.

'Your date's here,' she barks.

'I didn't order a date. Don't let anyone in here unless you've checked with me first.'

'She's a pretty little thing,' she says, as though that's reason enough.

I scale the stairs, drenching the threadbare carpet as I climb. All the doors along the second and third floor corridors are closed. I don't see a lot of my neighbours, but I often see their sorry customers—shifty characters who shuffle out of the apartments dabbing sweat and shame from their cowed faces. When I reach the top floor, I pause outside my door.

'I see you've made yourself at home,' I say as I enter.

Jiko's sitting in my moth-eaten armchair with an expensive-looking drink in her hand. Her wet, flaming red hair is plastered down on pale pearlescent cheeks. She treats me to a cynical scan, starting with my sodden boots and finishing with my grumpy old mug. Her vixen eyes are swift and shrewd; piercing orbs of scorched mahogany. A navy bandanna is tied around her neck and a plain black t-shirt just about conceals the tattoo beneath her collarbone. Her leather trousers look like they're stitched to her skin.

'I was starting to think you'd been bumped off,' she says.

'I've been busy.'

I remove my sopping jacket, kick off my boots and head

straight to my tiny kitchen. I select an amber bottle from the top shelf, rinse a glass at the sink, and pour myself a generous dram. I hold it beneath my nose and savour the smell before taking a giant swig.

'You haven't been busy at all. You've been hiding out here, drinking yourself to death. That's not the Dag I know.'

'Then maybe you don't know the real me.'

Jiko puts her glass down on the coffee table. 'I heard you were tagged. It was Ryoko Nishi, wasn't it?'

I glance at my ankle, but it doesn't answer for either of us.

'Why did she do it?'

'She's the prime minister. And I wasn't exactly innocent in everything that went down this summer. People died, Jiko.'

'That's not why they tagged you, Dag. Everyone knows Nishi wants to bury all of that.' Her eyes narrow. 'It's because you're after your girl. Your daughter. And Nishi doesn't want you to have anything to do with her.'

I sink another slug and feel the burn in my throat.

'I'm guessing you're no closer to finding her, then?'

Instead of answering I watch the bumbling advance of a mosquito above my head; slow and graceless, flight hampered by the bulk of someone's blood. Mine or Jiko's, I'm not sure.

'I get it, Dag. I do. You're frustrated. You're tagged. You can't get any answers. But can't you just let it go? Focus on the things you *can* control.'

I muster a sceptical smile. 'I've got a daughter out there that I've never met, and her aunt happens to be the most powerful woman in Sonaya. What exactly *can* I control?'

'You've got friends, Dag. People who count on you.'

'Who counts on me?'

'Shinji, for one. He won't say it, of course, but he misses you. He needs you.' She hesitates, picks up her glass and drops it again. 'And me. I need you, too.'

I glare at her and wait for the sarcastic follow-up. It doesn't come. All I get is a straight face and a penetrating stare.

'You still trying to change the world?' I ask.

Jiko stands and strides to the window. She folds her arms and sighs. I can read her expression through the back of her head.

'What happened?'

'One of my girls was captured and cuffed,' she says. 'Two days ago. We were gonna burn down Sakura.'

I chuckle. 'A pretty ambitious plot. The biggest Homework Club in the Rivers.'

'Someone blabbed, a working girl, maybe. We warned them, told them to clear out so they wouldn't get hurt. The police arrived right after we did. Most of us got away, except one.'

'Who?'

'Her name's Suzie. You might remember her. Frizzy hair, bush baby eyes. You met her in The Heights last year.'

'My second honsool date, how could I forget? I bet she's pleased to see her cell again. What about the rest of you?'

'The cops haven't come for us. At least not yet. But I know Suzie. She won't talk.'

'No problem then,' I say. 'What about the Roses?'

'Haven't seen them in weeks.'

'So the Rivers are yours.'

I raise my glass in salute, but Jiko replies with a shake of her head. 'There's a new gang in town. The Nightshades. The Roses were kittens by comparison.'

'Let me guess: black helmets, purple flowers, a lead lady in violet.'

Jiko nods. 'No one knows who they are, but they've told us to clear out. My guess is things'll kick off, and soon.'

I savour a long sip. 'I'm glad you've been busy.'

'You don't know the half of it, Dag.' Suddenly her voice is laced with a bitterness that belies her eighteen years. She drains her glass and crosses the room, stops before me so I can smell her damp hair, the whisky on her breath. 'Maybe when you wake up, you'll be of some help. Before everything comes crashing down again.'

She exits without so much as a goodbye, slamming the door behind her, and I'm left alone with the stillness of my sad splintered walls.

My relationships aren't what they used to be, but one has proved profitable. We've been seeing each other for six weeks now and things are going pretty well. She doesn't mind my drinking, and I don't mind that she's plastic.

All around the world countries are fighting overpopulation. A long time ago China implemented the one child rule; later they introduced a gruelling application process, and now only the elite are eligible to spawn their own miniatures. I don't know why they don't simply send their kids over here. Japan and Korea have had sink populations for decades, and our little island's right between them, alone in the middle of the East Sea, sucking up the worst of their debris. Since Japan cut its apron strings and let us loose, the government's thrown everything it can at the ageing population: incentives, bonuses, and the one that messed up my life, the handsome tax. But nothing has changed. Sonayan men still believe that pixelated women make better girlfriends than women with brains and real flesh and blood, and women have realised that careers are better companions than red-eyed suits who sink all their wages into shot glasses.

That's where my beloved cup comes in. Before my arrest I used to be someone, but not anymore, not with this ankle tag hindering my hopes of employment. Old Kosuke's got plenty of lowlife work for friends, but I'm too old to be a full-time mutton delivery boy. I ran a few jobs for him recently and they paid well enough, but I couldn't stand the way people looked at me. The customers were all high-rankers, plastic-faced smugs in swish apartments by the Pulse or the strip. I'd roll up at their doors with a special delivery and they'd eyeball me as if I'd skinned and sliced the Hokkaido sheep myself, slam the door in my face and hastily hide the contraband. Arseholes.

So I've started ignoring Kosuke's carrier pigeons; the cup will do. The hospital pays by weight and concentration, and I've got a decent production line somewhere down there. I won't pretend I haven't thought about the consequences; dozens of little Dags skiving and slithering in the backstreets. Maybe since I found out I have a daughter my paternal instincts have kicked in. I could be the last Kawasaki of my line, and when I'm five whiskies in, that thought doesn't sit too well. So I sink five more.

When I'm done with my latest donation I'm ready to drink. It's dusk now, and the sky starts to brown at the edges like a well-baked pie, the moon basking above a sleek government skyscraper. Little Sister's slipped off to Seoul, and she's left behind a perfect path all the way to heaven.

I cut into the Rivers to sample the smells seeping out from kitchen back doors, and as I pass the steady stream of restaurants, I realise I haven't eaten yet. Breakfast is usually two coffees at sunset, followed swiftly by two shots of something stronger, just to wake me up. I can cook well enough but I find the hard stuff fills the hole. Tonight, though, I feel like lining my stomach.

I know a place nearby where I can get a cheap meal, buried under a Chinese pharmacy crammed with paper lanterns and jars of root and powder. I push the door open but the familiar entrance bell doesn't jingle. The lights are off and wood smoke tickles my nostrils, intensifying as I descend the wonky stairs. All the tables are overturned, the corner sofa buried beneath broken bar stools torn from the floorboards. I step over the debris and lean across the counter but there are no fish waiting to be carved and dipped in wasabi; there aren't even any knives to do the slicing. All that remains is broken glass, spread over the counter like confetti scattered by a pissed-up priest.

I check the fridges and freezers, the store room and tiny toilet. Nothing. No sign of my old pal Ganzo. I don't need to guess what's happened; I already know. Gangs don't leave fingerprints, they send warnings and leave symbols, like dogs spraying piss against walls. A collage of petals is sprinkled on the floor between the furniture fragments. I pick one up and place it in my palm.

Purple and yellow.

○

Nakata is standing on the wrong side of the bar and she doesn't bat an eyelash when my tag sets the alarm off.

I straddle a barstool and eye her up. Wrapped in a blouse the colour of midnight, she blends in to her dimly-lit den like a bat against the night sky. Her short black hair is streaked with metallic grey and it brings out the dark velvet pools of her eyes.

'I just went to Ganzo's,' I say.

A scowl sculpts new lines into Nakata's forehead. Without looking at me she wipes down the bar stools like she's trying to wear away the leather, while a machine in the corner releases tendrils of smoke that smell like nostalgia.

'Is the big panda all right?' I ask.

'Now you care, do you?' Her voice is deep and rich, like the husky purr of a panther. 'The Nightshades raided him a week ago. He ignored their warnings.'

'How is he?'

She straightens up and puts a hand on her hip, her wind-chime earring swaying like a nagging finger.

'That bar was his world, Dag, how do you think he is? He's not hurt, if that's what you mean. He's staying with a sister near the Pulse.'

She moves behind the bar and grabs a glass. 'You going to sit here all night without a drink?'

'Stout,' I say.

She nods and pours from the tap.

'So you got tagged,' she says, passing me the glass. 'It must be hard to find places to drink.'

'Most people have other things to worry about.'

'Damn right. I'm guessing you've heard about the latest policy?'

I wet my lips with the stout. 'I haven't been keeping up with the news.'

'The Borrowing from the Philippines finally went through, which means that dealers and addicts are shot dead on the spot. Just in time, eh? A couple of weeks before polling day. One last attempt to win over the dumb sheep who worship the PM.'

'And what do the wise citizens of Sonaya make of it?'

'They're scoffing it down,' she says, curling a lip. 'The ones who aren't on drugs, anyway. Religious nuts think Nishi's some kind of saviour, cleansing the streets. Another three were knocked off last night, just around the corner.'

'Shot?'

'Like dogs,' she says, removing a record from the shelf. Doris Day smiles at us from the sleeve, all yellow hair and white teeth. She wouldn't be smiling if she knew where she was now. Moments later the basement erupts with the sound of Secret Love. Nakata closes her eyes and inhales deeply, contentment washing over her face as if she's sucking the music straight into her lungs.

She ducks beneath the counter and takes a seat beside me. 'Where the hell have you been, Dag?'

I glance around at the empty stools and naked tables, bereft of drinks and drinkers. 'Business been slow?'

Nakata stares through the artificial smoke. 'Typhoons and murders don't make for good business. *They* were in here a few nights ago, too. The Nightshades. Came in when the place was full. Ordered everyone out. Demanded payment. I gave it to them. They're gonna put half the Rivers out of business.'

Alcohol licenses aren't cheap, and I don't know a soul in Sonaya who has one. It used to be that a few bucks in the right palms kept the cops away, but now the Roses' petals have been ripped up, and it sounds like the Nightshades smell even less sweet.

Doris Day finishes her endless love spiel and starts on Que Sera Sera.

'What will be, will be,' I say, echoing ol' Doris.

'Don't get cute, Dag. Are you going to help your friends or not?'

'Help them? I'm a jobless ex-con with a cup for a girlfriend. All I ever do is drag the people I care about into my steady stream of troubles.'

Nakata scoffs and snatches my drink. 'Don't you dare pretend you're avoiding everyone because you care about them. As if you care about anyone other than yourself.'

She pours half my pint down her throat and glares at me.

'You remember that kid? The little carrier pigeon who followed you around like a lap dog? Shinji, wasn't it?'

'Remember him? I'm still getting his smell off my clothes.'

'He's been in a few times. No messages to deliver, just broods silently in the corner. He doesn't come here looking for me, Dag.'

'So what?'

'So I'm guessing you haven't spoken to him, same as you haven't spoken to anyone else. He stopped running messages for Kosuke weeks ago, and if he's not doing that anymore, I don't like to think how he's getting by.'

I reclaim my drink and sip. 'He might be running jobs for someone else.'

'Who's going to pay more than Kosuke? I don't like it.'

'I don't like it either. I don't like its dirty old cap, or the way it followed me around, or the endless lies.'

Nakata stares me down.

'Get the hell out of here, Dag,' she says. 'You're like a wet dog, you're bad for business.'

'There's a lot that's bad for business these days.'

Nakata aims a boot at my shin and I feel it more than I've felt anything for days.

'I'm serious. Sort yourself out. And don't come back till you do.'

I raise my hands in feigned innocence and trump back up the stairs, leaving Nakata with Doris Day and the smoke. I venture a smile as I emerge into the night air; at least I don't have to worry about Nakata.

Shinji's new place is in a decrepit red brick building with a seafood stew joint on the ground floor. I can still smell the rotten mussels as I ascend the stairs and examine the battered wooden doors on the upper floors. Shinji's door might not have a number, but it makes up for that with an exhibit of scratched graffiti. Swear words in three languages, and most of them spelt incorrectly. I knock on the door, and a full thirty seconds later it swings open.

Shinji's wearing an ancient baseball cap and his old tattoo's still there, too: a small rose on his neck that's already fading. His face looks different, though: acne, and a lot of it, spreading over his prominent cheekbones in a big red rash.

'Look who it is,' he says.

He turns and leaves the door open. I guess that counts as a welcome. I follow him inside and scan the room: wooden floorboards covered in dust and tumbleweeds of pubes, a window with one of its panes boarded up, and a mound of blankets piled in a corner. A sink slowly rusts beside a couple of grimy hobs, and cobwebs collect in each corner. My head almost grazes the mouldy ceiling. Somewhere outside a street cat screams through its death throes.

'Didn't fancy staying with Jiko's biker girls then,' I say, eyeing the walls.

'Women,' he says, shaking his head.

I shrug. When I was fourteen I would've done anything to live with half a dozen biker girls.

'How'd you afford this place? Pigeon jobs picked up, have they?'

Shinji shrugs. We're having a shrug party tonight. 'I got onto a good job.'

'From who?'

'From someone who pays well. Where have *you* been?'

'Why? You missed me?'

'Like I miss my haemorrhoids.'

'That's a good one. If you weren't missing me, why were you skulking around Nakata's place?'

Shinji fixes me with an expression I can't quite read. His soot-black eyes are flat and cold, like long-extinguished furnaces. Duplicity is the only thing that keeps him interesting.

'You got something to tell me, kid? Or are you getting ready to sell me out again?'

Shinji answers with a scowl.

'You remember the last time you double-crossed me? You ended up with a gun at your temple and piss trickling down your skinny legs. I saved you. You forgotten that?'

'I'm not selling you out,' he spits.

'Then what the hell are you playing at?'

Shinji chews the inside of his cheek. I don't know whether he's about to rush me or burst into tears.

'I can't tell you,' he says.

I reply with one of those loud exhales that some people mistake for a laugh. 'You can do better than that, kid.'

Shinji shakes his head. I'd feel better if he told me an outright lie. All these goddamn secrets. Things were simpler when I was shut up in my attic. I've got one last card to play, though.

'How's your sister?'

Shinji frowns. 'Don't think I don't know what you did.'

The boy's sister is a ten-week-old little bundle of sheets with a purple face. Her mother was an addict, and a determined one. Shinji swiped the little one away from the needles as soon as he could, and she's been holed up in a hospital ward ever since. It's true that lately I haven't done much of use, but getting Eiko adopted by a doting couple has to go down as one of my masterstrokes. And people say I don't care.

'What makes you think I had anything to do with it?' I say.

'They're friends of yours, the ones with the yacht. They've got money.'

I push out my bottom lip. 'Money doesn't always mean happiness.'

'No, but it means a roof over Eiko's head once she's out of hospital.' Shinji inflates his chest and approaches me. He extends a hand and I watch it hover between us. 'Here,' he says. 'This is me saying thank you. It's probably the only time you'll hear me say it, so enjoy it.'

I consider the kid and make him wait. A face full of acne and an extra inch in height; suddenly this little punk could pass for a young man. I don't like it. It makes me feel old.

'Just tell me what stupid mess you've gotten yourself into,' I say.

Shinji clenches his jaw.

'Save your thank yous for when your sister's fully recovered,' I say. 'Until then, stay out of my business.'

I turn and leave his hand hanging limply in front of him, free to grow moss for all I care.

'You're a coward,' Shinji says.

'We all knew that already,' I say, closing the door behind me.

17

Kosuke's new yacht makes the Arkansas look like a fishing dory. Her name is Homura. She's two hundred feet long, and it's no coincidence that she shares a name with my dear runaway mum.

It's a fine evening for a rich people party. The sun's slipping towards the horizon like egg yolk sliding down a soiled kitchen wall. With Little Sister long gone the sky is clear—a beautiful chalk blue with small sunburned scratches of cloud. It's not every day you see the sky above Sonaya; usually the sun and moon spin behind a dull grey ceiling like dancers trapped behind an unraised curtain. Kosuke has a knack for choosing perfect party nights, though. The boss-eyed bloater has a lot of money, and tonight it seems he's slipped a sweetener straight into heaven's back pocket.

The plastic folks are on deck with foaming champagne flutes and a young woman in a white blouse stands before the gangplank with a well-paid smile. She asks for a name and I oblige. A pen skims down her clipboard and freezes somewhere near the bottom. She peers up at me and her eyes linger on my misaligned nose, the tattoos on my neck, the ear that's not there.

'Mr. Kawasaki,' she says, extending a hand towards the yacht.

I bow and head on up. A tray of champagne flutes materialises under my nose as soon as my boots hit the deck and I clear my throat with cascading bubbles. I grab a second flute and commence a slow circuit.

It's been a while since I was anywhere so swish. A string quartet plays in one corner, concentrated smiles plastered on pained faces, their bows trembling to a classical waltz. The cockpit is draped in strips of white satin that stretch across the deck as silver fairy lights glisten from railings. The women wear silk dresses and dangling earrings that shimmer like chandeliers. I see a lot of smooth skin and long waxed legs and teeth so white I bury my blemished enamel behind closed lips. The men are sleek and spotless and they make sure their watches catch the light when they shake my hand. Some try to crush my fingers, too, but they give up when they see the look in my eyes.

Appearances are everything in Sonaya, and I have to be careful what I say in such a fine and fragile crowd. I'm the ragged wastrel who's snuck from steerage to first class, and my back alley ways aren't welcome. I lose the expletives and replace them with compliments stolen from overheard conversations. *Your nose job looks great, who was your surgeon? I hear you got a promotion, how much did it set you back?* I'm dancing on a deck of glass swans, trying not to damage delicate wings or smash a sweet face into thousands of shards.

Peter Stones looks half-cut already, his blotched pink cheeks glowing beneath steel blue eyes. He pulls away from a circle of suits when he sees me, a big white smile stretched between his greying sideburns. I shake the Yank by the hand.

'Dag, my boy!' he says, slapping me on the back. 'Where the heck have you been, you son of a gun?'

'What are you working on, Stones?'

'The demolition of his liver and nose,' Aimi Stones says as she appears behind us, a glowing vision of pearly skin and silky black hair. She entwines her sleek tanned arm with her husband's, a subtle smile on her luminescent lips.

'I wish you'd been around,' she says, her eyes twinkling at me. 'You might have kept him on his toes. He hasn't done a day's good writing since-'

She stops herself mid-sentence. I know what the 'since' is because it's the same 'since' I've been tormented by for the past two months. Since all the deception boiled over and exploded around us. Since my right hand man spewed fountains of blood. Since we discovered how safe and happy we really are.

'He's promised to quit,' Aimi says, recovering. 'For the baby. I've told him I'll take Eiko away if he doesn't.'

She sounds like a mother dangling chocolate in front of a naughty kid. Stones raises his eyebrows at me conspiratorially.

'How's Eiko doing?' I ask.

'Oh, she's an angel, Dag,' Stones says with bravado. 'I didn't know I could love anyone as much as this one.' He places a hand on the small of Aimi's back. 'But that little cutie's something else, believe me, boy.'

'She's got a long way to go,' Aimi says evenly. 'She's been in hospital ever since we signed the papers. But she has a real sparkle in her eyes.'

'Good to hear.'

Aimi and Stones have been sailing through icebergs for a while, and I figured it was only a matter of time before the hull of their marriage was pierced. They can't have kids of their own, but Shinji's baby sister was an easy sell; it was love at first sight. The sickly baby gets rich parents, the expat writer finds a reason to get clean. Two birds with two Stones.

He claps me on the back and downs his glass. Aimi and I watch him closely as his cheeks redden.

'I heard about the Philippines Borrowing,' I say.

'Oh, don't worry about me, boy,' Stones winks. 'The cops don't see pollen if their pockets are full. Besides, I'm getting clean. This is a party, though, and I'll be damned if I don't enjoy myself one last time before the summer gets swallowed by fall.'

Moments later he's swept off by a group of dapper youngsters with mischievous expressions. Aimi rolls her eyes at me and saunters off in the opposite direction.

I sink another flute of champagne and find myself stood beside a potato-shaped man in a lurid cream tux. The best friend of my Brooklyn-born dad, an immigrant diplomat who drank himself to death, Kosuke near enough raised me after my mum took off for her homeland of Honshu.

The years have been kind to the old man; thick grey hair sweeps over his crown and milk-white teeth sparkle above his multiple chins. He's covered in gold jewelry like a blind pirate pimp, and the young woman on his arm could be his granddaughter.

'I like the yacht,' I tell him. 'Homura. How did you come up with the name?'

Kosuke narrows his one good eye; the other gazes out to sea, searching for my dear old mum, stuffed somewhere inside her Tokyo office.

'I've always liked the name,' he says with a smile. 'Let me introduce you to Kiki. She's a writer. Stones thinks she has talent.'

I shake her hand. She's a couple of inches taller than Kosuke, with purchased pale skin and a bust that invites unsolicited stares. She smells like she's been fermenting in a perfume bottle.

'You look young to be a writer,' I say, more to Kosuke than her. He must realise because he answers for her.

'Kiki's at the university.'

'I'm sure she is. I hear tuition fees are pretty high these days, Kiki, it must be tough.' I wish I had a boss eye like Kosuke so I could keep one eye on each of them as I play. 'What do you write?'

'Young adult fiction,' she says.

'Of course you do. You've always liked young adult fiction, haven't you, Kosuke?'

Kosuke's second chin wobbles. 'Would you mind fetching my best Scotch, Kiki? It's in the master cabin, in the-'

'I know where it is,' Kiki says cheerfully. She plants a kiss on Kosuke's fat cheek and toddles off.

'She's doing well in those heels,' I say. 'Her first pair?'

'Enough of that,' Kosuke says shortly. 'I don't tell you how to live your life, Dag. Don't tell me how to live mine.'

'I'm happy for you. She must be good conversation.'

'It's a darn sight better than yours. All I get from you is grief and gloom. You're finally out of your slump, are you? Tired of crying into your pillow?'

'Yeah. I'm done.'

'Good, because your sullen dog act isn't welcome here. Look around you. See those things on people's faces? They're called smiles. People like them, and they're cheap.'

'They might be cheap for folk like you, but silicone's out of my price range.'

'You can do better than that, Dag. We go back a long way and there's a lot I can do to help you, but I can only do so much. You were *something* once, and it's about time you got back in the game. Some of the most influential people in the city are on this yacht and all you do is hide in the corner and poke fun at people's happiness.'

'I've got a tag on my ankle.'

'A tag doesn't stop you from sweet-talking, does it? You're Daganae Kawasaki, the ten. Go find an in. Look, right there, Jo Umatsu,' he points at a bearded guy surrounded by three women. 'Managing Director of Sonaya Bank. And there, Yoo-ri Baek.'

'Ah yes, the celebrated Borrower,' I reply. 'Excuse me if I don't ask for an autograph.'

Kosuke huffs as I glance at Sonaya's latest success story. Thirty-three years old, five foot eight, Baek beams at her adoring flock with the city's finest synthetic smile. The bridge of her nose is high and prominent, Western style; protruding from her Korean face like some kid stuck it on with double-sided tape. She's Sonaya's idea of the modern woman: slim, suited, and carefully sculpted. It's a shame her latest offering is a backward slice of bad news.

When I share my insights with Kosuke he sighs into his champagne. Just thinking about sweet-talking these fakers makes me sick.

'Fine,' Kosuke says. 'Keep running donkey jobs for an old man. See how happy it makes you.'

'Speaking of delivery boys,' I say. 'Any idea what happened to Shinji?'

Kosuke questions me with an arched eyebrow.

'One of your old carrier pigeons. The one with a rose tattoo on his neck; the one that double-crossed me.'

'Ah, *that* one. I don't deal directly with my pigeons, Dag, I've got people for that. But I hear he wanted out.' Kosuke waves a nonchalant hand through the air. 'It's not my business what those urchins choose to do with their lives. I pay them more than fairly, but if they want out, so be it.'

Two women pass by, flashing coy smiles. Kosuke bows and reveals a glimmer of gold teeth.

'I *do* have something for you, though,' the old man says, turning back to me. 'Or, at least, the German does.'

'Bernd? He here?'

'Working, I'm afraid. It's election season, and propaganda doesn't write itself. He'll be expecting you.'

'What does he have?'

'He seems to think he's got a lead on Silver Beard. You're still interested in catching up with him, I take it?'

I nod. The sharpest thorn of the Roses, Silver Beard was the one tasked with finding my daughter. He sunk beneath the soil with the rest of his rank garden, and my hopes of finding the girl disappeared with him.

Kiki returns with a tall amber bottle and three glasses. Kosuke pours and our glasses chime as they collide. Here's to us: the old man with a wandering eye, the student with dreams of literary life, and me, the aged stray from steerage.

We talk nice beneath the darkening sky until Kiki whispers something that makes Kosuke's good eye sparkle. They leave me with half-hearted goodbyes and venture off arm in arm. I head to the stern to survey the harbour.

The depths of Sonaya aren't what most people would describe as pretty, but the eastern coast is a treat for eyes exhausted by darkness. Yachts sway in the breeze as swanky hotels sparkle along golden sands. You can almost forget that the world went to shit. The harbour and strip are the shimmering tip of a rotting iceberg, but sometimes it's good to peek above the surface and pretend.

'You think he's a fool, don't you?'

Aimi appears at my side with two fresh drinks and the familiar shadow of doubt entombed in her eyes.

'Who, Stones? No, not at all. I think you love him,' I say, accepting a glass. 'And if I were you, I'd gather my loved ones and get out of here. It's not a good time to be an addict in Sonaya. It's not a good time to be *anyone* in this city.'

The moon paints a hazy line over the ocean which reflects in Aimi's eyes. She used to be a real livewire, a model. She thought she'd won the winning ticket when she married Stones, expected him to whisk her away from this godawful place. But she's twenty-seven, retired, and still stuck here. Richer than ever, but stalked by the same old problems.

'Listen,' I say, 'I chose you to look after Eiko because you're a good person. The kid's mother was a wreck, cared more for her needles than the needs of her kids. Shinji would kill me if he knew I'd passed Eiko into the hands of another addict.'

'I understand, Dag. He'll get clean, I promise.'

Suddenly the music stops. I'm only surprised it's taken so long. Kosuke's voice barks from the other side of the yacht.

Police, no doubt; after money or blood, and I've little of either to spare.

'Goodbye, Dag,' Aimi says, glancing over her shoulder. 'I'd make myself scarce if I were you. That tag makes you twice as likely to attract a sniper's sight to your chest.'

I nod. Stones might be a fool, but Aimi isn't. She heads towards the commotion while I hang back, contemplating a quick exit. I scrutinise the sea but can't say I fancy making a swim for it. Grime coats the surface, a thick layer of grease all the way from China, and the carcass of a seagull floats nearby on bloodied, misshapen wings. I decide to wait while Kosuke and Stones lighten their pockets to keep the hyenas happy. Once the going's clear, I'll return to my attic for a few final shorts of whisky and another sleepless night.

Laughter drifts across deck—laughter that's swiftly silenced by gunshots. Screams erupt like thunder after lightning.

I rush over to see what's happening and witness bodies dropping to the song of piercing screams. Maybe Stones was too drunk to count his notes properly. If the druggies have got themselves killed it's their own fault, but I'll murder Stones myself if something's happened to Aimi. I push my way through the panicking crowd and catch sight of the men in padded blue.

Bodies lie motionless on deck as the officers bellow orders to those still standing. Stones yells right back at the gun-toting cops while Aimi struggles to restrain him. An officer grabs her by the elbow and I step forward as the men in blue raise their guns.

I stand beside Kosuke and smuggle Stones behind me.

'We're all done here, officers,' I say, holding up my empty hands.

Kosuke takes Aimi's arm and escorts her away. I glance at the nearest corpse, a pool of blood painting the laminated deck. The anxious guests appeal to the sky for help; the richest cats punch pleas into their pagers.

'We'll decide when it's done,' one of officers says. He's built like a rhino and just as pretty.

'You've done your job well,' I say. 'Now get the hell out of here.'

The rhino curls a fat lip at me. 'Check him.'

The officers raid my pockets and discover Old Trusty, my Wharncliffe knife; better a blade than a bag of the white stuff. The other ankle receives a similar review.

'He's tagged, boss,' one of them says.

The rhino looks me over as I flash an innocent smile. I'm starting to wish I'd braved the oil-slick seas.

A flock of drones glides over the jetties. News drones, probably—the government likes to share how swiftly it can slay a drug deal. Officers aren't too keen to share their faces, though.

'You,' the rhino turns to me. 'Get out of here, or I'll make sure they find your bloated corpse in the bay tomorrow.'

They even return Trusty. Luck of the Dag. Another minute and I'd have been dead on deck with planted coke in my pocket and bullets in my back.

The drones hover over Homura and snap photos of the bust. Aimi falls to her knees in silence as Stones curses the cops and gawps at the fallen bodies of his friends. Kosuke is pale as paper and Kiki weeps into his heaving chest. I count three dead, many more injured.

'Call the fucking paramedics,' Stones cries.

Damn fool. These parties are all starting to look the same.

I head straight for Vino Ryusui, the basement bar run by Jiko's biker girls. It looks the same as before, only now it has customers. They're a young crowd, perched on stools or lazing in the leather booths, wine glasses held in two dainty fingers. They glance at me as I waltz down the stairs and immediately look away, like I'm not worthy of their esteemed attention. It doesn't feel good to be irrelevant.

I approach the bar and straddle the one free stool between a stream of solo drinkers. The woman to my left scrutinises me before sinking her nose into a glass of white. The goth to my right doesn't even flick her eyes in my direction. I tap my finger on the counter until the woman with purple hair arrives to brood before me.

'Bo-min,' I say. 'It's been a while.'

'Dag.'

Bo-min was always good with words. Her fringe looks like it was clipped by a guillotine, and black eye shadow pools around her moody eyes, which bore into mine with all the interest of a cat woken from its slumber.

'You're doing good business,' I say.

No reply.

'Is Jiko here?'

Bo-min shrugs. She could write a dissertation on shrugging, but she wouldn't read it to you.

'Wine?'

I nod. Bo-min pours something vaguely burgundy into a vaguely washed glass. It might be the worst wine I've ever tasted, but she doesn't ask me to pay. She watches me drink, ignoring the other customers waiting for refills. She's still gawking when the short blonde appears.

'No need to ask where you were tonight,' she says.

I like Su-young. She speaks, and sometimes in full sentences. She smiles, too, but not now. Her bright lipstick matches the pink hue of the mugunghwa tattoos that bloom along her left arm, and the vibrant yellow dye of her bob is like the warning colouration of a venomous animal.

'So you heard about the yacht party?' I ask.

'I thought they'd keep the expats out of all the drug bullshit,' Su-young says.

'They left Stones out of it.' I sip the wine and curtail my wince. 'Just wanted to scare him.'

'And kill half his closest friends. You'd best be careful around him, Dag. They'll have drones watching that yacht night and day now, and your tag's like catnip for them. I'm guessing Yoo-ri Baek was there?'

'She was. I take it you girls are fans.'

Su-young raises an eyebrow and I smile into my glass. When the Borrowings began everyone thought it was gonna put Sonaya on the map. 'A jigsaw puzzle of future thinking'—that was the motto the hyenas in government concocted. Fifteen years later we're still several pieces short of a pretty picture, and the pieces we do have are stained with spilt booze and stuffed in the wrong places.

The Borrowers have one of the most sought-after jobs in government. They travel to assigned countries, review their policies, and report their results. Then somewhere in a vast hall near the Pulse all the high-rankers vote on which foreign policies to adopt in Sonaya. It's relevant, rational, open-minded. It should have transformed our little island. It didn't.

'It's all bullshit,' Bo-min says.

'We should scrap the lot of them,' Su-young agrees, pouring herself a glass.

'You're young,' I say. 'It started with good intentions. The plastic tax from Finland, Germany's ban on vaping. For a while, it worked nicely.'

'That should be Sonaya's slogan,' Su-young says. '*For a while, it worked nicely.*'

She's not wrong. You can't transform a nation's mindset with a quick click of the fingers. The more forward-thinking proposals were rejected outright, especially when it came to working hours, holidays, the gender gap. A four day working week? Impossible; something's wrong with the stats. Equal pay for men and women? Slow down; tradition is tradition. The problem with having an overpaid herd of sweaty male suits in power is that they're careful to conserve the balance, one heavily weighted in their favour.

Yoo-ri Baek won a Borrowing nine years ago when she was still a rookie: free public transport in the form of our beloved Pipe. It came from Luxembourg, where the system thrived. The Sonayan government hired crews to clean the underground, maintain peace and order, and for a few short weeks it seemed like a masterstroke. But pretty soon the budgets were slashed and the Pipe fell into disrepair. Platforms drowning in puddles of piss, carriages crammed with the crude shelters of the homeless, and stations transformed into bases by low-level gangs. And while the Pipe remains free to ride, rollicking under the city like a decrepit rollercoaster squealing off the tracks, it ain't no Luxembourg.

The following year, Baek introduced a policy from the Middle-east: prison sentences for homosexuality. This government's been anti-gay for decades—discreetly, of course. A surge in Sonaya's population is the number one aim, and same-sex marriage doesn't fit with the agenda. But the mere mention of implementing such a plan triggered anger and unrest among the more liberal sections of Sonayan society. There were protests and warnings and threats, so Baek dropped off the radar and disappeared. Now, following several years of strategic silence, she's back, and this year's Borrowing is even more controversial.

The idea was swiped from Korea, even though they never implemented it. We often look to our Taeguk neighbours when it comes to population control. The Hermits first introduced family-planning policies when the country was piss-poor after the first Korean War, but the new strategies worked too well. After the digital boom Korea found itself with a dwindling workforce and a huge population of pensioners with no one to care for them. Japan wasn't much different, and any problems Japan and Korea face, we inherit as their bastard child.

But even by Sonayan standards, this one is out there. The premise for the policy is for sex workers to get paid for childbirths, *if* they can prove they're drugs-free. Moral implications? Who cares. The government just wants numbers, workers, people to bring Sonaya out of the ashes. And who's going to take care of these bastard children? Well, that's the second part of the plan. Foster parents will receive bonuses for adopting these poor brothel-born kids. Adoption is big business in Sonaya—you'd be surprised how many couples can't conceive—scientists say it's the electromagnetic waves we suck up, the microplastics buried in our bodies.

'At least it's good for the sex workers,' I offer.

'Don't be stupid, Dag,' Su-young bites back. 'This government has never supported sex workers—they have zero rights, zero protection. This policy doesn't support them; it *uses* them. It's insane. The plan wasn't even implemented in Korea, so how the hell has it won the Borrowing? It reeks of corruption.'

It doesn't help that Yoo-ri Baek is one the few Sonayan

politicians of Korean descent. To young women like Su-young and Bo-min, she's a role model turned monster.

'She deserves to be in prison, the backwards bitch,' Su-young says.

'Next time I see her, I'll tell her she's doing a wonderful job,' I say.

'Don't worry, Dag. We'll see her before you do.'

Even Bo-min almost smiles.

'Do I wanna know?' I ask.

'Maybe you do, but it would make you complicit,' Su-young says. 'Unless you want to help, of course?'

'I've got my own business to attend to.' I kill my drink and Su-young collects the glass.

'You're not staying?'

I shake my head. 'Just passing through. I'm off to see Bernd.'

Bernd is the old German who lives in the Rivers. Big guy, wrinkles round his eyes, big black beard with wild grey patches. He used to be a real writer, back when the city was young and happening, one of the first expats on the scene. He gave up fiction when Sonaya went to shit, and now he's been here too long to leave. He lives in a tiny attic room above a whisky house, keeps himself busy writing whatever the government tells him to.

'You looking to get a job in politics?' Su-young asks.

'I'm in no rush to return to work.'

'Yeah, we've noticed. The longer you're out, the harder it is to get back in.'

'I'll get back in, alright,' I assure her. 'When I've tied up all the loose ends.'

'Then you'll be out of work forever.'

I stand. 'Give my regards to Jiko. Thanks for the drink.'

'Hey,' Su-young calls after me. 'Jiko will be glad you dropped by.'

'I know,' I say as I leave Su-young and Bo-min to deal with the complaints of their impatient customers.

The whisky house is lively. I'd stop for a quick one but Germans don't like to be kept waiting. I follow the stairs to the attic and knock on the door. Manners cost nothing, after all.

'Who's there?' The voice sounds groggy and sore.

'Death,' I say. 'Sorry I'm late, but it's your time.'

Nothing but silence, until two heavy feet and a walking stick tread the wooden floor. The door swings open and Bernd has a shotgun in my face before I can even feel the draft.

'I thought Death would be better looking,' Bernd says, lowering the gun.

I hold out my hands. 'I'm new on the job. Give me time.'

Bernd turns and leaves the door open. I stroll in and smell the dust and the whisky. His dog hobbles over to greet me—a white Jindo with a missing foreleg and only half a tail.

'Found yourself someone at last,' I say, rubbing under the dog's chin.

'I got lonely while you were locked up,' Bernd says. 'Found her in the alley a few years back, made the mistake of feeding her some scraps. Couldn't get rid of her. Now I don't want to.'

'What's her name?'

'Hildegard.'

'Christ. What did she do wrong?'

Bernd sneers and sinks into his beaten armchair. I lean against a wall and the dog props against my leg. I glance at Bernd's desk; a kerosene lamp burns beside a pile of papers. Looks like poetry.

'You writing for fun again, old man?'

'None of your damn business,' he says, reaching for his decanter.

'On the rocks?' he asks.

'Very small rocks,' I say.

As Bernd pours our drinks I leaf through the documents on his desk. Letters from foreign ambassadors, interview notes, half-translated scripts; all of it dull. An old-fashioned telephone sits beneath a flickering lamp; it might look ancient, but these bulky relics are pricier than pagers. I spin the number wheel just for kicks, then pick up an old cigar box. I have it half open when Bernd snaps at me.

'Didn't your mother ever teach you not to touch other people's things?'

I shrug. 'My mother isn't that boring. What's the news, then?' I ask, returning the box to the windowsill. 'Kosuke said you might have a lead for me.'

Bernd sips his drink and I follow suit.

'If Ryoko Nishi knows anything about your daughter then she's not letting on. She probably thinks I'd tell you.'

'Maybe she overestimates my popularity.'

'Maybe she does. But your best shot isn't through the PM, anyway. The Roses might have disbanded, but that doesn't mean their work is done. Kenya Oh is an honourable man, as far as men in his line of business go.'

'Who the hell is Kenya Oh?'

'I thought you two were well acquainted. He's the leader of the Roses, or former leader, should I say. Pinstripe suit, eloquent speaker.'

'Ah, Silver Beard. I didn't know he had a name.'

'No, you wouldn't. Anyway, it turns out that before he died, Fujii left Kenya Oh some money. To protect the girl.'

Fujii. Even hearing the name makes the bile in my stomach boil. The man who tried to frame me. The man who replaced me in my lover's eyes and brought up my daughter in my place. The man who died choking on blood and secrets.

'And if I know Kenya,' Bernd continues, 'he won't have given up the hunt. He'll want to make sure she's taken care of before he ducks out of the game altogether.'

'That's swell, but like you said, the Roses are done. Their pachinko hall's closed down and as far as I know they're not even in Sonaya anymore.'

'People in their line of business know how to keep a low profile. I hear Oh's got a share in the Cow Shed now. You can probably find him there.'

'I'll check it out.' Hildegard rests her nose on my boot and I scratch behind her ear. 'You know anything about this new gang? Helmets, leather, half-decent bikes. Some kind of flower I can never remember.'

Bernd sips his whisky and for the first time tonight I see a smile emerge from the depths of his badger beard.

I tut playfully. 'Well, well, Bernd. You are full of surprises. Does Ryoko Nishi know you're working with an underground gang? It doesn't seem very safe for someone with a government pension.'

'Careful, Dag. I like you, but I don't have to. I've given you a lead and a glass of good whisky, and that's more than I give most people.'

I look at Hildegard and expect her to share her owner's dogged expression, but she just stares back at me, wide-eyed and curious. She licks her lips and lies down.

'You want my advice, Dag?'

I shrug. That means I want to hear it but I don't want to make a show of it.

'Forget the girl. What do you think will happen if you find her? That she'll run into your arms and the two of you will live happily ever after? You're a criminal, Dag. Kids don't like disfigured men who drink too much and hide knives in their socks. Ryoko Nishi's a good woman, whether you like her policies or not. More than that, she's the girl's aunt, and she's got the standing and finances to take care of her if she's found. If you've got any guts left, leave the girl with her.'

Guts. I've never lacked guts. But all too often I throw them after the wrong cause.

'Listen,' Bernd says, reclining in his chair. 'This isn't a good time to go snooping around. The elections are coming up, these ridiculous Borrowings are being implemented, and that's only the start of it. There's a lot more going on than you know, and I've got a feeling it's all about to turn ugly. You've already got a tag and a bad reputation. Get yourself to the port and smuggle yourself to Honshu, that's what I'd do. If you want, I can help you.'

'And miss all the fun? I've only just returned to the wild. And between you and me, I'm not hating it.'

Bernd bristles like a disapproving grandparent. 'Booze and women, I'll bet. You're not a kid, Dag. Make a fresh start, away from all this. There's nothing left for you in Sonaya.'

I sink the rest of my whisky and leave the glass on the table. I give Hildegard a final rub under her chin.

'I've got more than you think.'

Cicadas and me are like brothers. They brood underground for years, biding their time until they finally emerge for a few short weeks to piss the world off. You mostly hear them up on Broken Hill among the trees, but some also venture downtown to hiss away from places unseen. Tonight, as I follow the meandering lanes towards the Busy Stream, they serenade me like an itch at the back of the eyeballs.

The Cow Shed is a two-floor monstrosity on the main thoroughfare that runs through the heart of the Rivers. The front doors are flanked by two big bulls who snort through flaring nostrils and turn away everyone but the pretty girls. One bull dons a goatee that looks like it's been drawn on in marker pen, and the other has a head so square you'd need a ruler to sketch it. I stroll up to the doors and let them appraise me. Goatee grunts his displeasure and shakes his head, so I pull out a wrinkled note and casually slip it into his breast pocket. He lets the money sit there for a few seconds before removing a security scanner from his belt. He runs it over my body and we listen to it beep by each ankle. I remove Trusty from its sheath and hand it over.

'What about that?' Goatee jabs a sausage finger at my tag.

I lean in. 'The PM's got a soft spot for me. Doesn't want me to get away.'

The bulls glance at each other and roll their eyes. I fold up another couple of notes and slide them snugly into Goatee's pocket.

'In,' he grunts. He straightens up and scowls at the street. I reply with a small bow and pass between them.

'Next time,' Square-head says, slamming a hand on my chest, 'don't let your dog chew your boots before you leave the house.'

They guffaw dumbly. I consider hitting them, but decide to flash them a smile and push through the doors. I'm in.

I take a seat at the long LED-lit bar and soak in my surroundings. It's the kind of place I might have liked twenty years ago. Disco lights illuminate the circular dancefloor but everything beyond is dark. The dancers are young; most of them haven't even broken into their second decade. The guys are all in tight T-shirts and chinos, the girls in short skirts and heels unfit for dancing. The music's loud and lousy—club hits of the nineteen eighties.

Glazed eyeballs stare from shadowy booths around the perimeter. I scan faces, hoping to land on someone interesting, but I don't know a damn person. I'm twenty years older than everyone else and half as well dressed. The barman knows it too and he sneers at me while wiping down glasses that don't need wiping.

'You gonna order something or just sit there and perv all night?' he says.

I glower at him. His hair is slicked back with rock-hard wax and his shirt looks like it was ironed by his mum. He's got a narrow, cocksure face with plucked eyebrows and thin lips that barely move when he speaks. I glance down at my boots and wonder if they're older than the surly boy before me. I soon stop wondering because it doesn't make me feel any better.

'Give me a Senor Ramon,' I tell him.

He plants his palms on the counter and shows me how long he can go without blinking.

'You want trouble, old man?'

'I want a Senor Ramon,' I say. 'You gonna mix me one or not?'

'I don't know what the hell a Senor Ramon is. Order something off the menu or get out.'

I run my eyes over the menu; all the usual cocktails but no Senor Ramon, which is no surprise to me. He doesn't need to know it doesn't exist.

'If you don't know how to mix a Ramon, give me a Manhattan. Do you know how to mix a Manhattan?'

His eyes become pinpricks. 'I know how to spit in them.'

'I bet you do. Mix one up for me, without the spit. The bouncers are old buddies of mine, told me to come in and enjoy myself. They didn't say anything about people spitting in my drinks.'

His lips almost disappear. I can tell he doesn't believe me, but he nods sullenly and gets to work. Manhattans take time to mix.

'Your boss is a pal of mine, too,' I say to his back. 'Kenya. You probably know him as Mr. Oh. Or maybe you don't know him at all.'

The kid glances over his shoulder as he opens a bottle of rye whisky. 'You're right, I don't know him.'

'He's got a silver beard and wears a suit. Used to head up a group known as the Roses, until they split. That was after they got involved in my business. A couple of important guys ended up dead. You know him now?'

The kid turns to face me and slams the mixer on the counter. For a moment I think he's gonna throw a fist.

'You still have one ear, don't you? I told you I don't know him. But if you don't believe me, I can only think of a couple of ways to convince you.'

We stare at each other like warring lovers. I give out first.

'Okay, so you don't know him. Fine,' I say. 'Have you finished making my Senor Ramon?'

The kid laughs. Or it sounds like a laugh. Nothing in his face tells me he even knows what laughter is. He turns around and gets back to mixing, and five minutes later I've downed half my drink. It's a pretty good Manhattan, but I wince every time I take a sip. The kid stomps around like a spoilt brat.

When I'm almost done with my drink someone sits down beside me. I turn to see Square-head perched awkwardly on the stool.

'You look too old to be in here,' I tell him.

He tries to smile but his lips don't comply. Must be something in the water here. Or the kid's Manhattans.

'You got a death wish, arsehole?' he whispers. 'What the hell you doing here?'

'I came for a cocktail but I'm supping on some cherry juice your boy mixed up instead.'

Square-head glances at the barman and sighs. We watch him shake a cocktail for another customer.

'He's new, give him a break. He pressed the alarm to call me over. You been asking questions you shouldn't?'

'You tell me. I only asked to see my old buddy Kenya Oh. I heard he got himself some shares in this swanky new place and I wanted to congratulate him. Anything wrong with that?'

'What do you really want?'

'I'm looking for someone, the same person he was—and might still be—looking for. I thought we could help each other out, that's all.'

Square-head glances up at the balcony overlooking the dancefloor. I follow his gaze and see the old man sitting at a small table, watching us. He nods.

'You're in luck,' Square-head says.

'I usually am.'

He leans in to whisper into my one good ear. 'Behave. Or you won't be leaving here alive.'

He stands and grunts at me.

'I haven't finished my drink,' I say.

He grabs my collar and pulls me to my feet. I follow him along the bar and up the winding staircase on the far side of the dancefloor. On the semi-circular mezzanine we pass a couple of cosy-looking booths with cosy-kissing couples. Silver Beard doesn't assess our approach; his eyes are fixed on the dancefloor.

'Daganae Kawasaki,' Square-head announces.

I don't wait for an invitation to take a seat. Silver Beard studies me and finally nods at the bouncer, who retreats to stand between the bathroom doors.

Silver Beard's aged like hell. His silver hair, usually parted neatly to one side, is scruffy and wild, and his signature beard needs a trim. His pinstripe suit still looks expensive, but his top button's undone and his tie hasn't been strangled straight. I pick up his empty glass and poke my nose in.

'Rum. Christ, I didn't realise things were that bad.'

The old man smiles. Half-shrewd, half-tired. 'I thought you had disappeared,' he says. 'Finally emerged from your hole, have you?'

A waiter arrives with a fresh rum for Silver Beard. I order the same.

'Anything on your daughter?' he asks.

'About the same as you, from the looks of it. This'll damage your reputation, you know. People will stop hiring you if you can't even track down little girls.'

Silver Beard takes a long, slow sip, his sharp little eyes locked on mine. 'What does it matter? Fujii is dead anyway.'

'He left you money to look after her. That's what a protection racket's all about, isn't it?'

He shrugs. 'If your daughter is still alive, she's not in Sonaya. I did everything I could, now I'm calling time of death on the whole thing.'

'You're telling me you got nothing at all? What the hell have you been doing? Apart from nodding at people and drinking rum, I mean.'

'Well, I did get something, but I'm not sure you want to hear it.'

'I want to hear it.'

Silver Beard swirls the rum around in his glass. 'We all knew Fujii wasn't the greatest stepfather, and now we know why he left us money before he was killed. It was guilt money.'

'What happened? What did he do?'

Silver Beard runs a hand over his snowy beard.

'I asked you what he did.'

He takes a deep breath, looks everywhere but at me. 'I received word that he sent her to the Homework Clubs.'

I wait for more but it doesn't come.

'What do you mean?'

'I mean precisely what I said. While he was out getting drunk and picking up different women to bring home every night, he sent her out to Homework Clubs. Evidently he had friends who enjoyed spending time with pre-teen girls.'

Something in my stomach stirs and I feel my heart begin to race.

'Who?' I demand. 'Who the hell are these friends? I'll kill them all.'

'That I don't know, Kawasaki,' Silver Beard replies. 'If it's any consolation, physical contact isn't permitted in those places. It's simply old men pretending they're not.'

'Leering at my little girl. She's twelve years old, for fuck's sake. I should have gutted that cop bastard myself. Did you check the clubs?'

'Of course. They refused to talk. All the girls use fake names, and they look out for each other.'

'Didn't Fujii give you a photo?'

'He did, but Ryoko Nishi sent a troop of clowns to destroy our pachinko hall and confiscate our possessions. I could draw you a sketch, but I'm no artist.'

The waiter returns with my rum. I down half of it in one.

'You should have come to me earlier,' I say. 'We could have worked together.'

Silver Beard shakes his head. 'It wouldn't have made a difference. Nishi doesn't want either of us to have anything to do with your girl. Just follow my lead on this one, Kawasaki. Give it up.'

'And what about the Roses? You calling time on them, too?'

Silver Beard holds his glass to his lips, his breath slowly clouding the rim. 'Let's just say we're shy on support. The government doesn't want anything to do with us anymore, not since we got mixed up in *your* dirty laundry. Elections, you see. Now we're just another troublesome gang in the Rivers.'

'I don't see what made you different to begin with.'

Silver Beard dabs a napkin on his lips. 'The government backing our plays, that's what made us different. But I refuse to let go so easily. Do you know how hard I worked to gain control of the Rivers?'

'I can tell how hard you worked from the quality of your suit. What about these new boys? The pricks in helmets.'

'Aha. Yes, they're doing rather well.'

'Any idea who's behind them?'

Silver Beard considers me for a moment. 'Of course I do.'

'You and Bernd have a lot in common. You both look smug as shit when you're in exclusive charge of secrets. You gonna let me in on the joke?'

'There's no joke in the world funny enough to make *you* laugh, Kawasaki. The Shades aren't bothering you, are they?'

I let a swig of rum burn my throat and think of Ganzo's trashed basement.

'Just ignore them.'

'Everyone's sniping at me for staying away, but as soon as I start asking questions, I'm told to stick my head back in the sand. Sometimes I think nobody gets me at all.'

Silver Beard grins. '*I* get you, Kawasaki. That's why I'm

going to let you walk out of here alive, and I won't even have Mouse follow you home. But the last time you started poking around my business it cost me dearly. That *will not* happen again.'

We stare at each other.

'The music here is shit.' I stand and finish my drink. 'And the cocktails stink.'

'Take care, Kawasaki.'

Mouse escorts me down the stairs and the barman glares at me as I pass. I drop a coin into the tip jar. 'Thanks for the cocktail, Senor.'

Once we're at the front doors Mouse shoves me in the back with his gorilla hand and I stumble out into the street. The bouncer with the goatee laughs as Mouse falls in line beside him.

'Have a nice time in there, tramp?' Goatee asks.

I straighten up and brush my hands down my shirt. 'You wouldn't know, would you?' I say. 'You fucking doorstop.'

I turn and disappear into the bustling Busy Stream.

JIKO

When I see Su-young's face I know she believes in it more than I do. My stories are nothing compared to hers, and that realisation makes me feel like an imposter. She bites her lip and fixes me with the look I've come to fear—the look that tells me I can do no wrong, that she'll follow me to the end.

Maybe that's why I'm lurking in shadows in the dead of night, breathing into a bandanna. I grasp the throttle of my bike and wonder how it came to this.

I never wanted to run a gang or own the Rivers. I never wanted revenge or righteousness. After my dad put a bullet in my mum's brain and one more in his, what *I* wanted didn't enter the equation—I did only what was necessary to survive. But now I question where I'm leading them to, how this will finish. Does this end in The Heights? In death? Sometimes I wonder if I should cut and run, like Dag keeps urging. But I know he doesn't expect me to. He looks at me through neon-tinted glasses and sees only a fearless anarchist who'll fight to the end. I should have told him off the bat that he's got me wrong; that I'm not who he thinks I am, that I fell into this by accident. I'm not the hot-headed rebel destined to save Sonaya and make him young again. I'm just a drowning girl who's in too deep.

'They're coming out,' Bo-min says. She readjusts the sash that holds her purple hair, tightens her leather riding gloves. That's when I know she's nervous.

We stare at the restaurant door—a seafood place behind the strip that serves vats of creamy soup stuffed with oysters and decapitated octopuses. Half a dozen suits spill out. Four men, two women, red cheeks all round. Even from the alley I can smell the booze on them. They exchange endless handshakes and bows and finally split. Three of them head for the subway station for the short ride back to their luxury pads on the Pulse. Two men stumble towards the beach and the motorbike taxis; maybe home to their wives, or more likely to the seedy diversions of the pleasure quarter. The remaining woman disappears into the backstreets that lead to the old town. We leave our bikes and follow on foot.

The old town was built during the rush—traditional houses for the suits that oversaw the great revolution of Sonaya. Now it's home to the elite, a picturesque corner of a rotting island, complete with waterwheels, cobbled paths, and streams slaloming between cosy cottages. A small unit of officers patrol the lanes in pairs, making sure Sonaya's undesirables don't spoil the peace.

Yoo-ri Baek glances over her shoulder. She removes something from her designer handbag and I take that as my cue to rush her from the shadows. I muzzle her mouth and drag her into darkness. Su-young wrestles the pager from her hand as I pin her against the wall.

'*Help*,' Su-young says, reading the message. 'Was that the best you could do?'

Baek's eyes dance like pinballs, absorbing our bandanna-wrapped faces. Her quick, warm breaths moisten the palm of my hand.

'Make a sound and my friends will end this real fast.' The girls beside me respond with suitably menacing expressions. 'I had to convince them not to kill you tonight. I told them you were smart, that you'd do the right thing and that no one needed to die. Was I wrong?'

Beads of sweat glisten on Baek's forehead. Bo-min retreats to keep watch.

'You're going to reverse the bill,' I tell Baek. 'You're going to make them change it back.'

Tears pool in her eyes.

'You're not going to scream, are you?' I ask. She eyeballs the knife in Su-young's hand and shakes her head.

I remove my hand from her mouth and watch her splutter and cough.

'I—I can't,' she says. 'It's been approved already, and I'm only the Borrower. I don't have the power to reverse decisions like that. Please, I can't do anything.'

'Then perhaps my girls were right,' I say. 'Perhaps we *do* have to kill you.'

Su-young steps forward and brandishes her knife.

'Please! Don't!' Baek cries. 'I'll try. I'll do what I can.'

'*What* can you do?' Su-young snaps.

Baek's eyes search frantically for answers on the stone walls. 'I'll tell them I fudged the data, that the policy will tank. They'll *have* to withdraw it.'

Bo-min whistles; someone's coming. I raise a hand to silence Baek and we all hold our breaths. I hear footsteps, muted voices.

'We're going to disappear now,' I whisper to Baek. 'You had a pleasant evening, you understand? You ate dinner, had a few drinks, and went straight home. You didn't meet or speak to anyone.'

Baek nods.

'And tomorrow?'

'Tomorrow I'll tell them about the dodgy data. I'll tell them to retract the bill.'

'Yes. I knew I was right about you.'

A drone drifts over the rooftops nearby.

'Let's go,' I command.

We run full pelt through the alleys, out of the old town, back towards the ocean and our sleeping bikes behind the strip. We mount and speed off, my hands shaking as I guide my beloved Ducati through the backstreets, careening around corners and diving deeper into the darkness of the Rivers.

Comets of light catapult past me, transforming the Rivers into rushing streaks of colour as hot air assaults my eyes, drawing tears from my arid insides. I lose all sense of direction, as if I'm hurtling through the haunted tunnels of my mind, where light and sound have lost all meaning.

They call us Bosozoku, but *they* don't know shit. I used to swell with pride at the symbols of Japan plastered on my fuel tank, think I was connected to some great tradition of rebellion. But I was ignorant and idiotic. Just because I hate the government doesn't mean I'm not Sonayan. The Rising Sun on my chest still burns bright, but now my bike reveals the new me. A big black sun on a bed of red and white, Sonaya's flag of independence now takes centre stage on my Ducati. I lean forward and let my body bond with the purring beast beneath me, and only then do I find clarity about what I've done.

I threatened a government official.

I try to replay every action, make sense of every moment, but it's all a blur. The words I spoke emerged from someone else, the hand clamped down on Baek's mouth controlled by an unseen puppeteer. The only thing that feels real is the bike beneath me, a solid slice of truth sailing through a sea of grand illusion.

Someone calls my name. Gradually the world falls into focus, the smell of burning rubber and sound of roaring engines assault my storm of senses. I hear my name again and remember that I'm not alone.

I pull over and find myself beneath a warped fire escape barely hanging from a decrepit apartment block. I dismount, lean against the wall, and breathe. The girls pull up beside me and the fog inside my mind begins to slowly dissipate.

'The drone saw us,' Su-young says, tugging the bandanna down beneath her chin.

I shake my head. 'Our faces were covered.'

'They'll recognize our bikes.' She gestures to our rides— lime, purple, and red. 'They'll *know*.'

'They didn't see us do shit,' I say, trying to convince myself. 'As long as Baek keeps her mouth shut we've got nothing to fear.'

'We should've killed her,' Su-young says.

I glance at Bo-min, statue-still and silent.

'Well,' I say. 'I guess we'll find out tomorrow if we made the right decision.'

'Jiko,' Bo-min whispers.

I follow her gaze to a brick wall slimed with algae and realise she's not looking at all—she's listening. I hear it, too. They're closing in, and I know who they are before Su-young tells me.

'Nightshades.'

I catch glimpses of them in the alleys ahead, their black bikes burning through the concrete blocks like glimmering mechanical ghosts. Their roaring engines echo off the crooked walls like haunting howls.

'What a fucking racket,' Su-young says.

I almost manage a smile. 'You jealous?'

Su-young rolls her eyes and mounts her bike. Bo-min follows suit.

'What are you doing?' I ask.

Su-young smirks. 'Someone needs to remind these helmets whose hood they're in. *And* get them back for Ganzo. Come on, hurry up.'

I look between them and feel myself collapsing before their expectant eyes.

'There's only three of us,' I say. 'And at least twice as many of them. If we're gonna take them on, let's wait until we've got a full roster.'

'We've faced worse odds before,' Su-young says.

She revs her bike and Bo-min follows suit. I see the flicker of doubt in Su-young's eyes, a hint of disappointment. I feel the cowardice seep from me like a bad smell.

'Jiko,' Su-young says, with a hint of caution.

I have no choice. I swallow my fear and doubt. I've been careless, permitting my mask to slip away. I rapidly re-arrange my features into strange shapes I hope exude fearlessness, anger, leadership.

'For Ganzo,' I say, mounting my bike.

Su-young and Bo-min beam and take off after the Nightshades without another word.

Once more the night dissolves around me, but it feels good to let myself be led, to trail on someone else's tail. I focus on the tail lights of Bo-min's purple Honda and time evaporates as we ride this midnight carousel. I'm transported back to the harbour road of three years ago, when I first joined Ume and her band of outcasts. I remember every minute detail of my first ride: the beautiful neon streaks painting rainbows on the tarmac, the salty wind caressing my young and nervous cheeks, the flaming tail lights of our angry army, burning like bright beacons through our shared Sonayan night.

Back then I thought I was untouchable. I had the protection of the pack, of Ume. They planned and plotted and spoke of revenge, and even though I banged my fists in rhythm with my biker band, the reasons for our rage were lost on me. I was simply happy to be free, to ride beside my friends, girls who'd lived through ills like me. But the old gang's all gone now. Locked up or dead, or back within the buildings they once swore to burn into the ground.

And now I'm all alone. I might have my girls, but I can't tell them how I feel. I can't tell them all I see is blood every time I close my eyes. I can't tell them I picture my bullet bursting a man's brain, again and again. I can't let them know how weak, or scared, or human it's made me.

The illusion of my past crashes fast as Nightshades' motors growl up ahead. I pull up between Su-young and Bo-min, the tired head of our small triangle. We're on Ginkgo Lane, the boulevard leading south towards the uni. The ginkgo trees have dropped their vomit-fumed nuts and the unscavenged remnants have been crushed into the concrete by clumsy feet. Seven motorbikes face us in a V formation, their riders all dressed in black—except their violet leader.

I dismount along with Violet, and we converge like generals meeting before battle.

'Take your fucking helmet off,' I say.

Violet doesn't react.

'The Rivers belong to us,' I say, but even I can hear how hollow my words sound. I don't mean it, and I never have. Ume didn't care about power and control; she just wanted to destroy the industry that imprisoned and exploited us, the establishment that crafted this cruel city. But all the myths and rumours have moulded us, transformed us into something we're not. And now I've said it, the old mantra, like a draw-string doll blurting bullshit.

The rider shakes her head.

I glance over my shoulder. My girls are watching, waiting for a signal. They believe in me, and their faith is both an armour and a loaded pistol at my temple.

The violet rider flips up her visor to reveal eyes of liquid bronze and smooth ebony cheekbones.

'Well I'll be damned,' I say.

'The boys behind me might have other ideas,' she says. 'But you and I share the same goal, Jiko: to bring down the crooked suits that rule our city. We don't have to be enemies.'

I stare into her mercury eyes. 'Does Dag know?'

'Dag always knows less than I expect.'

'I've discovered that myself,' I say. 'But I've got a reputation to maintain. I can't return with news that I've conceded the Rivers to a new gang.'

'Nor can I, but maybe neither of us have to. I'll make sure my boys won't touch your turf, as long as your girls reciprocate. Call it a truce. You do what you do best and leave me to focus on the big players.'

I put as much spite into my laugh as I can. 'The big players? You make us sound like we're kids you can just brush off—we go play with our toys while you adults take care of business.'

'Well, forgive me Jiko, but I'm not exactly sure you even have a plan. All you have is a history of botched arson jobs. You're supposed to be the face of rebellion, but your face isn't even on the wanted wall of City Hall. Correct me if I'm wrong.'

'Oh, I have a plan, and it's *our* plan. You'll find out more in the morning, take my word for it. And you better think carefully about offering truces, especially when your boys put Ganzo out of business. I won't stand here and make deals with people who fuck with our friends.'

She tilts her head. 'I offered Ganzo plenty of chances to tell me the truth. He didn't take them.'

'The truth about what?'

'You'd better ask Dag about that. I told you, while you girls brood in basements and play with matches, I'm plotting to bring the big wigs down. The streets of Sonaya are haunted by a storm of hidden secrets, and I'm finally finding trails to truth. If you're smart, you won't get in my way.'

She removes her right leather glove, spits into her naked palm, and extends it towards me. I stare at it.

'We can help each other, Jiko, before the end. Trust me on *that*, at least.'

I bore into the black abyss of her eyes, searching for truth. I don't need more enemies. I don't need more friends, either, but the Nightshades are a poison I'd rather not swallow.

I spit into my palm and we mix an old-fashioned biker cocktail.

The rider pulls down her visor and returns to her waiting gang.

As I return to mine, my heart hammers in my chest, alive and angry.

There's only one place to find the panda when he's parted from his knives. I slip into the giant pachinko arcade north-west of The Cross and I'm greeted by a deafening circus of bouncing balls, clattering coins, and glazed, empty eyes. Countless rows of silver stools and ancient arcade machines form a labyrinth beneath the dim blinking lights, but Ganzo's easy to locate. He's superstitious, always uses the same machine. I find him in a corner on the second floor, still sporting his white sushi coat. He doesn't even look up when I fall onto the stool beside him.

'How's the luck?'

Ganzo shakes his head, his pug-like cheeks wobbling around his goatee. His fat thumbs are strumming the spring-loaded handles, flinging balls around the obstacle course of copper wiring. The panda always wears gloves to shield his skin from a world of poison and protect tomorrow's fish.

'Sorry about your bar,' I say.

Ganzo doesn't blink. His eyes are fixated by the chaotic dance of bounding balls. One of them lands in an on-screen cup—jackpot—and a cascade of virgin balls tumbles out into the tray below.

'Don't worry about it,' he replies. 'I found a part time gig in the eastern web. Decent place, decent people. Sometimes the fish is fresh, too.'

I know it must kill him to work for someone else, especially after all these years. I've never seen a man more faithful to his fish than Ganzo.

I turn to the machine before me. We're in the classics section; ancient apparatus from a time before the flashing screens of anime-themed slot machines. I insert a silver ball and flick the handle. The ball pings around the metal coils and disappears into the hole of death. I don't get the appeal.

'It's not gonna be forever,' Ganzo says. 'I can save some money, open something new. Now I know what I'm dealing with.'

'Did you see their faces?'

'They don't reveal their faces, that's their thing. I managed to hold off the Roses, but this gang is different. A guy comes in when I'm closing up, demands the usual payout to keep the badges from checking my licence. I told him I don't pay random strangers for random guarantees of shady service. When the Roses split, I expected a few new gangs to fight for the open turf. I just didn't expect anyone to mark their territory so quickly.

'They returned the following night during peak service. Six of them, all in leather biker gear and blacked-out helmets. Started smashing the place up. My customers ran up the stairs screaming. I grabbed my knife, but where was that going to get me? Six to one. They knocked me out, and when I woke up my place was trashed. Purple fucking petals everywhere.'

Ganzo tears his button eyes away from the machine and looks at me.

'I always thought I'd put up a fight,' he says. 'But I just let them ruin everything I've worked so hard for.'

'You did the right thing. They would've killed you otherwise.'

Ganzo shrugs and peers glumly at his gloved hands. I slam the handle and the ball briefly bulldozes around before disappearing into the hole again. Nothing.

'I wasn't there for you,' I say.

'You've got your own problems. Any luck finding your daughter?'

'Silver Beard said she was in the Homework Clubs. He went snooping but no one talked.'

'You know that Homework Club girls don't spill to outsiders. But you could try Bull.'

'Bull?'

'Remember the old gangs? Bull was one of the big boys, but now he's old and alone. I've heard he's spending his twilight years pretending he's fifty years younger. If you want info on the Homework Clubs, he's your man.'

'And why would he talk to me?'

'He probably won't. But the kids who work in those places look out for each other; they're not going to hand out names and addresses to one-eared beasts like you. Bull, though … well, he's closer to your age. Maybe if you can convince him your intentions are honourable …'

Ganzo's ball drops into the black hole. He turns to me.

'I heard you'd left the island. I wouldn't have blamed you, you know. Little Sister might have split, but it seems you're still at the centre of the storm.'

'What the hell does that mean?'

'I thought Fujii's death would mark the end,' Ganzo says, 'but I don't think the past is done with us yet.'

'*Us*? What are you talking about?'

Ganzo rubs a ball between his thumb and forefinger. He frowns at it, like he's trying to stare it out of existence.

'The Nightshades,' I say. 'They only wanted your money, right?'

Ganzo meets my eyes and blinks.

The unmistakable sound of gunshots echoes across the familiar crash of clashing metal. I stand and search out the source until I see a little girl with a buzz cut, sprinting through the aisles. Armed cops follow close behind.

'Leave Sonaya?' I say, dropping my balls into Ganzo's cup. 'No chance.'

I leave Ganzo blinking dumbly as I launch off and chase the dogs down the winding stairs. The floor below is just as rammed with pachinko zombies.

'Everybody down!' an officer screams.

The zombies comply with the command, but the clamour of steel balls hardly ceases. I crawl on my hands and knees to the end of the row, peek round the corner. The cops are scouring the aisles. One of them approaches me and I press my face against the fetid carpet; I sense the barrel of the gun aimed at the back of my head. The cop steps over me and moves on. When I look up again, I see the crown of a small shaved head. The Dove.

I risk a whistle and the girl looks up, terror tattooed on her young face. We shuffle over to each other on our elbows. The orchestra of steel is quietening, but the background noise continues to compete with the clamouring commands of the searching officers.

'The hell are you doing here, pigeon?' I whisper. 'Don't tell me they're after you.'

The girl shakes her head. Fear burns through her retinas.

I glance around for the cops. Good job the arcade is so damn huge and loud as hell. Someone makes a run for the stairs. A new player. The cops bellow orders and gunshots pepper the machines. I crane my neck and find the fire exit.

'Ready to fly, little dove?' I ask.

She's frozen to the floor with shell shock, elbows stuck to her sides. She might need my help to spread those wings.

'Three …' I start. Countdowns are my thing. 'Two … One … Fly.'

I grab the girl by the scruff of her shirt and we dash for the door. We burst through and emerge breathless into another neon night. I keep my hand on her back and drive us on. We turn into a narrow unlit alley two blocks down. We face each other, struggling to catch our breaths, her hazel eyes scanning the walls, avoiding mine.

She looks the same as before; baggy clothes hang from her skinny frame, hand-me-downs from Jiko and her girls, no doubt, her scabby scalp peeking through her close-cropped hair.

'What happened?' I ask. 'You shit on the wrong statue?'

'I was making a delivery,' she says. She might be scared, but her voice is bold and brazen. 'A bunch of junkies on the third floor.'

'Coke?'

She shrugs. 'It pays well.'

'Damn right it does. Didn't you hear about the Borrowing? They're not fucking around anymore. You get caught carrying, you die, and little pigeons aren't exempt. Don't go near that shit again, you hear me?'

The Dove nods, but it looks like she's already stopped listening. The monotonous drill of English grammar seeps from an open window above—a cram school class in full flow.

'You still boarding with the Bosozoku?'

'Mostly,' she says. 'But they're always busy, and they don't have much work for me.'

'You're still a kid,' I say. 'Why don't you go to school and learn something?'

'Are you serious? They'd lock me up in one of those homes. You never wonder why the streets are full of us? Those places are dives. Twenty kids to a room, no food or water, and beatings every day. The whole welfare system's fucked. I've learnt that much.'

I laugh out loud. 'Jiko been teaching, has she?'

The Dove doesn't answer.

'What happened to your parents, kid?'

She fingers her nostril absentmindedly and smears the result on her shirt. 'Never knew my dad. Mum was a drunk. Sold her body for a ferry ticket and left in the middle of the night. She's probably lying in some gutter in Tokyo.'

I nod. Familiar story.

The Dove looks like she's itching to get away.

'Are the girls feeding you enough?' I ask. 'You look skinny.'

'And you look fat.' She jabs a finger into my gut. 'You drinking too much?'

'I drink just right, and we're not talking about me,' I say. 'Let's get some food in you before you fade away.'

○

There's no sign of the cops as we emerge from the alley, but we're on the end of some funny looks as we wander the labyrinth of backstreets towards the business district. The Dove realises it too and falls behind me, but I stride on, glancing back at her at intervals like I'm being stalked by a stray cat.

'Can't you just walk beside me?' I bark over my shoulder.

'You walk too fast,' she says. 'I can't keep up.'

I turn to face her. 'You're not falling further behind, which means we're walking at the same speed. What's wrong? You embarrassed to be seen with me?'

The Dove simply stares at me with her hands stuffed in her pockets.

'What do you wanna eat?' I call over my shoulder.

The Dove shrugs.

'You like log?'

'Sure.'

I lead her to a cheap take-out place near the Pulse, a tiny shack crammed between two goshitels, with smoke seeping from the open doors and a line of customers complaining outside. We join the queue and the fragrance of fake meat invades my nostrils.

'You seen Shinji recently?' I ask.

'Once or twice. Why?'

'He's up to something dodgy. Same as always.' I glance down at the girl's wide eyes with a feeling dangerously close to fondness. 'He's not like you, he doesn't speak before he thinks. And I know when he's lying, because words come out of his mouth.'

'He quit flying Kosuke's messages,' the Dove says.

'I know that much. What I want to know is *why*.'

'Is this why you're buying me food? So I'll tell you about Shinji?'

'I'm buying you food because a wine bar's no place for a girl to grow up, and a biker posse aren't ideal guardians. You need … proper food … nutrients.'

'If you think log has any nutrients, it's you that needs to go to school. It's just mushed up soy proteins, and do you know how many MSGs they pump in to give it flavour?'

'You sure you don't go to school?'

The Dove smirks briefly.

I order two portions of barbecued log which arrive in steaming paper cups, impaled by tiny toothpicks. The Dove dives in before I've even settled up.

'Listen, I've got a job for you,' I say. 'One that won't get you killed.'

The Dove glances up as she devours her meal.

'I'm looking for a man named Bull. Apparently he's a regular at the Homework Clubs. You know him?'

'How much is it worth? My rates have gone up.'

'I'm not asking you to carry pollen. I'll pay my usual rates.'

'I don't have many contacts in the Homework Clubs anymore,' the Dove says, avoiding my eyes and burrowing into her log.

Whatever fondness I briefly felt for this pigeon is rapidly fading. 'Fine,' I snap. 'Name your price, but I'll only pay if I get results.'

The Dove peers into her empty cup and glances greedily at mine, untouched and smoking hot. I sigh and hand it over. 'You know where to find me. Now get out of here. Fly back to Jiko's coop.'

The girl dissolves into the darkness without a single word of thanks, chewing on my steaming dinner. As I watch her disappear a fleeting shiver slithers down my spine; summer has expelled her last warm breath, and Sonayan nights are cooling. I feel the crisp breeze caress my neck as I return to join the queue; I should fill my belly before the heavens open with their nocturnal shower of sweet liquor. Just as I'm about to order, the sound of gunshots pierces my peace.

For a moment everything stops. Motorbikes skid to a halt, the riders scanning their surroundings for the source of the ferocious sound. Faces appear at windows, peering out to scour the streets below for a spectacle of red. The rest of us—the lonely drunks and dregs, nowhere to be, no one to see, the sorry and the soulless—scrutinise each other, searching for humanity in the bleary bloodshot eyes that stare back. Drones descend like sentinels sent from a scrapyard in the sky, their flashing lights causing us to avert our eyes, guilty of our secret sins.

A battered ambulance chugs past, its rasping siren failing to disperse the gathered swarm of idle bikers. After cars were banned in Sonaya, the streets adapted to a two-wheeled ecosystem, but now they're overgrown and wild, like a jungle left to flourish. We watch the cab's pained progress, an agonising crawl for an impotent relic.

Word soon filters through the streets. A drug bust at a pachinko hall followed by a thrilling chase and shower of bullets. A wave of relief washes over the anxious mass of mixed spectators. Faces disappear from windows, bikes return to burning rubber, and us faceless street-folk resume our nightly wanders. Don't worry, everyone. It's just another corpse or two. Just the police doing their job.

I'm woken by the sound of knuckles rapping on my door. I growl into my pillow and try to sleep, but the knocking won't cease. My mouth is dry and tastes like death. I drag myself from bed and open the door.

'What the hell are you doing here?'

The Dove glares at me. 'You gave me a job,' she spits back. 'Most pigeons would charge double for a turnaround this quick.'

I rub my face and let her in. 'What time is it?'

She stomps over to the window and forces it open. 'Past midday. It reeks in here.'

I squint as hazy daylight pours into the room. 'I don't get up this early.'

'I can see that. How much did you drink last night?' She scans the battleground of bottles beside my mattress.

'I don't need life lessons from a kid. Wait here.'

I stumble to the bathroom downstairs and relieve my bladder. A painful sight peers at me from the mirror, bloodshot eyes and blotched dry skin. I splash my face with water but the towel is scarred with suspicious stains, so I trudge back upstairs with a dripping face to find the Dove rinsing bottles in the sink.

'What did you find out?' I ask, shouldering her aside to fill the kettle.

'Payment first.'

I huff and raid the tin beneath the sink. Every minor movement of my head feels like a drilling operation. I place a couple of notes onto the Dove's open palm, but she doesn't flinch until I add another to the pile. The kettle squeals.

'Lucky for you,' the Dove says, 'it turns out Bull has a strict routine. He's been going there for years and he's something of a celeb among the girls. They say-'

'I didn't ask for his biography,' I say, stirring my coffee.

The Dove clenches her jaw and glowers at me. 'Fine. You can find him in Angel Eyes tonight. That good enough for you?'

I sip my coffee and burn my lips. My head is pounding. I take a bottle of whisky from the shelf and drop a dram into my coffee. 'What?'

The Dove stares at me the same way I stare at the tangle of hair in the shower drain.

'I'm not running jobs for you anymore,' she says.

'Why not?'

'Because you're pathetic.'

I'm not surprised by her judgement, but I am surprised by the blaze in her eyes. Alcoholic mother—bad memories, I guess. She crosses the room, snatches the whisky bottle from the counter and pours the remains down the sink. She yanks the door open and pauses.

'Oh,' she says, her voice laced with venom. 'Jiko said she needs to see you. Tonight.'

'Tonight?' I say. 'What about Bull? You've double-booked me.'

I don't need to look up to feel the Dove's ferocious glare. 'She'll be in the Catfish at ten. There. Now me and you are done.'

She exits with a dramatic slam of the door.

I sip my Irish coffee and begin the process of feeling somewhat human. It'll take a while.

○

My stomach growls as I descend the worn stairs. The boarding house spills its familiar hollow sounds. Floorboards creak beneath stomping feet, pipes gurgle through warped and peeling walls, arguments flare behind battered wooden doors. The old landlady is boiling tea in the lobby and offers me a cup as I slog towards the front door.

'How many times do I have to tell you about letting people in to see me?' I complain.

'You want me to stop the pigeons from bringing messages now?' the crone answers without looking up. 'What a fine idea. Then you'll complain that you didn't get your messages because I didn't let them in.'

She's not a pigeon, she's a dove, I want to say. But all I say instead is, 'Just ask them to write it down and leave it with you down here.'

'I'm not running a post office. And you're behind on rent.'

'Later,' I say, stepping out into the waning afternoon. A brownish haze shrouds the concrete cityscape, the air choked by the dirty deposits of China's farting factories. Signboards hang sadly above closed doors, unlit and ignored, and blocks of blank stucco stare back at me. I've got two appointments and an empty stomach, and a painful root canal in progress somewhere behind my eyes. I'm in no condition to tackle this evening alone.

I rap my knuckles on Shinji's graffitied door and he greets me with a sour expression and a sea of speckled acne.

'What do you want?'

'Charming. I want a sidekick. Someone to make me look big.'

His stare is loaded with suspicion. 'Why me?'

'You've got experience. Sometimes I feel like you get me. And, to be honest, I don't have any other options.'

'Not tonight. I'm heading out to check on Eiko.'

'I'll make it worth your while.'

Shinji glances over his shoulder and adjusts the mangy cap on his head. 'Fine.'

He follows me out and I lead us through the web towards the pleasure quarter. We take a path illuminated by swinging paper lanterns, my evening eyes assaulted by their garish glows, and duck into a ramen bar. It's small and smells like oak and wasabi and miso. The proprietor is a squat woman wrapped in a navy kimono, her wiry hair pulled back into a brutal bun. She glares with beady eyes as Shinji and I sit at the counter. The flashing red light above the door doesn't seem to bother her; we're her only customers, and a tagged man's money is as good as anyone else's.

'What do you want?' she asks, deadpan.

'Miso,' I say.

'Soy,' the kid says. 'With log.'

'Pork or beef?'

'Pork.'

The woman's nostrils flare like we've asked her to throw in a free tap-dance. She turns her substantial back to us and busies herself with fire and water. Shinji cracks apart his wooden chopsticks and picks at the side dishes on the counter.

'We haven't done this in a while,' I say, watching him attack the bowls.

'I haven't missed it,' Shinji replies, spraying the counter with morsels of half-chewed radish. 'I've been doing just fine since you disappeared.'

'So I see,' I say drily. 'You gonna tell me who you're working for, or you gonna keep holding out on me?'

Shinji turns and gurns with a mouth full of kimchi mush.

'You're such a little shit,' I say, averting my eyes.

'You're the one who walked away without even shaking my hand. Then you turn up three days later asking me for help. Typical Dag. And now you want information too—*for free.*' He points his chopsticks at me. 'Want my advice? Stay the hell out of my business. Stay the hell out of everyone's business. Go back to your attic and wallow like a pig in shit. That's what you do best, and it makes life easy for the rest of us.'

We stare at each other. The woman drops two ramen bowls before us with such force that the soup spills out onto the counter. I wipe the mess with a napkin and watch Shinji violate his noodles. Soup dribbles down his chin as he tears through chunks of pork-scented log.

'It must hurt,' he says, wiping his chin with the back of his hand.

'What?'

'Not being needed.' He swallows and balances his chopsticks on his bowl. 'Being needed—that's important, right?'

'I need you like a dog needs ticks.'

Shinji shakes his head. 'Eiko needs me and I need her. She gives my life purpose. Jiko needs her girls and they need her. That's what keeps us going.' He stares at me cautiously, like he's determining whether or not to free the words waiting eagerly on his tongue. 'But no one needs you, do they?'

I dig into my sloppy noodles and ignore the eyes boring into my face.

'You've got a daughter, somewhere out there, but she doesn't give a shit about you,' he continues. 'And if she *did* know who you were, she'd probably run a mile.'

'Don't pretend you didn't miss me. I know you were sulking in Nakata's place, hoping to bump into me.'

Shinji laughs. 'You? Listen, I'm big enough to admit that for a while we had a decent thing going on. You helped me, I helped you. But you lost all of that when you slipped off the face of the earth. Yeah, I needed someone. I'm fourteen. I can't do everything on my own. Sometimes I need help. But you think that's from you?' He shakes his head again. 'Dag, the mask has slipped. You're not the hard man I thought you were. There's a new game going on now, and you're not playing. You're not even on the board.'

I drag my eyes from my food and watch his upper lip curl.

'Hell,' he says. 'You've fallen so damn far, you're blind to it.

It's a good job you haven't found your daughter, she'd be ashamed-'

In a flash I'm on my feet, gripping Shinji by his throat. The bowls crash to the floor in an explosion of steaming soup and shattered porcelain. The woman beats me with a dishcloth but I brush her off as my fingers tighten around Shinji's skinny neck. He coughs and splutters, spewing spit and soup over my knuckles, his face glowing red, fingers clawing at my clasp.

Tears pool in his eyes, his face screws up, and he cries like a kid.

A kid.

The mist dissolves and I throw Shinji to the floor with one last thrust. He topples over the stool and lands in a grave of soup and shattered crockery. He curls into a foetal position, starts sobbing and drooling into his trembling hands. It's the sound that hits me. The gurgling, wounded squeal of a broken child.

The woman thrusts a kitchen knife at me and orders me to leave, but I barely hear her. I stand over Shinji, my heart racing, and watch his slow, gasping breaths. He turns his head to look at me, and his eyes cut me deeper than any knife ever could. Pure pain. Fear.

I turn and leave before the image burns itself onto my brain.

○

Darkness descends like a silent curtain, dropped by the drunk puppeteer who pulls Sonaya's frayed and ragged strings. But I don't see it fall. I see nothing but the advance of my boots on the cracked concrete paths that sprawl through the pleasure quarter in jagged, snaking streams. My mind has absconded to another plane, the memory of the last hour retreating to the teeming vaults of repressed remembrance. Time evaporates as I trudge blindly through the seedy labyrinth, hounded by raging searchlights blazing purple and bright pink.

Angel Eyes is a custard-coloured hub of hideous crumbling brick. I gaze numbly at the door, blinking myself back into existence. Crass graffiti stares back between peeling posters of girls dressed as maids and posing with feather dusters. The door swings open and in a flash my arm is clasped by a teenage girl in a billowing skirt and blazer. The lobby smells of candy floss and the walls explode with anime. Sweet-talking teens flash gummy smiles across the counter, but a sudden high-pitched alarm swiftly ends their greeting. These places cater for all breeds of weirdos, but tagged men like me are a step too far.

'Bull,' I say. 'I'm not here for your services. Where's Bull?'

The girls exchange nervous glances and one of them looks close to tears. Destruction Dag, destroying the dreams of kids across the city.

'Room 12,' one of the girls tells me in a voice that's barely a squeak.

I dart up the stairs and burst through the door of room 12. I'm greeted by the familiar and depressing sight of an old man sat opposite two schoolgirls. The man is pushing seventy, but he's dressed in skin-tight leathers, his skull tattoos glaring at me from his wrinkly neck. He stands and curls a lip in my direction. 'The hell do you want?' he growls.

'You Bull?'

He doesn't answer.

'My name's Daganae Kawasaki. I'm looking for someone and I heard you might be able to help.'

Bull glowers at me.

'Give us three minutes,' he tells the girls. 'Get yourselves something while you wait.' He hands them some bills and they squeeze past me out the room. With a wave of his heavily inked hand Bull invites me to sit down.

'You had a bad day, or you always look like that?' he asks.

When I don't answer he tries again.

'What's this about? Who you after?'

I glance at the textbooks and notes on the table. I pick up a sheet at random and scan the handwriting. Dates, names, bullet points; an outline for an essay: *Despite the protestations of many, particularly those in Tokyo, it can be argued that the restrictions on internet use and the ban on mobile phones in Sonaya, first introduced in 2031 and 2033 respectively, have positively effected Sonayan citizens. In this essay ...*

'Your three minutes are going fast, boy,' Bull says.

'I think this is the first time I've seen a Homework Club being used properly,' I say.

Bull scratches his white moustache with skinny, tattooed fingers, so many little letters inked on his skin I'm unable to decipher a single word. 'It keeps me busy. Now talk—fast.'

I eye the bottle of scotch on the table. Something to bring me back to life.

'Do you mind?'

Bull blinks. 'Not if you can neck it in two minutes.'

I stand and cross the room, passing through the stench of Bull's worn and rusty leathers. I pick up two glasses but Bull shakes his head.

'I quit,' he says. 'Now hurry up.'

I fill my glass to the rim and return to my chair. I sip my drink. The whisky's better than most of the stuff you get in these places.

'I'm looking for my daughter. She's twelve years old. Name's Maaya. I'm told she was sent to these places by her stepfather.'

Bull rubs his stubbly chin. 'Her stepfather did that? And what did you do to him?'

'I would have killed him if someone else hadn't beaten me to it.'

Bull grins and I catch a glint of gold.

'I have to admit, I don't recognise the name. You got a picture?'

I shake my head. 'I didn't even know she existed until recently.'

'There aren't too many girls that young in clubs like this.'

I take another sip of whisky. It no longer tastes good.

'This is Fumiko's patch,' Bull continues. 'That prune-wrinkled pimp's a piece of work, but one thing I'll say for her is that she doesn't recruit them *that* young.'

Fumiko Muira. A seventy-something bag of hollow bones who plays puppeteer to the marionettes of the pleasure quarter. A vile old thing for sure, but I've seen brief glimpses of light between her rotten rolls of wrinkled skin.

'I figured as much,' I say.

'That's not to paint a pretty picture of her, mind. This is a nasty business and most of the people involved in it are nasty, too.'

I glance at the skulls on his neck. 'And what about you?'

Bull pins me with such a sour stare I almost regret the question.

'I hear you were a big face a long time ago,' I say. 'One of the original Sonayan Bosozoku. Have you softened in your old age?'

Bull eyeballs me. For a moment I think he might hit me, but then his taut expression softens.

'My missus died in thirty-six,' he says evenly. 'She was a bitch sometimes, but she was a fucking comet, too. A vast chunk of stellar rock catapulting through Sonaya. I've never seen a woman look so mean and sexy on a motorbike. We were the biggest gang in Sonaya, and she held it all together. Oh, I was by her side, sure, but she was the one everyone feared. Her bike roared like a beast from the underworld, and her tits were bigger than her head. Fuck, those were good ol' days.'

I finger the condensation on my glass. Bull stares at something over my shoulder, as though a window to the past has replaced my missing ear.

'She had just turned fifty, but reaching the half-C destroyed her, that and the booze. And on the eve of her big party, while I dived into a drunken coma, she threw herself off the roof.'

He meets my eyes with a dogged expression.

'I'm the only one of the old gang left. A man gets lonely.'

I gesture to the mess of papers on the table. 'So you get kicks out of this, do you? Talking to teenage girls?'

'That's all it is. Talking. They get help … and so do I. You think there's something wrong with that?'

He massages his tattooed knuckles.

'I don't know anymore,' I admit. I finish my drink and stand. 'If you hear anything...'

He looks at me blankly. As I head for the exit he picks up an essay and begins to read. When the door closes behind me, I swear I hear the sound of paper being torn.

I like to see the hands that sculpt my sushi. I like to see the gleam of the knife as it skins and fillets my fish. If it's not Ganzo, I want a wizened veteran with crow-feet wrinkles and grey hair. I want them to slide a thumb over the tuna's scales and tell me how many brothers and sisters it left behind.

You don't get any of that in the Catfish. It's the biggest sushi chain on the island with all of two stores. They're both as shit as each other, but someone must like them. This one's in a pitiful corner of the northern Rivers, a few blocks south of the Pulse; a dingy basement under a comic book shop full of sweaty fat suits who slaver over cartoon tits.

The booths are tiny and only sit two people. It's a simple set-up: a table, a bowl of miso soup, a pot of soy sauce to soak your wasabi. There's nothing to look at apart from the rickety conveyor belt that hauls sushi around the restaurant in an endless sad parade.

I drop onto a wooden stool and assess the scrolling fish. The squid smells two days old; the eel looks like it was attacked by a maddened cat; the plate of salmon roe looks like the morning after a dodgy curry. I slurp my miso soup and wait for something that might have been swimming in the ocean this week.

The couple in the next booth have been arguing ever since I sat down. The girl's parents are shipping her off to the Hermit Kingdom; they must be loaded to afford tuition in Seoul. The guy is begging her not to leave, whining like a deflating balloon. I picture him in five years' time, wanking in the corner of the comic shop upstairs. Soon they stop talking altogether, until they finally get up and leave. All that remains is silence and a sour mood.

I'm done waiting on the belt to bring me some edible sushi, so I pluck a plate of salmon and drown it in soy sauce to disguise its sickly brown hue. I'm still chewing through my first mouthful when Jiko stealthily slips into my booth. She's wearing a baggy beanie that hides her hair and without asking she swipes a nigiri.

'Is this eel?' she asks through a mouthful of mushed rice.

'I wish it were.'

Jiko grimaces then swallows hard.

'You're late,' I say.

She shrugs and bats her eyelashes. The mush inside her mouth looked cuter.

'Why are we meeting here anyway?' I ask. 'You get a kick out of food poisoning?'

'It wasn't *my* choice. *I've* got taste.'

'I do too, or at least I did before I came in here. I can't remember what it was like.'

Jiko stirs my soup with a chopstick and takes an uninvited swig.

'You remember I told you about Suzie?' she asks, smacking her lips. 'The one who got locked up?'

'For your failed attempt at making a bonfire of Sakura.'

'Right.' Jiko plucks a dish of nori-wrapped roe from the belt. 'We got a message from some pigeon, a real filthy kid, said if we wanted to see Suzie again we'd better show up tonight. So here we are.'

I drop my chopsticks on the table. 'What do you mean *we*? What the hell does this have to do with me? Why didn't you bring your girls?'

Jiko's grin brims with mischief. 'I did. Su-young and Bo-min are upstairs. I thought we could do with a little extra protection.'

I blow a bitter puff air from my cheeks. 'And I thought you wanted me for my company.'

'Your company hasn't been much fun for a while now, Dag. I don't drink with old men out of pity, you know.'

I yank a yellowtail off the belt and confront it. I can take a lot of insults, but smearing the quality of my company? She's probably right. Maybe I *should* make an effort.

'What's wrong?' she asks.

'What's *not* wrong? It feels like I've spent my entire evening pissing people off. Shinji said some things I didn't like and … well … let's just say I fucked up.'

'So you saw red.' Jiko slips a hip flask out of her boot. 'The sake here is overpriced,' she says, unscrewing the lid and swigging. 'How did things end?'

'With Shinji snivelling on the floor and me feeling like the world's biggest scumbag. You should have seen me, Jiko. I scared myself.'

She sizes me up, eyes narrowed. I can almost see a sly dig being held back.

'We all fuck up,' she says finally. 'Don't beat yourself up about it. Shinji's a tough kid. Maybe he just said some home truths you need to take a closer look at.' She hands me the flask and I practically drain it. 'Wow, look at that, he *does* remember how to have a good time.'

Something about my reaction makes her smile and she grabs her flask and swigs, her eyes firmly fixed on mine.

'This little gathering wouldn't have anything to do with Yoo-ri Baek by any chance, would it?' I ask.

'Why would you say that?'

'Su-young and Bo-min have a lot of fine qualities, but subtlety isn't one of them. Are you sure you're not aiming too high? This isn't like taking out an anonymous Rose. If something happens to a Borrower, no one's going to look the other way. Your faces will be all over the front page, and with your gang as colourful as a rainbow's bright turd, you'll be in cuffs before you can even rev your engines.'

Jiko munches mutely.

'You know I'm right. Suzie's locked up in The Heights, so who the hell's in a position to threaten her life? Whatever you've done, you must have upset someone with a lot of influence.'

She looks up and pouts like a teen tired of being told off. 'I'm always upsetting people, Dag, it's how I get what I want. And right now I want a shit load of sake that doesn't come with a lecture. Do you think I can get one tonight?'

I stroke my beard to hide my stretching lips.

'By the way,' Jiko says, 'have you seen Ganzo since his bar got trashed?'

'Last night. He seems to be taking it well enough. Why?'

'I heard a rumour that the Nightshades wanted something from him, that he wouldn't talk. Your name was mentioned.'

'Ganzo?' I shake my head. 'What information could he have, other than how to undress a flounder? Where'd you hear that anyway?'

'I'm more resourceful than you think. Don't be surprised if you see me among the First Bands tomorrow.'

'Damn, I'd forgotten about that.'

It's been weeks since the people of Sonaya took the National Intelligence Tests, the government's genius method of distributing votes to a nation of morons.

'What? You think the whole idea's dumb? Jiko asks. 'Or are you scared for everyone to see how low you ranked?'

'I'm reserving judgement,' I say. 'Till I see how many votes I get.'

Jiko smirks and removes her beanie, and I watch as red hair falls over her shoulders. When I glance back at her the smile is gone.

'What is it?' I ask.

I follow her gaze to the sushi belt. The dishes continue to

circulate, but I don't recognize what's on the plates. It doesn't look like any fish I know. It's pink and raw, all right, but it's unlike anything I've seen before, especially in the Catfish. We watch half a dozen dishes go past before I grab one. I remove the plastic lid and sniff. I frown and pass it to Jiko. She shakes her head. Then she glances at the belt again and covers her mouth.

'Oh shit, Dag.'

I grab the dish before it disappears and I don't need to remove the lid to know what it is: a thin, tanned finger, nail painted black.

Jiko heaves and retches and rinses her mouth with sake.

'Who did that belong to?' she manages to ask.

I've got an idea. I'm sure Jiko does too.

The conveyer belt stops with a sudden jolt and the final dish is empty bar a tiny scroll of paper. Jiko stares at it like it might explode. I pick it up and carefully unroll it. Handwritten.

'Thank you for coming,' I read. 'I did say you'd see your friend again if you did. Unfortunately, we couldn't fit her onto a single plate, so we improvised. This is what happens when you interfere.'

The colour disappears from Jiko's face. Tears escape her eyes and slide down her pastel cheeks.

I drop the scroll, unsheathe Old Trusty, and charge out of the booth. We burst into the kitchen and the stench hits us straight away. The kitchen is bathed in blood, abandoned and empty, apart from the rest of Suzie's mutilated body.

Bo-min paces between the tables, her fists clenched. Su-young slumps over the bar, black mascara slaloming from her eyes. Jiko stares at her drink, her complexion still faintly green.

Vino Ryusui is closed for the night, the customers kicked out early as flickering candles paint trembling shadows across the walls. A ponytailed Bosozoku girl with green eye shadow refills my glass; the others sit around their tables glumly, glancing now and then at Jiko as if awaiting her instruction.

'We shouldn't have left her there,' Bo-min says.

'We didn't have a choice,' I tell her. 'Did you wanna end up dead?'

Bo-min stops pacing and glowers at me, her eyes burning with hatred.

'Listen,' I say. 'We couldn't stay there. I don't know who did that to your friend-'

'Suzie,' Bo-min interrupts.

'Suzie,' I say. 'I don't know who did that to Suzie, but you can bet the cops will be there right now, slapping police tape over the door. And after your little chat with Yoo-ri Baek, you're all lucky you're not banged up. So sit down, and let's think.'

In a flash she's close enough for me to count her lashes, her thin fingers locked around my collar. Bo-min talks better with her eyes, and her blinking words beat through loud and clear. I concede and raise my hands in apology.

'Sit down, Bo-min,' Su-young says in a resigned voice.

Bo-min releases my shirt, shoots me a look laced with pity, and turns away.

'They could have killed or cuffed us there and then,' Su-young says. 'So why didn't they? They set a trap and we walked into it. Why bother warning us when they can finish the job and toss our ashes into the Pulse?'

'I'm wondering the same thing,' I say.

'*They*,' Jiko says. It's the first thing she's said since we arrived. She lifts her eyes from the wine and looks at each of us in turn. 'There's no such thing as *they*. When you look at City Hall you might see a solitary building, but we're not fighting some united army. Ryoko Nishi, Fumiko, the Nightshades, they all work for themselves, and that cesspool of a government has a dozen different factions all engaged in their own dodgy dealings. Any one of them can order a hit. Any one of them can hire a squadron of cops for the night. Baek might be a government drone, but we don't know who she answers to. If she was on the straight and narrow, she would have reported us directly to the top, and then we'd have been greeted by cops instead of … instead of Suzie. Whoever Baek works for didn't want us dead, at least not yet.'

We all sip our drinks and absorb her words.

'Fumiko,' Su-young says.

Jiko dismisses the suggestion with a wave of her hand. 'Fumiko wouldn't have done that to Suzie.'

'Fumiko would do *anything* to protect her business. And Baek's Borrowing is good for business.'

Jiko looks doubtfully into her glass and then drains it.

I glance around the room at the defeated, frightened faces. Some of these girls are younger than Jiko, and none of them look anywhere near as brave. The ponytailed bargirl refills our glasses with a trembling hand, her eyes glazed and unblinking. The chubby brunette next to Su-young chews on her nails like jerky while the pink-haired girl beside her beats the table leg with her boot.

'Whoever it was,' I say, standing, 'you've reached the end of the road. A warning is never the final word of a conversation. Someone out there is gunning for you, and you can bet the government will go public with this—especially now the elections are looming. And you're all sat here brooding in the one place they know where to find you.'

'So what do you suggest we do?' Bo-min asks venomously.

'Pack your things, prep your bikes. Leave the wine. Come polling day you'll have half the drones of Sonaya looking for you, maybe sooner.'

Jiko, Bo-min, and Su-young exchange glances. This isn't a game anymore, and finally, they realise. I make for the stairs, trying to veil the fear and sadness that churn in my stomach like a fast-growing tumour.

'If I were you, I'd cocoon myself, and fast,' I add, looking at each of the girls in turn. 'And once you're all transformed, head for the port. It's time to say goodbye.'

Once I'm out on the street I let the night air fill my lungs and try to blink away flashbacks of the blood-stained kitchen. I slip into an alley and vomit, and my whole body shakes as regurgitated wine slides down the wall in violent rivulets of red.

10

SHINJI

The lights of the Pipe flicker like fucked up fireflies. I close my eyes but the flashing strobes slice through and flashbacks beat my brain like lightning bolts; his hairy knuckles under my chin; his flaring nostrils; the mad whites of his eyes.

I swallow and touch my neck. It's like his fingers are still there, choking the air out of me. I open my eyes, stand, and move through to the next carriage. A gang of kids lounge on the shabby seats, their eyes finding mine as the door clatters shut behind me.

'Toll,' says the biggest of the group. He's short and wide, his face an ugly mess of blackheads begging to be burst. As he waddles over, his friends hang back and try to look menacing.

'I don't pay tolls,' I say, squinting in the carriage's bleak yellow light. I lean on the door and dig my hands into my pockets. The kids smirk. The shortest one, a punk girl of seven or eight, pounds her fist into her grubby palm.

Spotty sticks a finger up his nose. A trail of brown sludge follows his finger from the nostril, and he flicks it in my direction. I watch it splat on the floor beside my feet.

'No toll, no ride,' he says. 'Last chance. Turn back or pay with blood.'

I don't move. Earlier this evening a murderer fixed his fingers tight around my neck. After he split, the old bat that owned the joint tried to prize me off her floor, but I was glued to it like gum. I heard nothing she said, saw nothing but my shaking hands, tasted nothing but my own pathetic tears.

I don't remember leaving. I don't remember where I went. I've no idea how long it took for the fog to lift, for me to finally think clearly. Dinner with Dag didn't teach me anything new. My mum was permanently pierced with more needles than a porcupine—and after you escape a mess like that, you learn not to have high hopes, or set high standards for shit people.

Spotty steps toward me, and I finally snap out of my trance. I spit on the floor and spin my cap backwards. I think of Dag's fingers around my throat, my mum's drugged up body on a bed of junk, Eiko fighting for her life, alone. I think of all the tears I've shed, and I think I'm done with thinking.

Seconds later Spotty is squirming on the floor, blood streaming from his nose as pain pounds my knuckles. I jump the second biggest kid, throw a right hook across his jaw and send him clattering into the handrail. I kick the next one in the gut and watch her stumble like a rag doll into the seats. The two smallest kids back off.

'I don't pay tolls,' I repeat, sitting on the bench between the crying kids. I turn my cap around and massage my aching knuckles. Spotty cups his hands under his bleeding nose and rushes into the next car, his little lackeys swiftly following suit. I'm left alone with the soothing sounds of the Pipe's rattling ride beneath the Rivers. The ancient wheels squeal on the tracks as handholds swing above the seats with rhythmic moans of metal.

I close my eyes again and this time darkness wins out.

Sonaya's an assault course of hard living, and I've completed enough circuits to learn how to survive. Not many people know what I've been through, and none of them know how strong it's made me. Dag's the dumbest of the lot. In his whisky-washed eyes I'm a loyal hound that comes to heel at the click of his fingers. Hero syndrome. He thinks I look up to him, that I think he's someone special. He thinks that if someone aimed a gun at him I'd attack them; that I should be grateful to him for handing Eiko over to an expat with a pollen problem. But I've had enough of addicts. I've had enough of drunks, too. I've had enough of all of them.

What Dag doesn't get is that Eiko's the only family I've got left. I'll do anything for her. *Anything.* And as soon as Ryoko Nishi delivers on her promise and pays me, I'm getting my sister out of hospital and we're gonna leave this stinking hell hole. Eiko *will not* live a life like mine. I forbid it.

The Dove's chewing kimbab in the window of a convenience store that's covered in Chinese graffiti. When I push through the door and make the bell jingle, the fat chump at the counter watches me saunter through the aisles like I'm some deranged and dangerous animal. A couple of years ago he caught me shoplifting, but I guess he doesn't remember. I must have changed a lot since then.

'What is it?' I ask, taking the stool next to the Dove.

'Tuna,' she says through a mouthful of rice. She offers me some, but it reeks of rotten fish. 'It was past its sell-by date, half price. What happened to your neck?'

'Nothing, don't worry about it. How was your final donkey ride?'

The Dove shakes her head. 'I almost got pinched at the pachinko raid. But I'm done with all that now.' A grain of rice flies from her lips and splats on the counter. She scoops it up with her pinky finger and returns it to her tongue.

'I told you not to do that shit anymore. Soon you'll have all the money you need. You won't need to take care of yourself anymore.'

'No harm in being prepared,' the Dove says. 'Done any more pigeon jobs lately?'

'This is my last,' I say. 'You ready?'

The Dove looks at the remains of her kimbab.

'You can't back out now,' I say. 'This is your only chance for something better. You know how many kids would kill for this opportunity?'

'I know. But-'

'No buts. We've paid our dues, and now's it's *our* time, our chance to escape. You with the old man, me with my sister. This is it.'

I don't like the look on her face. Of course I get it. She's scared to leave Sonaya behind, to slip away and start afresh. But what has she got to lose?

We peer through the grimy window at a row of rusting scooters in the street. A woman in ragged clothes inspects them like she's looking for a lost key. I bang on the glass and she stares at us with empty eyes. She scans the scooters a final time before giving them up.

'This isn't a good place for kids to grow up,' I say, watching the woman skulk off.

'It's *him*, isn't it?' the Dove asks.

So she knows. It seems like everyone knows but the man himself. There's no point denying it.

'When did you realise?'

She points to her hazel eyes.

'You'd think I'd have realized sooner,' she says. 'You'd think *he* would, too.'

'You never told anyone the truth about what happened to you. If you had, we might have pieced it all together.'

The shopkeeper appears behind us, hands on his hips.

'Can we help you?' I ask.

'You gonna buy anything, kid?' he says.

'I'm with her,' I say, motioning to the Dove. 'We're eating dinner. So if you don't mind ...'

He tries to stare me out, but eventually snorts and wanders back through the aisle of instant noodles. The Dove continues to chew on her kimbab.

'I didn't sleep for two nights when I found out,' she says, staring blankly out the window.

'You don't need him. Once we're out of here you can forget about him. Forget about all of it.'

Without blinking, she finishes her tuna roll slowly.

'Tomorrow night, when everyone else is celebrating,' I say. 'Just be ready. It'll all be over soon.'

She looks me in the eyes. Kid to kid. 'Shinji, promise me this is the right thing to do.'

I chew on my bottom lip. In my fourteen years I've lied a lot, but I don't lie to the Dove.

'If it isn't,' I say, 'I don't know what is.'

The hospital is one of the best in the city and only ten minutes from the harbour. The wide stucco walls are almost white and the acidic smell of disinfectant beats out the stench of death. I've got to know my way around these past few weeks. Without a word the frumpy receptionist waves me through and I ride the elevator to the thirteenth floor.

I scan the face of each baby: scrawny, helpless little things, all wrinkles and mottled skin. I wonder how many of them have parents, where they'll be in ten years' time. This one might run pigeon jobs in the alleys; the next one might dig through bins on Broken Hill; and this might be the one to find a loving family, go to school, get a job. Maybe. Or maybe they'll all be dead before they even learn to talk.

I stop in front of Eiko's incubator. I always forget how small she is; three months old and no bigger than the day she was born. Her eyes are scrunched shut, her mouth open in blissful sleep.

I'm bewitched.

Every tiny motion of her trembling chest is like proof of pure perfection, every breath so beautiful my heart turns to mush. When I think how my mum looked the last time I saw her, gazing at Eiko makes me believe in miracles.

I drag a chair over and tell her about my day. I tell her about the life we'll live when we finally leave Sonaya. Every time I visit Eiko, time itself dissolves. I don't know how long I've been talking for when I realise night has fallen. There's a knock on the door. Aimi Stones.

'Hello Shinji.'

She pulls up a chair and sits beside me. Together, we adore Eiko. Eventually, the silent spell is broken.

'Where's Mr. Stones?' I ask.

Aimi sighs. I understand.

'I've made a decision,' she says finally. 'As soon as Eiko's better, we're going to leave. I've been thinking, Shinji. As much as I don't want Eiko to grow up in Sonaya, I also don't want to separate her from her family. And *you* are her family.' She turns to me and leans in close, pinning me with her eyes. 'I know we're far from perfect, but I swear to you that I'm going to make sure Eiko lives the best life possible. If you want, you can come with us. We can arrange to adopt *you*, too. That way you and Eiko can stay together, and you can both have a real home.'

Aimi is intoxicating; her perfection is a spell. The sparkle of her nail polish, the gleam of her skin, the silky shimmer of her hair.

'What about *him*? Your husband?'

'I won't let Eiko be raised by an addict. I won't, I swear it. If he can't quit, we'll leave him behind. Eiko and I will disappear. And you too, if you want.'

I let the proposal hang in the air, imagine the three of us together, across the sea, in a real house, safe and smiling. No drugs, no gangs, no running messages to survive. Aimi would drop me off at school. I'd kiss Eiko on the forehead and promise to study hard. Wave them off as they headed for home. Home.

Aimi's perfume is so strong I sneeze violently into my hands, which shakes the images from my mind. I turn back to Eiko.

Fuck it. When you've lived on the streets as long as I have, you become immune to false hope. You spot the flaws in every plan, see how easily every dream can crumble apart. I try to force the illusion away, furious at myself for briefly falling for it.

But Aimi's eyes bore into mine, fierce and determined. I do everything I can to mistrust her, to convince myself she's a fool, a pretty handbag for an expat drunk. But somewhere in those sparkling eyes I sense the truth: if she wants it bad enough, her dream can turn into reality.

Maybe I can drop the deal with Nishi. Maybe I don't have to do this on my own anymore. Why should I convince the Dove to leave if she doesn't really want to? She's survived on her own so far. We're survivors, me and her, and survivors know the rule: look out for number one.

Aimi places a hand on mine. We watch the stirring shape of my beautiful baby sister, both of us imagining a future that seems at once so close, and yet, so far.

I really need a pager. I'm tired of waiting for pigeons and searching out mangy kids. It's even harder now the Dove's fallen off the map. And Shinji ... well, I can't see him talking to me anytime soon. Thankfully there's an aviary near my attic, and I welcome the opportunity for fresh air. Stuck at home, all I see are suspect sushi plates circling my skull like a carousel of nightmares.

A short walk through the maze and I reach the north-west corner of the Rivers. Squeezed between an elementary school and a block of goshitels lies the sandlot, a decrepit baseball diamond enclosed by a jagged wire fence. It's been there for as long as I can remember, used to be jammed with hordes of truant kids playing ball. Now the ground is full of potholes and the bases have long since disappeared, together with the youthful grins and games. A group of glowering teens have claimed the court as their own—they lurk in a corner, conducting dodgy deals beneath worn baseball caps, spraying graffiti on the school and threatening students.

I slip through a hole in the fence and walk right across the infield. The teens watch me carefully, and once I'm close to the pitcher's mound they dig their hands into pockets and make their slow approach.

'You got no business here, grandpa,' a tall teenage girl declares.

There are five of them in total, each in different states of teen decay: acne explosions, baggy clothes, expressions ranging from melancholic to menacing. The tall girl removes her cap to reveal a mop of greasy hair and a pair of spaced out eyes. I'm not clued up on modern drugs, but she didn't get that way by guzzling candy.

'I'm looking for the aviary,' I say. 'That one, right?'

I gesture to the tallest goshitel in front of me, a colossal eyesore with bruised walls and rusty streaks trailing from each window.

The girl's face softens immediately. 'Go to room 302, ask for Hee-chan, my kid brother. He's a fucking genius. He goes to school.' She says the last sentence like it's something unheard of.

'I'll do that,' I say.

I get my head down and exit through a different hole in the fence. I walk around to the front and enter the goshitel. There's no one in the security office so I head on up the stairs. The entire building reeks. Like every Sonayan goshitel, it's bursting with the destitute: struggling single mums, pensioners without pensions, the unemployed and underfed. The only difference with the aviary is that most of the rooms are occupied by kids. Orphans, runaways, rogues and rascals, the unruly children of the Rivers.

I stop on the second floor and watch the comings and goings of the corridor. It's developed its own ecosystem. A shared bathroom at the far end spills foul smells, a small kitchen beside it is crowded with screaming kids engaged in chopstick swordfights. A couple of women spoon out rice from steaming cookers. The doors along the corridor are all ajar, slamming against each other as kids run in and out of rooms. A fun house without the fun. Hardly anyone notices me—they simply charge on past, squeezing between me and the wall with wailing war-cries. The odd one stops to ask if I need a pigeon for a job, but when I shake my head, they instantly lose interest.

The third floor is much the same. I kick aside two dead

cockroaches and knock on the door of room 302. I'm granted permission to enter so I pull the door open as far as I can and hold my breath.

Even by goshitel standards, the room is tiny. Two tatty mats are laid out on the floor, atop of which sits a woman and her kid. The woman is about my age, thin with unkempt hair, pale skin, and dark circles beneath her eyes. The kid is short and chubby, about twelve years old. He's holding a book in his lap, and his grip tightens when he sees me glance at it. The walls fester with patches of mould and fetid stains, and the stench of body odour reigns supreme.

'Can we help you, sir?' the woman asks.

For a second, I'm struck into silence. The state of the room, the smell, the reality of life like this … I swallow and croak a reply.

'Are you Hee-chan? I'm after a pigeon, a reliable kid for regular jobs. Your big sister recommended you, said you were a genius.'

His mother beams, her face suddenly stretched and skeletal. She runs her fingers through her son's hair, showering his shoulders with flakes of dandruff.

'Oh, he is. He's a good boy, a clever boy. His teacher said he's the best in the class.' The kid blushes and his lips jerk into a shy smile. 'He's gonna be a politician or a doctor, aren't you, love?'

Hee-chan just smiles and looks at his book.

'Yeah,' I say. 'Well, if you're good to start straight away, I've got some jobs for you.'

Hee-chan looks up at his mum with such a beaming smile I've half a mind to gather him in my arms and squeeze him until his stuffing pops out. They sit there smiling at each other, like nothing in the world could matter more.

'He can't miss school, you understand,' his mum says, a flicker of concern flashing across her face. 'He's doing ever so well, aren't you, love?'

Hee-chan blinks at me hopefully.

'I wouldn't worry about that. I'm more active out of school hours. There might be a few night jobs, but I'll pay extra if they're after midnight. That alright?'

His mum nods at him encouragingly and he closes his book and hands it to her. She clutches it to her chest as tears well in her eyes. Hee-chan stands and extends a pudgy hand. I take it; it's clammy and feels like it might fall off if I shake it for too long.

'Come on then, kid,' I say, stepping out into the corridor. 'Let's get you started.'

His mum gets up and plants a kiss on his rosy cheek. Hee-chan follows me down the stairs with beaming button eyes.

Once we're back in the Rivers I begin to worry. The kid has said nothing this whole time.

'You can talk, Hee-chan, can't you?'

'I can,' he says brightly.

I wait for more, but it doesn't come. He hums beside me like I'm taking him for a picnic in the country. I scrutinise his face as we approach the boarding house, but he shows no sign of disappointment. I guess it must look like a palace compared to his goshitel.

'This is my place,' I explain, leading him up the stairs. 'You need to reach me, try here first. Got it?'

He nods, smiling absently at each door we pass. He wouldn't smile if he knew what kind of characters lived behind them. Once we're inside my attic I pour him a glass of water and offer him a seat.

'Two messages this evening, all right? The first thing you need to do is go to Kosuke's. You know Kosuke's, don't you? The big silver tower near the harbour.' A blank smile is the only response I get. A genius, they said; maybe I didn't appreciate

Shinji and the Dove enough. 'You go there and you make sure Kosuke's got my suit ready, okay? I'll be there before the party starts to collect it and get dressed. Don't worry, they'll deal with you in the lobby, just tell them my name. Daganae Kawasaki.'

Hee-chan bites his lower lip and his eyes narrow in concentration.

'Second, you're going to a Homework Club called Angel Eyes. You're gonna find a customer called Bull, an old guy dressed in leather and teeming with tattoos, and you're gonna ask him if he's got any news about Maaya.'

Hee-chan's baby face crinkles, his little eyes blinking like he's trying to photograph every word of my instructions.

'Have you ever done any pigeon jobs before, Hee-chan?'

'I have.' Proud as punch. 'I delivered a message for my sister. Took her money to a man who gave me a package in return. Then I handed over the package to my sister and her friends. They said I did a real good job.'

'I'm sure you did. Can you remember everything I told you? You know where you're going tonight?'

He stares at the floor, his cheeks reddening with strain. Then he looks up at me apologetically.

'Okay, first job for the night. See that coffee table?' I say. 'Fetch me a pen and paper.'

Jiko's got a pretty face, but plaster it across the outside of police headquarters and suddenly it doesn't look so good. Her mugshot stares out over the Pulse with both menace and moody indifference. I study the image, her name emblazoned above her red hair, a generous reward flashing beneath. I wonder whether she's transformed yet, or if she's cut and run, whether she knows her mug is about to be one of the most recognisable in the city. Moments later the projection of her face fades as another fixes into focus: Su-young, her cherry-red lips curled into a contemptuous smirk. Soon the bright blonde hair is replaced by purple, and Bo-min glares morosely over the centre of Sonaya.

I grab a newspaper from a crabby guy in a frayed flat cap and stroll the sepia-tinted promenade of the CBD, the high-rise offices towering above me. I buy a watery coffee from a battered kiosk and search for a suitable spot to perch along the Pulse. A man-made stream that was once a river, the Pulse flows west through the city, transporting crumpled beer cans and cast-off junk towards the sea. I carefully sit beneath a ginkgo tree, between dried splats of pigeon shit and trampled orange ginkgo nuts. I open the paper and blow my steaming coffee. The news of Yoo-ri Baek's attack by three masked women has got some decent column space, but it's not the top story. The National Intelligence Test results have been released, and almost every page is loaded with analysis and 'expert' interviews.

I head straight for the centre pull-out, which lists the names of everyone who made the top two bands. It's a hefty tome, but it doesn't take me long to locate the only Kawasaki recorded in First Band. Surprised? Not terribly, but vindication is always valued. I search for the names of friends. There's no sign of Kosuke, nor Ganzo or Nakata, but I find familiar names in Second Band: Fumiko Miura, Aimi Stones, and Jitsuko Ryu. I can't say I'm shocked. Old Fumiko has more guile within her wrinkles than most of Ryoko Nishi's cabinet, and Aimi's always been too smart to be the trophy wife of a drunken hack. Jiko—well, Jiko has a decent brain for a teen who's spent more time on a Ducati than in a classroom. It's a shame she won't be allowed to put her precious votes to use; not a great time to become Sonaya's most wanted.

I sip my coffee and consider my companions on the steps: a group of suited office slaves fresh from work; a silent couple sharing a box of bean mush; a homeless woman cradling a can of government beer. I wonder if any of them came close to the top two bands, or if they'll even bother voting.

A breeze strokes the branches of the ginkgo tree as the promenade lights snap into life. Sonaya always looks its best at dusk, when the city's lights flicker into existence and cast their glow below an indigo sky. I recline against the bole of the tree and stare at the flowing stream, gently let my new responsibility sink in.

One vote for the abstainers; five for the lowest scorers; ten for the ordinary chumps, twenty for the also-rans, fifty for the white-collars, and a hundred for the Second Bands, some of Sonaya's brightest minds. In a city of three million, only three hundred made First Band. The best of the best, the silver stags in their high towers, the top 0.0001%. A thousand votes for Dag the Wise, the wily, misread genius.

Sonayans have been complaining about the elections for a long time. Democracy's all well and good, but what happens when the moron majority decide a nation's destiny? Thirty years ago America collapsed under Trumpocalypse, the UK went broke with Brexit, and neither has recovered. That's what an uneducated democracy delivers.

The intelligence test seemed like the perfect solution. Imagine a beefed-up IQ test, but infused with historical questions and general knowledge, then sprinkled with equations and riddles. Of course, every average sap believes they're smarter than their neighbour. I'm not sure how they'll feel when they discover they're at the bottom of the pyramid.

In three days' time the polls will open and the schmucks of Sonaya will cast their votes to choose our next saviour, but three days is a long time in the world of politics, and Ryoko Nishi isn't stupid. There are three hundred First Bands with a thousand votes each—if Nishi slips them sweeteners, suddenly she'll have as many votes as three hundred thousand abstainers. And Nishi's not the only corrupt candidate with deals to offer.

I finish my coffee and smile.

I'm one of the three hundred. Commence the bidding for my ballots.

I'm Dag the in demand, and I might just have some demands of my own.

It's almost time for Sonaya's latest soiree, but it's not fashionable to be early. The evening's new and full of possibility. I buy a box of sake from a 'liquor locker'—a booze vending machine—and drink my way through the smoking passages of the Rivers; brushed by flashes of brilliant neon, caressed by the growing crowds. Maybe it's my imagination, but it feels like lingering eyes converge on me, far more than usual. I soak it up. Let them look. I'm a First Band now, and tonight's gonna be one hell of a party.

I'm deep into Sonaya's heart when I find Fumiko sat in her usual chair, like a statue in the centre of a square. Shoulders slouched over her cane, her wizened eyes scanning the passing crowds of The Cross, the Rivers' biggest backstreet junction. Scooters and bicycles buzz around her like insane insects, spinning a web of toxic fumes and blazing lights.

'Kawasaki,' she barks. 'A thousand votes, my arse.' She has quite the vocab for a dame her age. 'Who have you been paying?'

I flash her a smile. Man of the people, me. 'Not jealous, are you?'

'I got a hundred votes of my own,' she says with wrinkled pride. 'I would have matched your score with ease, if my mind was what it used to be.'

'Heaven forbid.'

A phlegmy laugh explodes in her throat. 'You're going to Kosuke's party, I assume? Who's going to get stabbed in the gut this time? Not your turn, is it?'

The old vulture's still got her wit, at least.

'I need one of your girls to smarten me up,' I say. New Dag, new face. My beard's been growing wild for months and tonight's an occasion to impress. I am a First Band, after all.

Fumiko grills me from head to toe with her scythe-sharp eyes. 'I've got a new intern who can do a job on you.'

'Just the shave,' I say.

'Of course, Kawasaki.'

She leads me to her basement lair where grimy passages diverge in the darkness, peopled by posing girls and pigeon kids who scurry about like worker ants. The queen herself escorts me through the candle-lit tunnel, the smell of her unwashed grey bun invading my nostrils, her feeble arm intertwined with mine. Discordant screams and cackles seep through unmarked doors and Fumiko grins with gummy pride. A man built like a bulldozer limps towards us, his entire face concealed by coils of bloodied bandages, except for a single deformed eye. He salutes Fumiko and glowers at me like a giant mutated mummy.

Fumiko pushes me through a door and into an empty cave-like room. A smeared mirror sits before a grotty sink, a beat-up barber's chair, and a stainless steel table of tools that a surgeon would envy. A blinking chandelier swings from the ceiling and illuminates the room with stuttering flashes of feeble light. I sit down and examine myself in the mirror. An unruly mop of hair above a rugged, greying beard. Damn, this makeover is overdue.

Fumiko briefly disappears and returns with a dark, skinny young girl. She can't be much older than Shinji. Her large black eyes gawk at me in terror. I study her face in the mirror and have half a mind to scram. I think of all the stories I've heard from Jiko and her girls and wonder why I haven't changed my barber.

'Where are you from?' I ask her. The girl glances at Fumiko and I do the same. 'Where's she from?'

'No idea,' Fumiko replies. 'Can't speak a word, Japanese or English.' I try to stand but Fumiko places a claw on my shoulder and forces me back down into the chair. 'Don't worry,

Kawasaki. She's well taken care of, and I don't start them out this young.'

'She ever done this before?'

Fumiko hands the girl a knife. 'We'll find out, won't we?'

The girl's hands are shaking so I sit absolutely still; I can't go to an elite party with tissue spots on my face. Fumiko watches from a chair in the corner, hands crossed atop her cane. She bellows instructions, but it's clear the girl doesn't understand. When she's done sculpting my hair into a respectable crew cut, she lathers up my cheeks and chin. Taking the knife to the foam, her hands move so slowly it almost looks painful.

'I hear you're still chummy with the Bosozoku,' Fumiko says. 'I suppose you've heard what they've been up to.'

I'm in no rush to talk, especially with a knife running over my jaw.

'Jiko was always smart,' Fumiko continues, 'but threatening Yoo-ri Baek wasn't a shrewd move. Now her pretty little face is plastered across Sonaya. She's probably in a cocoon right now, washing the fire from her hair and pumping fat into her bony cheeks.'

As the girl rinses the knife in the sink I take the opportunity to flex my jaw.

'You're worried about her,' I say.

Fumiko smiles. I watch her ancient face in the mirror, eyes squinting through the dark, like she could drop dead the next time she blinks.

The girl lifts the knife to my upper lip and scratches at my moustache.

'Ume was the same,' Fumiko says, staring blankly at the floor. 'A moral crusader. If it were up to the Bosozoku, I'd be enjoying my retirement from the top floor of The Heights. But the best thing about this government is that there are always people in high places willing to take your money. And you know what, Kawasaki? My money keeps a lot of people alive.'

I look at the girl's reflection in the mirror. Her face is a picture of concentration as she prepares to slice my sideburns.

'It didn't keep Suzie alive,' I say. 'I'm guessing you heard about that too. They cut her up in a Catfish kitchen like she was a fillet of fish.' I study Fumiko's face. 'Jiko and her girls have a crazy idea that you're involved. They think that Baek's Borrowing is good for your business. What do you think about that?'

The girl moves the knife to the base of my throat and slowly scrapes my skin.

Fumiko reveals her purple gums and says something in a language I don't understand. The girl stares at my reflection, her eyes wide and shivering in their sockets. Fumiko barks again, louder, and this time the girl presses the blade against the base of my Adam's apple. I swallow as slowly as I dare.

'Maybe if languages were on the NIT I'd be a First Band like you, Kawasaki,' Fumiko says. 'Cambodian, this one. She'll obey my every order, even if she pisses her pants doing it.'

The girl's eyes are frozen on the knife at my throat. She looks just how I feel: shit scared.

'There's no escape from sweet Sonaya, Kawasaki,' Fumiko continues, calm as ever. 'You should know that better than anyone. I've been around longer than most, I know how it goes. Sonaya's a well-oiled machine, and if you throw a spanner in the works, it's the spanner that breaks, not the machine. Jiko is just another spanner.

'Even if I wanted to make a change, it wouldn't make any difference. The weasels in office like things this way. That's the problem, Kawasaki—all they want is money. Money and power.' She extends a bony finger and rotates it slowly in small circles. 'They want the wheels to keep on spinning. I've always liked you, Kawasaki, but if you accuse me of something I didn't do one more time, I'll turn your head into a strawberry smoothie.'

She barks another Cambodian command and the knife softly cuts into my skin. I watch blood trickle over the blade and down towards my collarbone. Tears varnish the girl's young eyes.

'This is a war, Fumiko,' I say through clenched teeth, moving as minimally as possible. 'You admire Jiko and those girls, I know it. They're fighting everything *you* should be fighting. Everyone you never had the guts to fight.'

'Guts?' Fumiko's lips wrinkle into a sneer. 'Times have changed, Kawasaki. If I'd attempted what they're trying now, I'd already be long dead.'

'People die for their beliefs. *If* they believe enough.'

Fumiko keeps her razor-sharp eyes on me, the wrinkled smile frozen on her face. The girl's hand still shakes, the blade embedded in my flesh.

'Suzie died for what she believed in, and what's changed?' Fumiko says. 'The only reason Jiko didn't die with her was that *you* were by her side. Yes, my little pigeons have been busy. From what I hear, Baek reports to someone far more powerful than the PM. And whoever it is doesn't want you dead—at least not yet. That guardian angel of yours must be working overtime.'

Another Cambodian instruction follows, and the knife drops into the sink. The girl stares at the fresh blood on her small fingers. I look at Fumiko.

'Tidy yourself up, Kawasaki. The night is waiting for you.'

12

Kosuke is the only man in Sonaya with the clout to throw two parties in one week. This one is billed as a celebration of the test results, but everyone knows there's more to it than that. Throw a bunch of top bands in a room with rich politicians and the result is an auction for votes. Everybody wins: Kosuke gets a round of silver handshakes and the fantasy of friendship, and the politicians get a shot at buying their way into power. And me? I'm just looking forward to seeing how much I'm worth.

There's no need to hire a venue when Kosuke's place is a town in itself. His apartment block towers over the harbour; the only taller building is The Heights, which looms to the south like a sullen older brother.

We're not on the roof this time, and that's good news. The last time I saw my reflection in the rooftop pool I was being framed for murder. Tonight we're down on thirty-four; a seldom-used floor, though you wouldn't know it. The marble floor sparkles beneath two dozen tables draped in silk cloth and blinding silverware that winks at the crystal chandeliers. A buffet table with shiny silver platters full of salmon hors d'oeuvres hugs the window which runs floor to ceiling, and a raised platform along the adjacent wall awaits this evening's band.

This crowd makes the folk at the yacht party look like paupers and posers. All the men are dressed like penguins, black suits and silk ties and cuff links speckled with diamonds. The women pose in designer dresses of red, black, or gold, their hair draped in sumptuous black curtains or fixed by jeweled hair clips that could be traded for small countries.

It's my first time in a suit since I was a twenty-something hotshot. Kosuke got one tailored for me, a stylish midnight black with a plum pocket square and a matching tie held fast by a diamond clip and chain. I'm clean-shaven and sharp, my tattoos and the cut at the base of my throat the only minor blemishes; if I had two ears I'd be in serious danger of fitting in.

I'm on a table with six straight-backs who flinch at the mention of the Rivers. I'm the centre of attention, of course. The former lush and criminal who's finally come good. I'm a novelty in their little world, like new money, a mysterious outsider with an edge and a story. They ask me how I like my caviar. I say I like it to stay on the plate, and they laugh like it's the world's finest joke. They take turns filling my crystal glass. Cabernet Sauvignon is followed by Pinot Noir and Malbec. We kill four bottles before Kosuke stumbles to the stage and the clink of cutlery on crystal calls for quiet.

'Ladies and gentlemen.' He beams at the room with the tipsy affection of a proud grandparent. Someone has squeezed him into a smart Armani ensemble, but the shirt buttons look ready to pop off like plastic bullets. 'What have I done to deserve such fine friends?' A self-congratulatory laugh passes between the tables. I wonder if there's anyone in this room who *hasn't* received a backhander from Kosuke.

'We're here, of course, to celebrate the release of the National Intelligence Test results. Although perhaps some of us shouldn't celebrate at all.' Kosuke looks with mock-accusation at the sea of watching faces, prompting another round of titters. 'I noticed that quite a few of you were missing from the top two bands.'

'This coming from a fourth band!' Stones yells from across the room. Aimi rolls her eyes good-naturedly as nearby tables laugh along.

'Yes indeed, Peter,' Kosuke says. 'A measly twenty votes for this pompous windbag that stands before you. I shan't pretend to be surprised. In fact, I'm grateful for the twenty. I'm not sure I could have faced you with any less. But I must add,' his face turns serious, 'some of you haven't revealed your result to me yet, and this makes me truly suspicious.'

The biggest laugh yet, and even a smattering of applause. Hell, rich people are easily amused.

'I'll wheedle it out of you by the evening's end, mark my words!' Kosuke barks over the laughter, waggling a bloated finger. 'But for now, let me leave you in the capable hands of some old friends of mine. The Savoy Six, everyone.'

Kosuke opens the applause himself and steps aside as the jazz band takes the stage and bow at their rapturous reception. As soon as the sax begins to sing, the waiters replenish the wine and champagne as diners begin to stand and mingle.

I take it as my cue to ditch the duds on my table and find someone worth talking to. I start with Aimi and Stones. The waiters can't clear their table of bottles fast enough. Aimi looks stunning in a sleek dress of golden sequins, her hair elegantly fixed in a bun, her olive skin radiant. Stones has already ditched his dinner jacket and his shirt is blemished by red wine.

'Congratulations on making Second,' I say to Aimi.

'Congratulations yourself. A rebel with a brain, who would have guessed?' She smiles teasingly as Stones loudly protests.

'I would've been First Band too, you know,' he proclaims to the table. 'If foreigners were allowed to vote, I'd have put you all to shame.'

He says it in jest, but our companions' smiles are forced. Self-deprecation is the name of the game in Sonaya; American brashness doesn't go well with the caviar.

Stones starts telling the woman beside him about his work in progress: a political satire set in Sonaya. Aimi takes my arm and escorts me to the buffet table. The harbour is all lit up and the strip is pulsing with its glorious parade of neon as the ocean shimmers with fluorescent reflections.

'How's he doing?' I ask.

Aimi replies with a raised eyebrow. 'Catastrophically. I hear you've been hitting the sauce pretty hard yourself. I thought your dog days were over, Dag.'

'Turns out they've only just begun.' I watch Aimi fill a plate with dainty strips of avocado.

'Your daughter?'

'That's why I'm here,' I say. We turn and appraise the room. A pair of waiters clear away the central tables to make space for the dancefloor. Stones is still remonstrating in the corner.

'I'm leaving him,' Aimi says, her voice clinical and decisive. 'He's not the man I married. I've given him plenty of chances to change, and he's traded them all for bags of pollen. I have to think of Eiko now. Can I speak frankly, Dag?'

'I thought you were.'

'I've met a lot of addicts. Look at Peter closely. That's the end game. And that's where you're headed if you let it beat you.' Aimi places a hand on my shoulder and holds my eyes. 'Don't spiral. Once you start, there's no stopping.'

With that she takes her leave, strutting confidently back to the final chapter of her ruinous marriage.

I find Kosuke with his stomach squashed beneath a table and Kiki by his side. Her dress looks like it's been hacked by hungry scissors, but from her glowing smile I assume it's intentional. She gushes about her studies while Kosuke beams approvingly, placing his pudgy hand on hers. Finally the old man, tipsy and red-cheeked, congratulates me on my votes.

'This is it, Dag, the opportunity you've been waiting for.' He leans in conspiratorially. '*Use* it. Do you understand me? This is your way back in.'

I can hardly hear him. I'm distracted by the look in Kiki's eyes when the old man speaks. It takes me a while to recognize it, and even longer for me to believe it. Maybe I've been too cynical. Maybe I'm the only one in this circus incapable of love.

The lights dim, the Savoy Six up the tempo, and the booze flows forth. When Kosuke and Kiki take to the dancefloor, I'm approached by a number of slurring suits who take an interest in where I'm planning to cast my votes. I ask for recommendations.

The Secretary of the Liberal Democrats thinks I should get back into the world of work. He has a ton of contacts, he tells me; all I have to do is say the word and I'll be stationed in a high-rise cubicle by the end of the month. The Communists are shocked to discover I don't have a pager or a landline; they promise I'll never see a pigeon again should they come to power. The Republican treasurer whispers into my wrong ear that intelligent men like me shouldn't be paying such atrocious taxes. It's despicable, he adds, that a free man should be humiliated and forced to wear an ankle tag.

I like everything they say. I nod and smile and don't pour myself a drink all night. But there's something missing. The one person I really want to talk to isn't here—the only person who might have the single thing I want.

'You've got every lowlife minister here apart from the blasted Conservatives,' I complain to Kosuke. 'I thought you had influence. Where's the PM?'

'Oh, you know Nishi,' Kosuke says with a dismissive wave of the hand. 'These women in power, they care too much what people think. She's not the hothead teen you used to know, Dag. She thinks she's too good for all of this now. Can't be seen enjoying herself while Sonaya's going to pot.'

He rolls his eyes.

'I've never been able to get through to that woman,' Kosuke continues, slurring slightly. 'But worry not, there are plenty of capable men in her cabinet. *Malleable* men.' He stabs a stubby finger over my shoulder. 'Do you see that man talking to Yoo-ri

Baek? That's Zenzo Goto, the Minister of Finance. Dependable fellow; he's the one you want to talk to.'

I leave Kosuke in Kiki's loving hands and crash the conversation. If Baek knows I'm drinking buddies with the girls who threatened her, she doesn't show it. She's wearing an elegant rose dress with a beige pashmina draped over her shoulders and her plastic face is glistening so much I can almost see my reflection in it. The man beside her is a barrel-chested bull with square jaws and a sleek moustache. He looks about as malleable as a brick wall.

'Mr. Kawasaki,' Baek says, with a fake and frigid smile. 'Have you been introduced to Mr. Goto?'

The man grasps my hand with such force my fingers crack. I hold firm and gently caress his wrist like a secret lover. He drops my hand like it's made of fire.

'Congratulations on winning the Borrowing,' I tell Baek. 'With any luck we'll have the population back up in no time. And a new generation of teenagers stationed on our street corners.'

The plastic in Baek's face freezes. If I held a candle beneath her chin, I'm sure she'd melt all over the floor.

'I just identify the policies, Mr. Kawasaki,' she says with a smile that could cut glass. 'It's parliament that votes them in. I do hope your tag hasn't hindered your colourful lifestyle too much. We've all heard stories of your ... *frivolity*. I wish I were equally adept, but I'm afraid I grew out of all that once I graduated. I am glad you find the time to enjoy yourself so much.'

I stare at her. I'm starting to wish Jiko *had* slit her throat.

Zenzo Goto punctures the silence with a thunderous clearing of his throat. 'If you would give us a moment, Ms. Baek.'

Baek bows and flashes a final plastic smile. 'Gladly. Don't drink too much, Mr. Kawasaki, you don't want to go *shooting* anyone again.'

'I may yet,' I reply to her departing back.

'Ignore her,' Goto says brusquely. 'We all know the Borrowing is a dud, but we need to look as though we're doing something about this goddamn population problem. It's a sure-fire crowd pleaser among the electorate.'

He must see that I'm taken aback by his candour.

'Don't worry, Kawasaki. Kosuke tells me you're a sensible man. You've done a stretch in The Heights, you know how the world works. Baek's the only female Borrower who came up with anything good this year. It's all about quotas, you understand, Kawasaki. We can't have too many male winners in a row, no matter how good they are. It's the outside world, you know. Political correctness gone ape, but if we make these small allowances, the monkeys stay off our backs.'

'Does that go for Ryoko Nishi, too?' I ask. 'Is that how she became Sonaya's first female PM?'

He raises an eyebrow. 'Politics is politics, Kawasaki. Nishi is a good, capable woman. I'm completely behind her.'

Spoken like a true politician.

'Listen, Kawasaki, let's bluff past the bullshit. We all know why we're here. Every minister in this room had to pay Kosuke for access to this pool of voting riches. I'm sure you've already had some offers tonight?'

'All of them very appealing,' I say.

'Of course. But you know that Nishi has a soft spot for you. You have history, after all.'

I meet his eyes and give nothing away.

'Don't worry, Kawasaki. Nishi's secrets are safe with me. But it's not your history that will deliver the best deal. Nishi has something you want, doesn't she?'

'I'd prefer to talk to her myself.'

'It's only right that you do. You're to meet her tomorrow. Somewhere a little more discreet. Trust me, Kawasaki, once you've heard what she has to say, you won't even consider any other offers.'

He raises his glass and we toast to our new friendship. We gaze at the revelers on the dancefloor, the conspirers in dark corners. The saxman starts a solo and everyone falls silent. The music is building, building. His cheeks glow red, his sax leaps wildly as though possessed by the rhythm.

The room holds its collective breath. Soon everything will explode.

13

I haven't seen a honsool since The Heights. I've heard they came from Korea. The Hermit Kingdom, experts in loneliness —and honsool bars are the loneliest of the lot. Who needs friends when you can have a private booth, a bottle of booze, and your own sad soul to drown?

This particular place is called Solo—just to rub it in. It festers in the basement of a run-down building that specialises in solitude in the heart of the Rivers. The third floor is crammed with tiny singing rooms; the fifth is filled with capsule PC rooms for gamer geeks who will not sleep; the eighth is home to tarot talk and endless cards emblazoned with death. Solo is probably the cheeriest place of the lot.

The entire basement is black, illuminated only by blushing blue orbs that line the corridor and blink above each door. At the base of the stairs I'm greeted by the silhouette of a gargantuan woman sat behind a counter. Her welcome consists of a whooping cough and a fat finger stabbing at the florescent menu.

'Any drinks?'

'Makgeolli,' I say. 'Does it come with a smile?'

'Not from me.'

She snatches my money and counts it twice. 'You're tagged,' she says, gesturing to the flashing light above her head.

'I'm harmless, I promise,' I say.

She doesn't respond until another note finds her pudgy fingers.

'Booth eighteen.' She removes a bottle of makgeolli from the fridge behind her and slams it on the counter. I grab my drink and disappear down the narrow corridor. The doors are stacked in twos, little cubby holes with ladders leading up to the doors above. I lose my shoes and duck into booth eighteen.

I almost gag from the stench, a putrid cocktail of mould, booze, and filthy feet. The room is a box, barely big enough to accommodate an adult, the furniture a foul-smelling cushion on the tatami mat floor and a table just big enough to balance my bottle. The wallpaper is a peeling mess of Hangul calligraphy, spoiled by vomit-coloured stains and lude graffiti.

I cross my legs beneath me and inspect the makgeolli bottle; a cheap brand imported from Busan—a strong, sour brew from a small mountain village. I shake the bottle, unscrew the lid, and pour myself a glass. Cheap liquor made from rice, makgeolli looks like rotten milk, and it doesn't always taste much better. My first sip coats the roof of my mouth in a sour film that will linger for several days, I'm sure.

The screen embedded in the wall blinks and invites me to create a profile. I type in a user name: *Ten*. Then I select an icon: a cocktail glass. I set my status to available and the board lights up with flashing profiles. It tells me that a dozen other booths are occupied, with many already in conversation. Even as I examine the different profiles, another pair of lonesome losers engage, the lights above their icons changing from green to blue. There are only three green lights remaining, including mine. One has a purple heart icon, user name *CandyGirl*. I select her profile and discover she's been inactive for almost an hour; probably pissed and passed out. The final icon is an animated devil brandishing a pitchfork. *AngryBitch*. She's been signed in for twelve minutes and is yet to make or accept a call.

But now she's calling me.

I clear my throat and answer the call as the devil icon

invades my screen. A voice filters through the speaker beside me.

'Hi.'

'Hi yourself.'

Speed dating for the 21st century. Like most of Sonaya's grand ideas, the honsools started out with honest intentions: judge on personality, not appearance. For the most part, they work pretty well. Sure, some freaks turn up and pleasure themselves to strangers' voices, while others only come to fire abuse to make their own miserable lives more bearable. But mostly it's just lonely people looking for an easy hookup, and in a city where the population plummets and relationships have shorter lifespans than mayflies, that's not necessarily a bad thing.

'You could have taken me to a fancy restaurant or a penthouse on the strip,' I say. 'Why here?'

Ryoko Nishi's husky voice comes through loud and clear. 'Too many eyes. The same reason I didn't invite you to City Hall for an official audience.'

'Or show up at Kosuke's party,' I add.

'Our relationship is a little more personal. So I thought we'd keep the meeting that way too.'

'I'm staring at a cartoon Satan. Is that what you call personal?' No reply. 'Okay, let's get personal. What do you want?'

'Do you remember our last conversation, Dag? In Ganzo's bar?'

'I remember it well. We agreed to stay away from each other. And yet here I am.'

'I told you to forget about Maaya. I told you to stop looking. And have you?'

'Of course not.'

I hear Nishi pour out a drink.

'I'm on makgeolli,' I say.

'Coffee,' Nishi replies. 'No rest for the wicked.'

'So this *is* business. Is it gonna start any time soon, or are we gonna small talk till I pass out?'

I can almost hear her sigh.

'You're a First Band, Dag,' she says slowly. 'I'm not sure what that says about the intelligence of the Sonayan population, but there you go. And First Bands are going to find themselves extremely popular during the next few days.'

'I'm already popular. It's a shame you couldn't come to the party, I made a lot of new friends. People whispered plenty of pretty things in my ear.'

'Anyone can promise, Dag. Few can deliver.'

I take a deep swig of makgeolli and smack my lips.

'I liked you more before you became a politician. You spoke your mind, and with a colourful vocabulary. Does politics suck the life out of everyone, or is it just the Conservative Party?'

No answer.

Makgeolli goes down like water once you're over the initial sour shock.

'Listen,' I say. 'I get it. You track down the top bands and, let's say, *encourage* them to vote for you. It's nice and simple— very efficient, really. But my question is this: why am I different? Why did you wanna see me personally?'

'The other First Bands are easy. We pay them, they vote for me.'

'I can be easy, too.'

'No. You're not quite that simple, Dag.'

The screen begins to flash and flicker. Video permission. I accept.

The devil dissolves and the profile of Ryoko Nishi appears in a grainy square, her eyes staring at me from beneath a baseball cap, her jet-black hair nestled behind two dainty ears. She's wearing a baggy lumberjack shirt which is open at the collar. The birthmark beneath her left eye is the only thing that reminds me I'm looking at the prime minister of Sonaya.

○

'A baseball cap and a makeup-free face. Is that all it takes for you to go unnoticed in the Rivers?'

'Cocoons are overrated,' she replies. 'The Rivers is a labyrinth of shadows, and most people glue their eyes to the ground. Maybe that's why it's the perfect place to place to hide.' She looks me over. 'You've looked better, Dag.'

I glance at myself on the screen. I've looked worse. Maybe Nishi still remembers the sharp young cop of the past, the cad who regularly broke hearts. But that was before her sister made an honest man out of me. Almost. The handsome tax and a lush lifestyle lost me my job, but Hana never gave up on me. Until my drunken dalliance with her sister, that is. The dumbest one-night stand in history.

'What did the others offer you?' Nishi asks. 'Freedom of the city? The removal of your tag? I can give you that. Easy.'

'You were the one who tagged-'

'And I can *un-tag* you, too. You want work? How about a return to your old office? Why not get back on the ladder, pick up where you left off all those years ago? You know I can provide all of that, Dag, but we both know that's not what you really want. Only I can give you that.'

I wet my lips. 'So you *do* know where she is.'

Nishi stares but doesn't speak.

'I want to see her.'

'As I told you before, I'm concerned about you playing a part in her life. She's my niece, and I want to keep her safe from all of this. And from you.'

'I'm her father. What do you think I'm going to do?'

'You're a fuck-up, Dag. I know what kind of life you lead.'

'And what kind of life *do* I lead?'

Nishi sips her coffee, eyes fixed on mine with a poise perfected by politicians worldwide. 'I think you lead the same life you led before you got locked up. You've become the wreck that Hana fought to save. The sack of shit who slept with her sister at the first sign of-'

'It took two people to hurt Hana,' I say. 'Don't pretend you're innocent.'

'We don't need to do this again, Dag. I've accepted my mistake and paid for it. I still pay for it, every day. But I was a kid, I was stupid. And I'm not stupid anymore. Neither am I a bitter alcoholic, bumbling into middle age, pissed up and pathetic.'

I take a swig to absorb her blow. Middle age? Nishi always knew how to press my buttons, and I can hardly blame her. After Hana died by my own wayward bullet, Ryoko's family fell apart. Her mum fell sick and swiftly passed away, and her dad— who was never my biggest fan, even before my biggest fuck up —abandoned the city to live like a hermit out in the sticks, or so I heard.

'You're not father material, Dag. Maaya doesn't need to know that you exist.'

'She has a *right* to know. I just want to see her. I can protect her, look out for her. Just give me a chance and I'll prove it. All my votes go to you. You have my word.'

Nishi thinks hard on it, or at least she pretends to. She must have known I'd ask for Maaya. It was probably her plan all along.

'I'll let you see her—*if* you can prove you're living respectably.'

I swig my makgeolli. 'Fine. I give you my votes, you let me see my daughter. *And* I lose the tag and get a job.'

'It sounds like you're getting a lot for giving very little,' Nishi says.

'A thousand votes is a lot in a city this size. You should have heard the offers I was getting-'

'But no other offer included your daughter. I'm the only one who can deliver on that.'

'Fine. What else do you want?'

'I'm sure you've heard of these little uprisings in the Rivers.' She waits for confirmation, but I remain silent. 'Naturally we're concerned about where it's headed. The attempts to burn down brothels and Homework Clubs—that kind of thing we can let slide. We even turned our heads when one of the Roses got his head blown off during Earth Hour.'

'The government has always turned its head when it's suited them.'

'But threatening a Borrower,' Nishi continues, ignoring me. 'I'm afraid it's become public knowledge now, and that's something we can't ignore.'

'Because it makes you look bad.'

'Because it jeopardises everything we've built,' Nishi says. 'I'm not going to pretend every member of my cabinet plays by the rules, and yes, there are some things I'd prefer to be kept … *discreet*—for the sake of Sonaya. But Jitsuko Ryu is someone I can't ignore, not any more. Not when she threatens the system.'

'And why should I care about Jiko? I've seen her face plastered all over the Pulse. Let your army of goons catch her, throw her in The Heights. She has nothing to do with me.'

'Don't pretend that you're only passing acquaintances, Dag. She's a slippery little thing, and the voters know it. I want her locked up before polling ends.'

'You mean you want a trophy—to convince the sheep of Sonaya that you're capable of butchering the wolves.'

She sips her coffee and chooses her words carefully.

'Take care of her, Dag, and things will turn out nicely for you. Think about it. Think about your daughter. Think about your old life, and the new life you could have. You could go from convict to cop in half a year.'

I return Nishi's stare.

'How do I know you're not lying? How can I be sure you know where Maaya is?

Nishi doesn't bat an eyelash. 'I swear it. I swear on Hana's grave.'

I'm good with eyes. I can look through pupils and dissect retinas like they're polygraph tests. But Ryoko Nishi's no regular sap. I can't assess this test. All I can do is take her word for it.

'Leave it with me,' I say.

○

Nishi logs out and leaves, slinking back to her high castle. I sit in silence for several minutes and mull things over. Sell Jiko to the big bad cats in exchange for my daughter? It might be the only option I have to see my only family. Sure, she's a friend, but what's loyalty in Sonaya? Loyalty is a slit throat when you sleep.

My makgeolli is almost done and I can feel the intoxicating dance of the soused rice rolling around in the back of my head. Now that I have a taste for the stuff, I'm gagging for another bottle, but I don't wanna stay in this rotten dump a minute longer. Groans and muffled thumps seep through the walls, leaving little to the imagination. Somewhere in this honsool a lucky couple have beaten the odds of the loneliest city on earth. Barriers broken, avatars abandoned; a joining of two desperate, sweaty creatures, revelling in the stinking, mouldy lair of these fetid cubicles. I gag at the thought and suddenly overcome, suffocating, I throw the door to my room wide open.

I tumble out into the narrow corridor and fall to my knees, coughing and gasping for breath as I struggle to keep the makgeolli down. The pungent reek of the stained and shabby carpet makes things worse. I close my eyes and try to take deep breaths.

It's not because I'm some prude, believe me. I'm human too, with needs the same as the next sad sap, but things haven't been the same recently. They haven't been the same in a long time. Dag the Ten, Dag the Lush, Dag the Hotshot Cop—those days are long gone, and don't I know it. I'm reminded often enough. The truth is, I haven't been with a woman since Hana died. It's not that I haven't thought about it, because I have. A lot. But thinking and performing are two different things. And without going into too much detail, I haven't felt sharp since I left The Heights. The cup was patient with me. Women? I'm not sure they'll be quite so forgiving.

The sounds of coital warfare cease, and a door at the far end of the corridor swings open, spilling a middle-aged woman who stumbles towards the exit adjusting her knickers. I drag myself up and catch a glimpse of light behind me. I turn just in time to see a capsule door close. Another lonely soul on the lookout for love? Before I'm back on my feet I hear a beeping sound inside my cubicle.

I inhale deeply and examine the screen. Another call request. I'm all set to ignore it and slink out of this shithole when I notice the profile name: *50% Bullshit*. The icon is a pencil. It can't be …

I close the door, settle back onto the tatami mat, and pour myself a final slosh of makgeolli. I take a deep breath and accept the call.

'Been a long time,' I say.

'Sure has.'

I know the voice well enough. American, smooth and cool, with pitch-perfect depth, like a spoon being hauled through liquid chocolate. It's a voice I haven't heard for months, and feared I never would again.

'I thought you'd left,' I say.

'They wanted me to. They even paid for my ferry ticket and escorted me to Honshu.'

'What did you do? Swim back across the East Sea?'

Her laugh sends shivers down my spine.

'One of the customs boys liked my bills. I got myself a fake passport and found a quiet cocoon for a little makeover.'

'There aren't many Black women in Sonaya,' I say.

'No, but the cops aren't looking for a Black woman, are they? Anyway, I haven't been showing my face much.'

I consider the last week and smile into my glass. I like it

when things come together neatly. 'I didn't know you could ride a motorbike.'

'There's a lot you don't know about me.'

'So you gonna tell me why you came back? I'd love to think it was for me, but I know you *that* well, at least.'

'My reasons for being in Sonaya haven't changed,' she says simply.

'You're still stuck in the past, then. Hell, let it go, Sara.'

'Sonaya's suffocating, Dag, and Hana's death was only one knot in the noose. Yes, it was your bullet that killed her, but we all know someone set you up. Finding out who that was—and why—is the key to decades of corruption. They wanted Hana dead because she knew something, Dag. I'm certain of it. And I'm going to find out what happened, even if *you* don't care.'

'Here's a newsflash for you,' I say. 'Politicians are bad. Have you ever heard of an honest one? I haven't. You can dig under City Hall for decades and you'll still never find all the skeletons.'

Sara Barnes says nothing. I hear her pour a drink and I look at my meagre dregs of makgeolli.

Suddenly I remember something Jiko said.

'Wait a second. Did you have something to do with Ganzo's bar?'

Her silence is answer enough.

'Then you don't know Sonaya as well as I thought. Ganzo doesn't keep secrets from me; I could have told you that without your Nightshades destroying his livelihood. You'll pay for that.'

'Ganzo knows more than you think. I do my research, Dag.'

'Fine. Then do what you have to do. But just to confirm, if I have to pick sides, I'm picking the side without helmets.'

'I'm not asking you to pick sides, Dag. I'm asking you to listen. I didn't come here for you. I've been watching Ryoko Nishi for a while.'

'Ryoko loved her sister. If you're trying to tell me she had something to do with Hana's death-'

'That's not what I'm saying. But for a young woman without

a job or any prospects, she sure flourished damn fast after Hana died. All I'm saying is that she knows more than she's letting on. Ganzo, too.'

'What the hell does Ganzo have to do with Nishi?'

'She was ostracised by her family and friends. She had no one and nothing but her visits to his bar. She drank. She talked. And Ganzo listened.'

'So what?'

'So he's keeping his lips sealed, and I don't buy his cute panda act.'

'You've lost it, Barnes. Did they damage your brain in that cocoon?'

'Keep those blinkers over your eyes if it makes you feel better, Dag.'

We sink into a bitter silence. I forgot how frustrating this woman can be.

'I guess you're still not telling me who hired you for all this.'

More silence.

'I didn't think so. Then tell me this. After they shipped you out of Sonaya, why didn't your agency just hire someone else? They could've hired another expat or someone from Tokyo or Seoul. Or even someone with half a brain who already lives here.'

Sara takes a nice long drink.

'This is my job,' she says. 'And this is *my* city. No one's taking it from me.'

My makgeolli is dead, but the aftertaste lingers like a sickening dream.

'Later, Barnes,' I say. 'I wish I could say it's good to have you back.'

14

SARA

The more they stared, the more invisible I felt.

I was anonymous, a hazy face in the crowd, ghosting through a world belonging to others. When they stared, they stared right through me. I wasn't one of them, and never would be.

That's how I felt when I first arrived in Sonaya. Now, with my helmet, I feel even less human. They continue to stare at me, but not at my face. Their hungry eyes devour my body— long, depraved gawps that violate. A few simply gape at my bike or helmet, their faces clouded by confusion, peppered by pity. I can see them wondering what's beneath the leather, who's staring back through the blacked-out visor, and contemplating how the world has wronged her.

Now I look at my reflection and ask myself the same question. It's amazing what they can do in the cocoons. My head has been shaved to the scalp on each side, a solitary strip of braids casually swept over my crown. Jewels twinkle from piercings in my nose, and my lips and eye shadow gleam with brilliant violet. I questioned whether the makeover was necessary. I rarely reveal myself in public, and when I do, all the citizens of Sonaya see is a Black woman.

When Sonaya was on the up, people poured in from across

the world. It's hard to believe now, but before the big industrial push this tiny island was a resort for the rich. There was an expanding international community and English soon became prevalent alongside Japanese. But the melting pot didn't last, for better or worse. Now this senile old city lurches dumbly through the 21st Century, and diversity is all but a distant memory.

I finish my whisky—the bottle is empty. I ransack my kitchenette, but the cupboards are bare bar thick layers of dust. I force open the cracked and battered window and a pungent blast of soybean stew assaults the room. My elderly neighbour has a penchant for fermenting and a passion for acrid odours. We're the only two tenants, each of us crammed into paltry apartments above a garage stuffed with motorcycle parts. The old dear will knock on my door soon; she always cooks too much, and the only thing she's starved of is company. The thought of spending another evening trapped in this box is suffocating.

I need a drink. I need to breathe, to feel the wind on my face. I exit the squat, leaving my helmet behind. My bike is stowed in the garage downstairs, and the pot-bellied mechanic strokes it with oil-stained fingers whenever I enter. I stride past him without a word, avoiding his desperate leer and ignoring the catcalls that follow me onto the street.

I pop into one of my regular haunts: a wooden-fronted izakaya three blocks away. I take a seat at the candle-lit bar, order a bottle of hot sake and several skewers of grilled log. It's supposed to taste like steak, but all I taste is bean mush licked by charcoal and flame. I keep my head down to avoid the gaze of the salarymen. Their sake burps resonate like the mating calls of tormented toads.

Not wearing my helmet doesn't relieve me of the suffocating hand around my throat. Between shots of sake I breathe simple and slow, but the lingering gazes of the flushed clientele feel like knives to my lungs, stealing shot after shot of my innermost air.

I didn't expect Dag to take notice. Some people only hear

what they want to hear, and Dag continues to lurch from one shortsighted errand to the next, ignoring the earthquake beneath his very feet. I shouldn't have revealed myself to him, I know. It was reckless, but I couldn't help myself. I've spent so long alone, and Dag, for all his faults, is the only one that gets me.

I'm halfway through the bottle when someone takes the next stool.

'I like what you've done with your hair.'

I glance sideways at the smiling young man. It's been almost a year since I picked him up in a bar deep in the southern Rivers. Handsome Korean features, a sculpted moustache and clipped stubble, a sleeve of tribal tattoos embracing a lean muscled arm. I return to my drink.

'I didn't think I'd see you again.' He leans on the bar and beams. 'You remember me, don't you?'

I swig hot sake. It burns my esophagus but the memory of that night remains. 'I want to be alone.'

He laughs. In my peripheral vision I notice him glance at my chest. 'No, you don't. I remember what you said that night.' He leans in and whispers, his sour breath tickling my ear. 'That you're lonely, you have no one. That you *crave* company. I haven't forgotten.'

I pause with the glass at my lips. It happens every few months: I get drunk, lose myself, reveal my secrets to strangers. A release; a deep breath before diving back to the depths of my solitary ocean. But the bargain I make with myself is to never see them again. Sonaya is a city of strangers—that's the promise.

'Let me get you a drink.' He calls for service.

I place a hand on his arm and he flashes another self-assured smile. I beckon him towards me and he leans in again. It's my turn to whisper.

'Get out of here before I shove this shot glass through your eye.'

He pulls back and surveys me with a smile that shrinks with each passing second. I can convey a lot with a look. He stands and leaves, cursing under his breath as he slams the door behind him. The salarymen at the bar avert their eyes as I shoot daggers around the room.

Bernd Schulte arrives when I'm halfway through my second bottle. He collapses onto the stool next to mine, reeking of musky cologne.

'You're late,' I say, not bothering to look at him.

'Don't start,' he says. 'I'm swamped at the office. You're lucky I'm here.'

I slowly turn my head and wait for him to meet my eyes. He runs a hand through his black and white beard, the skin between his fingers dry and flaking. The collar of his shirt is stained at the neck and his rank mustard tie clashes horribly with his tweed suit jacket; symptoms of a middle-aged man living alone. When his brown eyes finally yield to mine, they do so with equal regret and resentment.

'Lucky?' I say quietly. 'You're lucky you're not behind bars.'

He tears his eyes away and has the decency to affect guilt. I don't know if it's genuine, but until I get what I want I don't care. Justice *will* be served.

'I'm doing everything I can,' he says curtly. 'Do you know how much I'm risking for you?'

I maintain my sniper stare until Bernd swallows dryly and loosens his tie. Choking discomfort with only a look; it feels good to be the one holding all the cards.

'You're risking nothing,' I say. 'I'm your only chance to escape the tornado of crap you span for yourself. And even after you've given me what I want,' I lean in and lower my voice, 'I'm not promising I won't cut your dick off myself and feed it to your dog.'

Bernd briefly bristles before his face loses all color. He opens and closes his mouth like a gormless guppy.

I refill my glass. The German doesn't give me any more lip,

and after he hands me the files from his briefcase, I dismiss him with a wave of my hand. I'm feeling the first tingles of being tanked, and I'd stay for another bottle but I'm already late. I snake my way back through the outskirts of the pleasure quarter, watching the blank faces of Sonaya's wretched cast. A middle-aged woman barks expletives at a wall. A little girl issues leaflets from a seedy motel, a mangey old crow perched snug on her shoulder. I reach for a flyer but the girl withdraws her hand, her face screwed up in a scowl. The crow caws fiercely until I fade from its sight.

I grab my helmet from the squat, the smell of soybean stew now rife through the building, and barge into the garage. The mechanic drops his spanner, his lecherous stare distorting his face as he straightens up to greet me.

'Storage fee's gone up,' he says, his breath glazed with oil and liquor. 'People been asking about that bike of yours. And I ain't too good with secrets.'

'Then I'll take my business somewhere else,' I say, shouldering past him. I roll my bike into the alley and mount beneath the neon sign of a cheap Botox business. I slip on my helmet and exhale. Invisible again.

Kenya always chooses the cheapest places to meet. The red brick building is wedged between the empty shell of a cram school and a dilapidated motel called 24 Hours, which is closed. I head for the screen golf outfit on the third floor. A whale of a man slouches in a chair behind the counter attacking a cup of instant noodles, drops of steaming soup trickling down his beard.

'Mr. Oh's room?' I ask.

When he's done assessing my face he fires his answer at my chest. 'Room Six.'

The dimly lit corridor reeks of piss; the bathroom door is

wide open and yellow puddles spill out form rows of antique urinals. I enter Room Six without knocking and three people glance up from their golf clubs.

'Sit down, Barnes, you're late,' Kenya orders. The silver-bearded man is in his trademark pinstripe suit, reclining on a worn sofa that sags against a peeling wall. 'Shall we add you to the round? We're only on the third hole.'

'I don't golf,' I say.

'Shame,' he says, making room on the sofa. 'It's a good way to de-stress.'

I sit and stare at the sour-faced loons circling the tee—Higata and Lee. I prefer them with their helmets on. I've seen them threaten the weak and elderly, the poor and pained who cannot afford back-handers to keep their businesses running; I've seen them batter rival gangs with crow bars and hammers.

The first time I met them was at a private dinner above the Cow Shed. Me, Kenya, Higata, Lee, and a grinning surprise guest. I watched as Kenya smiled and poured him wine, and seconds later I watched him drink and die. As Higata and Lee dragged his body away, Kenya informed me that the man had been a rapist, and the victim's family paid a handsome fee for death and discreet disposal. I picked up the dead man's drink and sniffed the glass. Kenya smiled and explained that he'd decided on our new gang's name: The Deadly Nightshades. The flowers were painted on our bikes at sunrise.

Kenya hands me a can of Hitz from the ice box on the floor. Sonaya's cheapest beer: watered-down lager in a bland blue can. I crack it open and suck the bubbling froth. It's a dire step down from sake.

Higata weighs a five iron in his hands and adjusts his feet beside the ball. He takes a couple of practice swings while Kenya and Lee watch on. Finally he swings for real and the ball rockets into the screen like a bullet and weakly bounces back, rolling limply along the artificial turf. The giant screen shows an animated ball soaring through the sky above a lush landscape which looks distinctly un-Sonayan. Kenya claps and Lee looks sour.

'The boys tell me you spoke to the redhead,' Kenya says, turning to me. 'Jitsuko, isn't it? You made some kind of deal.'

'I wouldn't call it a deal,' I say. 'More of a mutual understanding.'

'We've garnered quite a reputation in a short space of time, Barnes. A reputation for ruthlessness. I wouldn't want to lose that because of a single act of weakness.'

'It wasn't weakness.'

'You told her we would stay off their turf. That sounds like weakness to me.'

'Those girls are no threat to you.'

Kenya smiles. I've worked with him long enough to know which smiles are sincere. He stands.

'What do you think, boys?' he asks.

Higata selects a five iron from the trolley.

'These streets,' Kenya says, accepting the club and examining it. 'These people. They are not controlled by money. They are not controlled by laws. They are controlled by *threats*. By rumour and fear.'

He lines up a shot and sends the ball thwacking into the screen. Higata and Lee nod approvingly. Kenya passes the club back to Lee and returns to his seat. 'The threat is in the threat. Do you understand, Barnes?'

'I don't have any interest in controlling the Rivers,' I tell him.

'You might not, but as long as we're working together, you will do what needs to be done.'

'It's *my* money,' I remind him.

'No, it isn't. But you *are* the person passing it on, which I respect. All I'm asking is that you keep up your end of the bargain. If you're going to wear the symbol of the Nightshades, you must act like one. No acts of charity.'

'I don't have any charity in me.'

This time Kenya's smile is genuine. 'I'd have to disagree with you on that.'

He drinks and crushes the empty can in his palm.

'What do you want?' I ask him. 'What do you *really* want?'

Kenya considers me with a hint of surprise. He furrows his eyebrows and measures his words carefully. 'Power is a drug, Barnes. This city … well, let's just say I have an attachment to it. You wouldn't understand.'

'Because I'm a foreigner? Trust me, I understand. I know what it means to love Sonaya.'

'Not like I do. I was born here. I've lived here my whole life. I've seen it all. The rise, the fall, and everything in between. These streets belong to the people, not to the government. I *am* the people. And I'm not letting go.'

He nods to Higata, who exits the room. I see Lee smirk.

'You are yet to reveal yourself to Kawasaki, is that correct?' Kenya asks.

I hesitate. 'Dag tends to get in the way of my plans.'

'Our Lee had an encounter with him in the Cow Shed. Took a liking to him, didn't you, Lee?'

Lee's stretching lips threaten to split his ugly face. 'He's got a way with words, that's for sure. It was all I could do not to poison his cocktail. I don't know if I'll be able to resist next time.'

Kenya chuckles as Higata re-enters the room, dragging a large body behind him. The figure is wearing a Shades helmet and his hands are tied across his bulging stomach. Higata leads him towards the patch of artificial grass and forces him down onto his knees before the screen.

'Recognize this bear?' Kenya asks, lifting another can from the ice box.

Higata prizes the helmet from Ganzo's head. The sushi chef opens his bleary eyes, squints as if suddenly waking from hibernation. Groggy but unharmed.

'We are working together, aren't we, Barnes?' Kenya says,

sipping his beer. 'You help us, we help you, that's how it works. The panda here has information you want, information he fails to share. We helped you destroy his bar, and we sold it on for a moderate profit. But it seems you're content to let him leave and live his life without obtaining what you wanted. Not a very efficient way to do business.'

Lee removes a club from the trolley and hands it to Kenya.

'I can't let that slide, of course. I know how badly you wanted Ganzo to talk, so here he is. After all, we're partners. It's what we do for each other. Now we can finish this chapter and move on to the next.'

Kenya twirls the club in his hands. He approaches Ganzo and presses the head of the club under his chin.

'Yes, he looks ready to talk,' Kenya says, gazing into Ganzo's eyes. 'But we wouldn't want it to interrupt our game now, would we? We're only on the third hole, after all. I believe it's your shot, Lee.'

Lee takes the club and places a ball on the tee, mere feet from Ganzo.

I step forward but Higata places a firm hand on my shoulder.

'I'll do this my way,' I say. 'Leave Ganzo with me, I can deal with him.'

'Oh, but I'm not convinced you can, my dear,' Kenya says. 'After that little incident with Jitsuko, I've decided you need reminding who we are.'

He nods at Lee, who obligingly swings with force. Ganzo slams his eyes shut, sweat glistening on his forehead. The ball sails past Ganzo's ear and bounces off the screen.

Kenya laughs. 'Bad form, Lee. You made the rough. Would you be so kind as to take my turn, Ms. Barnes? I'm afraid the beer has clouded my vision.'

'You've made your point,' I say. 'Let him go.'

Higata forces the club into my hands and Lee drags me towards the tee.

'Hit the ball, Barnes,' Kenya says. 'Hit it hard. Show me you have what it takes to keep this partnership going.'

I drop the club to the floor but Lee retrieves it and slams it into my chest, holds it there until I reclaim it. He manhandles me until I'm perfectly positioned beside the ball. Higata slides another club out of the trolley and swings it teasingly, malice carved into his eyes.

I stand over the ball, staring into Ganzo's pleading eyes.

'Like you mean it, Barnes,' Kenya says.

I crane my neck and glare at Lee. 'Touch me again, and I'll fucking kill you.'

Before his smirk can spread I swing the club into Lee's ribs and send him tumbling to the floor, gasping for breath. Higata leaps forward with his club and I'm about to swing again, but Kenya appears between us.

'Enough,' he commands.

I point my club at him as Lee howls from the floor. My eyes bore into Kenya, my lungs aflame, my muscles tense and poised to pounce. He merely smiles, amusement twinkling in his eyes.

'I think we all understand each other,' he says, stepping back. 'Take the bear and finish what you started, Barnes. Lee, stop your whimpering and get up. Higata, choose your club, we have a round to finish.'

I guide Ganzo down the hall and into an empty room. The lights are low, the screen scrolling course records. I remove the ties from Ganzo's wrists and he collapses on the beaten sofa, his face vanishing behind trembling hands.

My head begins to pound. Whisky, sake, and cheap beer. A bubbling cocktail of bad booze to heighten the hammering of my heart.

'Listen,' I say. 'I didn't ask for this, Ganzo, but you know why it happened. I know you want to protect your friends, bury your secrets in the past. . But the past isn't finished. It's still here, dragging Sonaya into the dirt. And it won't end until I get some answers.'

Ganzo's hands fall to reveal a clammy, frightened face. The dark circles beneath his eyes make him look more of a panda than ever.

'You hid inside a helmet and destroyed my bar.'

'I can't reveal myself to everyone, Ganzo. I know you know something, and your secrets could be the key. Everything you lost, you can get it back. You can have a bigger sushi bar, hire a horde of staff, anything you want.'

He pinches his button nose. I observe the big man closely; benevolent, harmless, polite. But when I boil it down, he's just another man positioned between me and my work. Kenya's words burrow like mites beneath my skin. I'm as far from answers as ever. Maybe he was right. Maybe I've been too soft.

I choose a club.

'I think Silver Beard and his goons got the message,' Ganzo says. 'You don't have to prove anything to me.'

'Kenya would have tortured you until you talked,' I say.

Ganzo eyeballs the club as I weigh it in my hands. 'You're a good person, Sara.'

I smile. 'Do you still think this world is split into angels and devils?'

Ganzo doesn't answer.

'Well it's not. We all have one on each shoulder, and it's our choice which one to listen to. I'm a private detective, Ganzo. It's my job to find answers. I try to do it nicely, all above board, but sometimes I'm not given that opportunity. According to records, I'm not even in Sonaya. I left two months ago after killing a former police sergeant.'

Ganzo runs a faltering tongue over his frozen lips.

'I consider myself a good person, mostly, but I've been stumbling through the dark for some time now. And my employers aren't going to be patient forever.'

'Silver Beard?'

'Kenya is not my employer. He's my ticket to the underground.'

The club whistles as I swing a practice shot. Ganzo's face drains of colour.

'I'm bored of being nice,' I say. 'It's time I stop being invisible and start getting results.'

When I return to the boarding house there's a pigeon waiting for me in the lobby. Not Hee-chan, or the Dove, or Shinji, but a boy I've never seen before, with lank hair to his shoulders and a timid expression in a thin, sallow face.

'He's been here for over an hour,' the landlady declares. 'I tell you, Kawasaki, I'll pay for a phone line in your room myself if it stops these street mongrels wondering in at all hours of the blasted day.'

'Thanks, I'll take you up on that,' I say as she leans over the counter and watches us. 'Can you give us a minute?' I ask.

'You've got a room, haven't you?'

I stare her down until she finally retreats out back.

'What have you got for me, kid?' I ask the boy.

He digs a hand into his pocket and pulls out a folded slip of paper. I unfold the note and scan the spidery handwriting. *Saju Market, 11p.m. F.*

I turn the paper over but that's it. I look at the kid.

'You needed paper for this?' I ask, but he just shrugs and extends a skinny hand. I drop a coin into his palm and he's out the door before he even remembers to thank me.

East of Korea Town lies Saju Market, a lantern-lit labyrinth erected on the former site of an apartment complex that was demolished and abandoned. A huge marquee houses rows of makeshift tents, each rented by a wizened pensioner weighed down by grubby bangles and shawls infused with incense. The sprawling market is controlled by a gang of middle-aged women called the Cosmos, a steely band of former convicts known for their unflinching business flair. Their racket in the eastern Rivers has remained untouched—maybe due to their modest earnings; or maybe because few crooks would want to cross them.

I haven't been here in years, but the bounty of aromas instantly transports me back in time. I pay a small fee to enter and soon the sounds and smells of this fortune-telling world engulf me. Incense, unwashed carpets, perfumed ladies. Vats of noodles simmering in steaming pans; peppers and mushrooms and perilla-wrapped parcels of rice, all lathered in batter and sizzling in deep-fryers. Sake and soju and makgeolli. A playground for Sonayan seniors.

I stroll between the tents—food tents, drink tents, but mostly fortune teller tents. I glance inside as I pass, observe blurred and distorted figures through the clear plastic tarps, catch glimpses of muted meetings. The tellers are hunched and ancient creatures—women with cheap perms and cheaper pearls; balding men with silk shawls and thick Confucian beards. They sit at plastic tables peering at their patrons—old women on new pilgrimages from Broken Hill—spouting shit about the future and flipping antique cards or glowering at warped wrinkles on endless withered hands.

I complete two laps of the maze before I spot Fumiko. Maybe I didn't recognize her away from her cocoon; I don't think I've ever seen her so far from her arachnid lair. I stare through the vinyl sheet that shields one side of the tent, try to listen to the spiel of the fortune teller. When it shows no sign of coming to a close, I push through the flap into the tent.

'Sorry to interrupt,' I say.

'Daganae Kawasaki, you found me,' Fumiko says. 'Two nights in a row, must be my lucky week. Sit.'

'What did you want to see me-'

'Just sit down, won't you?' Fumiko barks, pushing out the stool beside her. 'Mrs. Kwon was just finishing up my reading. I'm sure she wouldn't mind reading you too.'

'I don't believe in-'

'I didn't ask if you believed, Kawasaki. Just give the woman your hand.'

I sigh and drop my empty palm on the table.

Mrs. Kwon is a square-jawed woman in her fifties; a squat and sour face with frog-like lips and dark curly hair streaked with white. She takes my hand in hers like a metal vice claiming a small animal, and she eyeballs me with all the affection of a corpse.

'Please, don't be shy,' I say, but she ignores me and flips my hand over, slowly tracing the lines in my palm with a dirty claw-like fingernail.

'Your lifeline is short,' she confirms. 'And your life is full of trouble. There's more of it coming your way.'

'You surprise me,' I say.

Fumiko snaps her cane against my shin. 'Please, get yourself some food, Mrs. Kwon. I need to speak with Mr. Kawasaki in private.'

She slides a week's salary across the table and Mrs. Kwon smuggles the notes beneath her shawl. The teller stares at me with her amphibian face and doesn't let up until she leaves the tent.

'Fumiko, I'm surprised at you,' I say. 'A woman of your intelligence, a Second Band, believing in all this garbage.'

'I don't believe in anything apart from my own instincts,' the old woman answers. 'But I like to consider different viewpoints before I make my decisions.'

'And what did this old toad tell you?' I ask, leafing through the upturned cards.

'Much the same as you.' She laughs, that familiar gagging sound from her throat sending a shiver down my spine. 'Maybe she says the same thing to everyone, I don't know. But knowing the two of us, I wouldn't bet against her being right.'

I glance around the tent.

'You like all this, don't you? The old stuff, the nostalgia. You know it's bullshit, but you can't stop looking back. You're a soft old bitch, really, aren't you?'

I wait for a routine reaction, a barked response, a throaty laugh. None of them come. Fumiko lowers her eyes and her chin trembles. I look away, but what I really want to do is run clear of this sorry sight.

For what feels like an eternity we're firmly stuck in silence.

'The past,' she eventually says. 'The present, the future. It all collides right here. My wrongs—and I've wronged a lot, Kawasaki—my crooked life, my redemption...'

'That's what this is about, isn't it? What I said last night actually got to you.'

She slams her cane on the table with such force I almost fall off my chair.

'Of course it fucking got to me. You think I'm proud of everything I've done? You think I enjoy seeing Jiko on the run? I don't know what comes next, Kawasaki, what happens after we die. But I don't want to go out like this. Being hated. Forgotten.'

I want to say something to soothe her. I could tell her that she's loved, but that would be a downright lie. Admired? True for some, maybe. In the end I settle on the only thing I'm sure of. 'Well, you sure as hell won't be forgotten.'

For a brief second I think she's going to burst into tears, tumble from the stool like a rotting relic turned to ash. But then her gummy smile appears, the most awful and allaying sight I've seen all night.

'I always wanted to tell you ...' she says, placing her veiny hand on mine. 'I'm sorry.'

I resist the urge to pull away. 'For what?'

'For being the other woman. For being the one who tore your family apart.'

'Don't blame yourself for my father's sins.'

'I knew your mother. Homura. A good woman. A strong, successful woman who always had Sonaya's best interests at heart, unlike the other suits from Japan. I don't mind admitting that I envied her. When your father came to me, I reveled in it. I was the other woman—an *older* woman. It felt good—like I had something she didn't. So stupid.'

I listen to her tortured liberation and try to imagine what she looked like thirty years ago.

'I won't pretend to know what you've been through in your life,' I say. 'But I know you did what you had to do. And for what it's worth, for all your wrongs and faults, I still think you're a damn Rivers legend.'

She laughs. 'If I were thirty years younger, Kawasaki.'

'Let's be glad you're not, we'd be at each other's throats. Now stop talking like you're about to kick the bucket. We both know you'll outlive us all, you cockroach.'

'Do you think they'll ever forgive me, Kawasaki? Jiko, Bomin, Su-young … all the others.'

'Turn those cards over,' I say, pointing to the untouched pile in the middle of the table. 'And don't let someone else decide. Pick the ones you want. Choose your own future. You've earned that right.'

I stand and make for the exit. Dag the Sage.

'Wait.'

I turn back to see Fumiko blinking away her tears. 'I didn't call you here for advice. My little pigeons have been busy.'

'And?'

'That Yankee sleuth is back in town. Did you know?'

'Funny you should mention it,' I say. 'I spoke with her this evening. What about it?'

'She's working with Kenya Oh. They're re-imagining the Roses. And I believe they've got something that belongs to you.'

'What?'

Fumiko cackles. The vulnerability of two minutes ago has disappeared entirely. 'I'm afraid I'm not talking about your daughter, Dag—yes, I've heard about your little goose chase. I always have my little chicks keeping an eye on Kenya and his crew —you never know when they might make a play for my patch.'

'Pigeons, doves, chicks. I'm tired of all these birds, Fumiko.'

'That's because they're all beyond your reach. As usual you're flapping around on your own, losing your feathers in the shadows while the flocks migrate to keep up with the world. You're older than you think, Kawasaki, and you're behind the times. You're a flamingo in a world without colour, dancing the tango with your own ghost, lost inside a flurry of putrid pink feathers.' Her eyes narrow. 'Quit drifting in your flamingo mist. Open your eyes and join the migration.'

I chuckle despite myself. 'Suddenly you've got your finger on Sonaya's pulse, have you? Okay, give it to me. What have your little birds found out?'

'One of them saw Kenya's crew scuttle away with a certain sushi chef.'

'Ganzo? They've got Ganzo?'

'So it seems.'

'And why are you telling me?'

Fumiko picks a card from the table, examines it closely and discards it with a decisive flick of her ancient wrist. 'Just choosing my cards,' she smiles.

The bouncers of the Cow Shed have a few choice words when I appear before them. When they run out of insults about my ear, my boots, my clothes, and my mum, I ask if I can see Silver Beard.

'You've got some fucking nerve,' Mouse says, sneering.

'I do. Now go get your boss. It's important.'

'He's out. Playing golf.' They look at each other with insufferable smirks.

'No, he's not. He's here.' Silver Beard materializes behind me, a wingman at his side. 'What do you want, Kawasaki?'

'Business,' I say. 'Your doorstops need a lesson in good manners.'

Silver Beard chuckles. 'That's what makes them perfect doorstops. I'll give you ten minutes, but only because I'm in a good mood.'

'Get a hole in one, did you?' I ask.

'Something like that. Excuse us, gentlemen.'

The bouncers stand aside to let us through. Mouse spits on the floor as I pass, narrowly missing my boot. I stop and stare at his large and leering face.

'One speck of your saliva lands on me, and I'll cut your little tail off. *Mouse.*'

His face reddens and he grabs a handful of my shirt.

'Let him through, Mouse,' Silver Beard calls from inside. 'He's just playing.'

'Just playing,' I say, winking.

He releases me roughly and shoves me through the door.

The Cow Shed is quiet. It's just gone midnight and the dancefloor won't erupt until the early hours. I follow Silver Beard past the empty bar, a solitary bartender pretending to work.

'Where's the other guy?' I ask. 'The punk with the slick-backed hair and the face you wanna fist.'

Silver Beard glances over his shoulder as we ascend the stairs. 'He had an accident with a golf club.'

'Sorry to hear that,' I say, not bothering to hide my smile.

I'm steered towards a meeting room at the far end of the mezzanine, a large oak table occupying the centre and a long leather sofa surrounding it on three sides. Silver Beard takes his seat at the head of the table, his man to the left, me directly opposite.

'I'll have a Senor Ramon,' I say to the third wheel.

'Higata isn't a waiter,' Silver Beard says. 'Anyway, you've only got ten minutes. Hardly enough time for a cocktail. What do you want?'

'Ten minutes is time enough for two. No? Suit yourself. A reliable source tells me you've done some business with a friend of mine. A good friend. Ganzo.'

Silver Beard and Higata glance at each other.

'Reliable indeed,' Silver Beard says. 'But I'm afraid our business was concluded. We left him to a colleague. Rest assured he's being well taken care of.'

I instinctively search for a nearby glass or bottle or anything to wield, but the table's empty. Before I can reach down to Old Trusty, Higata is on his feet, opening his suit jacket to reveal his gun.

'Now, don't do anything hasty, Kawasaki,' Silver Beard says. 'Here, let's have that drink after all.'

He rings a bell and a waiter enters.

'A selection of wine,' Silver Beard says. 'The *best* selection.'

The waiter nods and exits.

'Does your best selection include two fat bouncers by any chance?' I say.

'Sit down, Kawasaki. Let's talk this through like gentlemen. Please, sit.'

I eyeball Higata and his gun, then return to my seat. Higata follows suit.

'We know quite a bit about your friend,' Silver Beard says. 'Real name Gun-soo Park. Nicknamed Ganzo for his love of knives. Born 2013, thirty-nine years old. Former owner of a sushi bar on 37th in the Rivers. How's that?'

'*Former* owner because a gang rocked up and ripped the place apart.'

'Calm down, Kawasaki,' says Silver Beard. 'I believe your

friend Sara Barnes was responsible for that particular bit of business. But you already know she's back, don't you? I'm afraid I struggle to keep a leash on that one.'

'She's not an animal,' I say.

'Of course not.'

The door opens and the waiter reappears with a tray laden with bottles and glasses. Red wine, white wine, champagne, sake.

'Let me guess,' Silver Beard muses, studying the bottles. 'You get enough wine in your regular cheap haunts. Sake, too. But you don't often get to drink champagne. Out of your price range, usually, isn't it?'

He opens his arms, gestures to each of the bottles, inviting me to help myself. 'Please, choose your poison.'

I think it over. I don't like being second-guessed; I prefer to stay unpredictable, so I opt for the red. It reminds me of Ganzo and our nights of noise and nuisance. Of Jiko and the Bosozoku's underground bar. I reach for the bottle and pour myself a glass. Silver Beard serves himself champagne; Higata goes for sake.

'We mustn't forget to cheers,' Silver Beard says, just as my glass is about to touch my lips. 'It's an old practice, but an important one.'

I lean over and clink glasses, watch them sip their drinks before sampling my own. Sweet red.

'In truth, Kawasaki, I think you needn't worry about your friend Ganzo. We handed him over to Ms. Barnes to do with as she wished, for her own purposes. She is a tough cookie, isn't she? But I doubt very much she would do anything to seriously harm your friend. She doesn't have the heart to be a true Nightshade.'

'And what are *true* Nightshades?' I ask. 'Cowards who hide inside helmets? You're one of them, aren't you?' I nod at Higata, who doesn't react. 'That arsehole barman, too. This is your headquarters, this shitty little club.'

'Kawasaki, please. Mind your language. This is a respectable establishment, and you're a guest. A guest with a fine glass of red.'

'Whatever. The Roses. The Nightshades. Different flowers, different members, same old shit. Same threats, same petty attacks on unarmed people, same coward at the head of the table, casually sipping champagne when he should be looking for my daughter.'

For a moment Silver Beard looks sour, but the contortion of his lips quickly cracks into a smile. 'Like you are, Kawasaki?'

'I'm doing everything I can. *You're* not. You've given up. You failed. You failed with the Roses. You failed with Maaya. The Nightshades will go the same way.'

There's a brief spell of silence in which I sip my wine. My outburst doesn't make me feel any better.

'You're in a foul mood because once again events are out of your control, Kawasaki. Your friends are fighting among themselves, and you can't do a thing to stop it. You're losing control, aren't you? How's the wine?'

Like a blinding pain that erupts when you see the wound, I begin to feel dizzy only when I look at the glass.

'I chose it myself,' I say.

'I'm good with people,' Silver Beard says. 'Words, gestures, suggestions. It's amazing what one can achieve with the simplest of techniques. Don't worry, Kawasaki, it's not going to kill you. As I told you once before, I don't kill for fun. I do what's best for my business, and I'm starting to feel that you're intruding a little too much.'

The room starts to spin. My vision blurs. My mouth opens and closes but I can't form words.

'Consider the wine a warning. From the *Nightshades*. Atropa belladonna—a beautiful plant. Careful now, Kawasaki, you're spilling it all over the table. Come now, sit up straight, won't you?'

And with that, everything turns black.

16

I awake with my cheek stuck to the floor. My head pounds and my mouth is a sour disgrace. It could be any hangover of the week, but I don't see any empties on the naked floorboards and I don't even remember getting drunk.

Last night's memories appear in faltering flashes. Nishi's plea to trade Jiko for my daughter; tarot cards wet with Fumiko's tears; Silver Beard's smug smile. Sara Barnes. Ganzo. Poison.

I drag myself up to answer the cries of my desert-dry throat. I drain a glass of water and swiftly sink another. Suddenly bloated, I trudge to the window and stare sullenly out over the Rivers. The outline of the sun shows through a blanket of cloud —early afternoon—and a light rain falls on the backstreets. Figures shuffle through the alleys with their heads down. Cadavers dragged into animation by the city's relentless quest for numbing routine. Ancient bicycles wobble round corners and scooters chug like smoking shells of scrap, the stark grey light of day stripping them of their sleek nightwashed cool.

I lean against the glass and close my eyes. A mosquito buzzes around my ears, desperate to interrupt my train of thought.

Silver Beard is no friend of mine, but I never saw him as an enemy. Until he poisoned me. Not lethally—clearly—but enough to make me lose the best hours of the night. How did I get home? Did one of his cronies drag me unconscious through the streets? I don't suppose it matters. I'm home and I'm alive, and the sun still hasn't set.

I fill the kettle. Coffee first. As soon as I have my wits about me, I need to check on Ganzo. I'll deal with the Nightshades later. But I *will* deal with them.

The resident mosquito launches an attack on my ankle. I slap it and curse as I spill hot coffee over my hand. The mosquito is now a mangled mess above the bone, and I stare with grim satisfaction at the stain of my own stolen blood.

Nagoya Nigiri is one of the better sushi shacks in the northern Rivers. The crooked ceiling is a collage of driftwood defaced by woodworm and supported by columns of contorted oak. Fishing nets hang between paintings of samurai, and lanterns swing over polished tables swarming with red-faced salarymen.

I stroll through the munching parade and holler at the kitchen. 'Ganzo!'

The Panda looks up from his work and glances at his boss.

The big woman shoots me an evil look but concedes. 'Two minutes,' she says.

Ganzo abandons his half-sliced salmon and escorts me through a beaded curtain. Our eyes meet over a table festering with puddles of soy sauce and wasabi-coated chopsticks.

'What are you doing here?'

'Those bruises on your face,' I say. 'That's why I'm here. Was it Barnes?'

His cherubic face relaxes. The blotches on his jaw and neck look like tattoos of splattered plums.

'These?' he says. 'You think Sara would do this to me? I can look out for myself, Dag. It's all taken care of, I promise you. I might even get my bar back.'

'I heard the Nightshades kidnapped you.'

'I'm telling you, Dag, it's all over. And you don't look too sharp yourself. Another heavy night, was it?'

'Drank something that disagreed with me,' I say.

He considers me carefully, his eyes dancing over every flawed inch of my face.

'Listen, Ganzo. We go back a long way. Between you and me, I don't feel too smart today. All this shit going on—the Nightshades, Sara, the Bosozoku—I'm out of the loop. And it's my fault, I get it. But I should still be able to protect my friends, shouldn't I? I just wanna know you're okay.'

Ganzo's only half listening. His face is pointed towards the sounds of the busy kitchen and raucous customers.

'Ganzo.'

He meets my eyes and blinks.

'I don't know what to tell you, Dag. I used to hear a lot of things in my bar. I was a shoulder to cry on. But now I'm out back, and you know what? I prefer it this way. I don't want to know what's going on. I don't want any part of that world.'

I finger the chopsticks before me and poke at a morsel of tuna. I once accused Ganzo of burying his head in the sand, and it didn't make me feel better about myself. Maybe he's right; maybe I should let sleeping pandas lie.

'Ganzo! Back in the kitchen!'

'Sorry, Dag. It's rush hour.' He stands and pauses before the curtain. 'Any progress on your daughter?'

'Ryoko Nishi,' I say.

'Nishi?' His face falls. 'She knows where your daughter is?'

'Apparently. All I need to do is give her my votes and … well, take care of something.'

I see the cogs turn behind his eyes.

'Ganzo! Get the hell in here already!'

'Sorry, Dag, gotta go. Listen, don't worry about me, okay? Focus on finding your girl.'

He places a hand on my shoulder and turns. I watch him

disappear through the beads and see his silhouette shrink back into someone else's kitchen.

○

'Do you trust her?' Kosuke asks.

'I've known her a long time,' I say.

'That's not what I asked. She's a politician. That means you can trust her like a lamppost trusts a dog. But what does it matter who you vote for? They're all as bad as each other. I say give Nishi your votes. What do you have to lose?'

'It's not the voting part I'm stuck on.'

'Ah, of course,' Kosuke smiles indulgently. 'The redhead. You're fond of her.'

'She's a friend. I can't just give her up, not after what she's done for me.'

'Well then, it seems you're in a pickle, aren't you, Dag? Nishi knows where your daughter is, and the only way to get her is to throw the redhead under the Sonayan steam train.'

'Thanks for painting such a vivid picture.'

Kosuke sips his cocktail and smacks his lips. We're sitting in the lounge bar on the eleventh floor of his apartment block, a study in brown leather and polished oak. He's already tipsy, fresh from a 'business' meeting. I saw the suited gentlemen leave, rosy-cheeked and rowdy, as I lounged in the lobby with a newspaper.

'I'm sure you'll work it out,' he says with an absent smile.

I glance around at the lacquered surfaces, the glass lanterns that glow golden from the walls, the bookcase filled with dusty volumes of Sonaya's past. I watch the bartender arrange bottles of imported liquors on the shelves, serenaded by the tinkling of piano keys. Maybe the man with everything isn't the best person to ask for advice.

'So there's nothing you can do? With all your riches?'

'Oh, riches don't mean much when it comes to Ryoko Nishi.

You want my advice? Give your friend up. She'll probably get out after a few months, all she did was threaten a Borrower.'

'And kill a Rose. Nishi was happy enough to bury it at the time, but she'll dig it up if it suits her. And cuffing a murderer will do wonders for her reputation.'

'You're getting soft, Dag. Wanting to see your daughter, I can understand. But sticking your neck out for a Bosozoku girl half your age?'

'You're one to talk, old man. But I guess Kiki's more like a third of your age... a quarter, even?'

'Watch it, Kawasaki. Just watch it.'

Kosuke seethes for a moment before barking at the bartender. Moments later two fresh mojitos sit before us. 'And bring two more down to the eighth floor,' he tells her. 'I've something to show you, Dag.'

He rises with our drinks and I follow him to the elevator.

'Hell,' Kosuke says, pushing for the eighth floor. 'Sometimes I forget what you've gone through. Back then,' he pauses to belch, 'you had it all in your grasp. You were so close to having it all.'

'I don't need reminding.'

When the doors open we emerge into a room I've never seen before. For a moment I think we're in a museum or a trophy room—rows of glass cases assemble before us.

'My private collection,' Kosuke announces with a wistful look in his eyes. 'Memories of Sonaya.'

He sips his mojito and advances to the first cabinet. I lean in and peer through the glass, where newspaper clippings and grainy photos spill Sonaya's past. It's a study of flags and handshakes and morose-looking men signing contracts.

A long time ago Sonaya was part of Korea, but Japan's invasion of the Hermit Kingdom changed all that. Still, it wasn't until the First Korean War that outsiders took any real interest. The UN helped broker a deal, granting Korea fishing rights and access to Sonaya's source of natural gas while leaving the island under Japan's jurisdiction. It was a disappointing deal for both countries, and Sonaya's inhabitants weren't happy either. They weren't Japanese, of course; they were Sonayan, and they had to wait almost a century to get what they wanted.

'Independence Day, 2035. Look at you.'

I peer at the photos through the glass. There's me, twenty-four years old, long hair, two ears; youth and a bright future ahead of me.

'That was before you met Hana.'

'After my first tax assessment,' I say, nodding. 'A newly-crowned ten. I didn't know how much it would affect my life. Damn, I enjoyed myself in those days.'

I study the photos. Parties, bars, picnics at the Hunting Grounds. Ganzo before he grew a goatee. Nakata with porcupine hair, before she came out to her parents and retreated to a basement. Kosuke, full stomached and smiling, looking much the same.

'You were different from all the others,' he says. 'The ikemen, they called them in Japan. Handsome playboys.'

'How was I different?'

'You didn't have it all handed to you on a plate, that's how. Once your father died and your mother returned to Tokyo, you had nothing.'

'I had you.'

'And I was careful not to spoil you. I made you work for everything you got. Your job, your life—I showed you the doors, but you opened them yourself. That's why you were so close to greatness; you never fell for it.' He opens his arms wide and whispers, 'The big charade.'

I sip my mojito and follow him to the next cabinet.

'Not to say you weren't proud of your looks—you were handsome and you knew it—but you weren't born into the club like the rest of them. You were essentially an orphan at sixteen, right when Sonaya was on the up. Industry booming, disposable incomes, the great rat race. It was all a game, and the winners were the ones with pretty faces. That's what happens when a poor nation grows out of the ashes; people become obsessed with the material. Looks, money, possessions. The money didn't last, of course—the boom was short-lived—but the obsessions remain.'

He stares at paraphernalia of the transition days, when Japan labelled Sonaya a 'special administrative region'. Smart phones of various sizes and brands; packs of cigarettes and cigars; a photo of a young Kosuke leaning on a sleek car.

'You haven't done too badly for yourself, old man. Or did you forget where you're living?'

The elevator doors open and the bartender enters with fresh mojitos. She stands to attention with the tray in hand, staring blankly ahead like a soldier awaiting command. Kosuke ignores her.

'I found my own way to beat the system,' he says with a twinkle in his eye. 'But I wasn't one of the darlings of Sonaya's social scene. There was a split in those days. The otaku went one way, the ikemen the other. The otaku retreated into online worlds to date pixelated partners. Or buried their heads so deep into careers they lost interest in sex altogether. The ikemen were the only ones getting any. That's why the handsome tax came in.'

'And which side did you fall on?' I ask.

Kosuke laughs with a hint of melancholy. 'I was a lonely man, nothing more.' He moves onto the next row. 'My point is that you deserved the life you had. That's what Hana saw in you that so many others failed to see. That's how she changed you from a poser playboy into a decent man.'

'*Almost*,' I correct him. 'Almost changed me.'

'Don't be too proud of that,' Kosuke says. 'I've gushed enough on your behalf. I haven't forgotten that you slept with Ryoko and lost the best thing in your life.' He sighs. 'Beauty is wasted on the young. No, beauty is the curse of humanity.'

Kosuke swigs, reducing his cocktail to a vase of ice and

sodden leaves. He clicks his finger and the barwoman relieves us of our glasses and hands over fresh drinks.

'You were a supporter, then?' I ask. 'Of the handsome tax?'

Kosuke exhales heavily. 'It levelled out the playing field, you have to give it that. Gave no-hopers like me a chance to keep up with the pack.'

'Keep up? Or break away?'

I'm surprised to hear the bitterness in my voice. Maybe it was the visit to Hee-chan's goshitel and the sight of families crammed into shoeboxes. Maybe it's all the time I've spent with Shinji, who wears the same three shirts on rotation. Maybe this is what happens when your friends live at opposite ends of the money ladder.

Kosuke cocks an eyebrow. 'You don't resent me this, do you, Dag? You don't resent an old man his comforts?'

'Ever since independence, since the handsome tax and all these bullshit policies, the rich have been getting richer while the poor get poorer.'

'And I'm to blame for that, am I?'

I shake my head and suck at my cocktail.

'I didn't know you had such an interest in politics, Dag. It never used to concern you.'

'That's because I used to be on the winning side.'

For a few moments we both stare into the past, gazing at the photos of our younger selves, remembering a world that no longer exists.

'Listen,' I say. 'I better get going.'

Kosuke frowns. 'Don't bog yourself down, Dag. Prioritize. You want your daughter, that's the bottom line, so do what it takes to get her. If that means a gutter gangster like Jiko has to pay for her crimes, so be it. Remember who you used to be. Nothing comes free in Sonaya—you have to work for it, like you used to.'

I stare at the old man for a few seconds, then I make for the elevator without saying goodbye.

A black motorbike purrs outside the boarding house. I've had so many meetings in the past few days, I'd almost forgotten all about the old man in leather and tattoos.

'You could have sent a pigeon,' I say. 'No need to come all the way over here.'

Bull steps off his bike. 'Any excuse to get outside.'

'So you *are* as lonely as you look.'

I'm disappointed by Bull's expression. I wanted a smart retort and a dressing down, but all I get is a sad, beaten look that's compounded by the falling rain. It's coming down in heavy splats now, cold against my skin, and Bull's leathers shine with glistening drops.

'What can I do for you, then?' I say.

'Your daughter. I did some research.'

'And?'

'I asked a few of my girls. One of them knew a girl called Maaya from a few months back. Twelve years old, like you said, but she went by the name of Echo back then. Used to be a bell girl down in the Fish Nets.'

'Echo? And what the hell's a bell girl?'

'Kind of secretary, you could say. Door girl, helper, whatever. They're usually the younger sibling of some kid who's working in the same place. Sometimes they're not. Sometimes they're sent in by druggie parents who don't give a shit how they get their fix. Sometimes the kids come in off the streets of their own accord, trying to find a way to feed themselves.'

'In the Fish Nets?'

'A place called Grade A.'

'You ever been there?'

Bull's lip curls. 'I don't go to the Fish Nets.'

'Why not?'

'Go there yourself and see why.'

Bull remounts and revs his bike, shining black in the evening shower. I reach into my pocket.

'I don't want your damn money. Do I look like a pigeon to you?'

'So what?' I say. 'Are you trying to prove something by telling me all this?'

'If there's a chance your little girl is still working in the Fish Nets, you'd better get there as soon as you can.' He studies my face. 'I'm not a ...' he says, but he can't find the word he's searching for. All he does is stare like he's daring me to disagree.

'I know,' I say.

He nods and I watch his bike disappear down the dark alley in a curtain of rain.

17

I turn left at the giant neon heart and avoid the desperate hands that claw at my clothes on Lovers' Lane. Pre-teen boys glare at me from a dark doorstep and catcalls rain down from open windows dressed with lace and lingerie. Before I went away these buildings used to churn out electronics. Now they only churn out STDs.

I've seen glimpses of Fumiko's slice of the pleasure quarter —lurid pink buildings that smell of candy floss and disinfectant —but tonight I'm venturing deeper into Sonaya's sordid depths. Just beyond the comforting glare of purple spotlights basks the Fish Nets, decaying in a rotten corner of a rotten district. Pitch-black passages spill putrid odours and even pimps blush at its web of kinky cul-de-sacs. This was the pleasure quarter before the boom; most was burned down by gangs when the big corps started redeveloping. But no one dared destroy the Fish Nets.

I'm no longer a wanted man, but I've still got my pride. I recruit my old fedora and pull its wide brim down towards my nose as I enter the first crooked row of hovels. I'm already half drenched. My trousers are stuck to my legs and raindrops dribble over the rim of my fedora, soaking my shoulders. As soon as my feet hit the Fish Nets' first puddles I'm face to face with a man twice my size. He plods out of the darkness, dabbing a dirty handkerchief at his sweaty red face. I back up against the wall to let him pass and he ogles me with pink piggy eyes before disappearing into darkness.

I venture through unlit alleys until I meet a small boy sat beneath a torn paper lantern.

'You know where Grade A is?'

The boy peers up at me with cowed eyes. His hand hovers nervously over his pocket like a gunslinger.

'Don't worry, kid, I'm just looking for someone. What's a boy your age doing here?'

He flicks his eyes towards the shuttered window over his shoulder. 'My brother's working.'

'Homework Club?'

He nods.

'How old is your brother?'

'Thirteen.'

I stare at the battered wooden door. Maybe it's all good. Maybe it's a retired professor drilling algebra, or a housewife explaining the causes of the Second Korean War. Maybe.

I feel the boy's eyes on me as I take off and scour the other shacks. Some are simple watering holes: tiny bars with grim customers perched on stools. Others have lists of names and prices pinned to the wall, and you can hear exactly what the customers are learning. I stop at a door scarred with the symbol of Homework Clubs across Sonaya: a pencil poised over a notebook. When I knock, the door swings open and almost re-breaks my nose.

A teenage girl squints out into the rain, her features scrunched up with suspicion.

'Yes?'

'Is this Grade A?' I ask.

The girl's pigtails run relays past her ears.

'Do you know where it is?'

'Third alley over, the one with the plant outside.' She tries to close the door, but I get a boot inside before she can return to the flickering candlelight within.

'You know a girl called Maaya? Or Echo? She's twelve years old.'

The girl studies my face. I know how this must look.

'She's my daughter.'

She squints and shakes her head again. 'If you find her, get her out of here,' she says before slamming the door in my face.

I cut through a narrow corridor between buildings, stepping over rat corpses and a pair of soiled underpants. In the third alley a half-naked man watches me as rain dribbles down his handsome face and ripped stomach.

'Fancy a go?' he says.

'Not tonight,' I reply, keeping my eyes down. I head straight for the potted bonsai tree, take a deep breath, and rap my knuckles on the door. It creaks open to reveal the timid face of a twelve-year-old girl.

Her long dark hair is matted and tangled in places, just like mine was before I went short. She stares at me with big, pretty dark eyes and a cute button nose.

'Good evening, sir,' she says, attempting a smile that comes out lopsided.

'Evening.'

I scan her features, trying to find some resemblance to me or Hana. I don't feel it.

'Are you coming in, sir?'

'I will.'

She stands back to let me through. It's a tiny place with a mezzanine squeezed in above the bar. I advance on the corner table and try to make myself comfortable on the stool. All I see on the second floor is a drawn curtain and two pairs of feet; one belongs to a girl, the other to a grown man. Between beats of background J-pop I hear the girl giggling and the man laughing gruffly.

The young girl hands me a menu. The first page has a list

of drinks and the next has photos of teenagers. I read the biography beneath the first photo.

Sasha, age 16. Likes: K-pop, J-pop, cats, hot chocolate with marshmallows, comic books. Needs help with: maths, English, everything!

I glance at the girl before me and try to match her to a photo.

'You're not on here,' I say.

'I'm just starting,' she says, her voice shaking.

I flip the menu over to scan the cocktails.

'Give me an Old Fashioned,' I say. 'And whatever you want.'

'The manager says I'm not to start yet,' the girl says.

'What's your name?'

'Cho,' she says.

'Cho. Choose something for yourself and make me an Old Fashioned, and then sit with me for five minutes.'

She eyeballs me like I've just asked her to dance the foxtrot. I don't know how to talk to kids. I'm so used to Shinji's smart mouth I forget what most kids are really like.

'Five minutes, I promise.' I put everything into arranging a smile.

Eventually she scuttles off, ducking beneath the bar and setting about my drink. She has to stand on tiptoes to look at the instructions on the cocktail menu. I watch the top of her head bob behind the bar as she raids the fridge and looks for bottles and glasses, all the while straining my ears to listen to the meeting upstairs. The man's voice is low and muffled. The girl must be an old hand; she laughs at everything that comes out of his mouth.

I stand and slip behind the bar, take the bottle from Cho's hand and start mixing my Old Fashioned. She looks down at her shoes.

'Don't worry,' I tell her. 'You're doing fine. What will you have?'

She raises her eyes to mine. 'Orange juice,' she says in barely more than a whisper.

I pour a juice and hand her the glasses.

'Now take these to the table,' I say. 'That's it.'

She spills some of the juice as she ducks under the bar. I wipe down the table and Cho pulls a mangy pink curtain around us.

'You don't have to do that.'

'It's the rules, sir,' Cho says, climbing onto the stool. 'That's what all the other kids do, I've seen them.'

She stares at me, looking terrified. I hear rain pattering on the tin roof above.

'Enjoy your drink,' I tell her. 'Relax. I just want to ask you some questions, and then I'm leaving.'

Cho sips noisily through a straw. She blinks happily at the glass after she swallows.

'How long have you been here?'

'This is my first week, sir.'

'Good,' I say. 'You're doing well.'

She smiles tentatively.

'And why are you here?'

Cho points at the curtain and lowers her voice. 'That's my sister. They made me come, so we can help mum with the bills. She's been out of work ever since the accident.'

I nod and take a swig of my Old Fashioned. It might taste good if I were anywhere else in the world. I need to finish this as soon as possible.

'I'm looking for someone,' I say. 'A girl who used to work here. Her name is Maaya, but she also goes by the name Echo.'

Cho takes another sip and shakes her head. 'I don't know anyone by those names. Like I said, I haven't been here long.'

'You wouldn't have any of those old menus, would you? Like this one.'

Cho shrugs. 'I can have a look.'

'I'd appreciate it.'

She pushes the curtain aside and I hear her rooting around behind the bar. She returns with a fat pile of menus and I start scanning. Looking into the girls' faces, looking for an Echo, thinking I'll recognise my daughter right away.

The front door swings open and Cho's eyes widen.

'Cho,' a man's voice calls. She quickly slips out behind the curtain, leaving me hidden. I can't waste any time; I thumb quickly through the menus.

'The hell you think you're doin'?' the man barks.

'He wanted to talk to me,' Cho whispers back. 'He paid up already, said he'd only be here five minutes.'

Some of the faces appear again and again on the menus, but there are a lot of one-timers too.

'Well his time's done,' the man says.

Then I see her. Half way down a tattered page, half-concealed by a whisky stain. *Echo*. Short neat hair down to her ears, a ruler-straight fringe, a morose expression. I *do* recognise her. I recognise her because I've met her a dozen times before. My heart hammers with such force I half expect my ribs to shatter and tumble down into my stomach. I quickly fold the menu and shove it inside my pocket.

The man draws the curtain aside just as I'm bringing the glass to my mouth in the most casual way possible.

He's big and handsome, just as I expected. Anyone running a place like this must have fallen on hard times, and in Sonaya it's the handsome men who fall the hardest. He's about my age, I reckon, early forties, with pompadour hair and a thick moustache.

'Time's up, friend.' He gestures to my drink and notices the pile of menus in front of me. 'What the hell's this about?'

He looks between me and Cho for an answer.

'I took them from behind the bar,' I say. 'Wanted to find a girl I used to see.'

'Does this look like fuckin' City Hall to you? Get the hell out of here.'

I remain seated and take another slow swig. When I'm done

I stand and fish inside my pocket for an extra note. I hand it to Cho.

'Nice place,' I say to the man. Then I shoulder past him and disappear into the rain.

As soon as I'm clear of the Fish Nets I remove the menu from my pocket and look again at the girl in the picture. I imagine her without the hair. I imagine her with black studs embedded in her ears. I imagine her in a black shirt and khaki cargos and a scrap of paper in her hand.

I can't believe how stupid I've been, how I didn't recognise her before. The eyes; the stubborn expression. How did I fail to recognise my own kin?

The Dove.

18

JIKO

Red. The colour of flame. The colour of passion. The colour of my bike. The colour of Jitsuko Ryu.

I watch the hair fall over my shoulders like tendrils of fiery smoke, lilting and spiraling to the floor. The scissors snip and chop with deafening bites that echo around the chamber, and the razor follows with vibrating teeth that scratch at my scalp like hungry mites.

As my reflection transforms before my eyes, I keep expecting to see someone different staring back. Someone stronger, maybe; someone who can tell me if this is the right thing to do. But all I see is the same scared girl, a bird of paradise with her feathers plucked, left naked in the dark.

'Lenses?' the cocoon weaver asks, offering a tray full of multicoloured contacts.

'Why not?'

I peruse the selection, take my time. I pick out caramel.

'Going for a colourful look, are you?'

'No,' I say. 'Only the eyes. Everything else is black. Everything.'

The weaver nods and gets to work on the rest of me. My skin is bronzed, my ears pinned back an inch. My eyebrows are reshaped above false eyelashes. New choker, new earring, new clothes. She starts work on my tattoo, a cover-up job that will take a few sessions.

When we're all done I examine myself in the body-length mirror.

'You look entirely different,' she says as I pay up.

'Funny,' I reply. 'I feel exactly the same.'

I sit in the lobby and wait for the others to emerge from their cocoons. The basement is cold and dark and sounds echo off the damp stones walls. I hear a woman crying, the sound of a drill penetrating bone, the rumbling purr of a razor, muffled screams. A cocoon weaver emerges from an unmarked door in a blood-splattered smock, his bloated face ablaze with panic as he races down the corridor clutching metal instruments coated red.

Silently I pray to some god I've never acknowledged, hoping the blood doesn't belong to one of my friends.

Su-young appears first, looking more confident than ever, and Bo-min follows soon after. We exchange appraising looks; new hair, minor amendments to the faces I've grown to know so well. I'm not surprised by their new looks—I knew every change they were planning—but there's something unnerving about seeing the transformations. Like there's no going back.

Half an hour later Kano emerges with a new bob, paler skin, and swelling around her eyes—she's had her eyelids done, something she'd been threatening to do for months. Mia comes last, her pink hair straightened and dyed black, a bandage and splint over her nose.

'I told you not to do your nose,' Su-young berates. 'You're not even on the wanted list.'

'Better safe than sorry,' Mia says, fingering the bandage. 'Suzie …' she starts, but she can't finish it. I know what she's thinking: if they found Suzie, they can find any of us. She clears her throat and shuffles on her feet. 'Anyway, my nose was too small.'

As I stare at my transformed comrades, I lament how we came to be so few. The others scarpered as soon as we cleared out of the bar, off to distant relatives on Broken Hill or friends deep in the Rivers.

'Well, what's next?' Kano asks, turning to me.

The others follow her gaze.

'You all know what's next,' I say. 'The bikes.'

We ride through the rain-drenched back alleys, and I guide my Ducati with the utmost care, crawling at a pace that seems unnatural. None of the others complain. This is our last ride together, and none of us wants to be parted from machines that are more like extensions of our souls. I feel the engine's melancholy vibration through my bones, like a dying cat purring on its owner's lap.

Eventually we reach our destination and I dismount slowly. The girls follow suit and we stare at each other through the rain, as if hoping for some last minute reprieve. None comes.

I first came here to pawn my bike a few months back, and not much has changed. A black-coated den glazed in oil and bursting with bike parts, it would be my idea of heaven if it weren't for the pot-bellied manager in greasy overalls.

'What do you want?'

He directs the question to my legs. When he finally glances at my face, there's no hint of recognition. At least the cocoon did its job.

'We've got five bikes to sell. You interested?'

He straightens up and runs a hand over his stubbled chin. 'Let's have a gander at them.'

He follows me to the alley where the girls are waiting. They're still unwilling to lose contact with their bikes. They lean against the fuel tanks, or else leave a hand on the seat or the handlebars. Raindrops filter through the canopy of wires above, falling quietly onto the bodies of my statuesque friends.

'Pretty old models,' the man says, caressing my Ducati. It's like seeing someone stroke your sleeping face while you watch from afar.

'Don't try to bullshit us,' I say. 'We know what these bikes are worth. If you can't pay us what we want, we'll take them somewhere else.'

The man continues as if he hasn't heard me. He inspects the bikes one by one, revving the engines, scrutinising the fuel tanks and tyres. We stand back and watch, feeling violated.

'I'll need to check them properly. It'll take a while.'

I see a movement in one of the second floor windows, but I don't let my gaze linger.

'We need a quick sale,' I say, 'and paint jobs as soon as possible. We'll take a discount for the trouble.'

The mechanic grins. 'On the run, are you? Yes, look at those bandages, you're fresh out of the cocoons. Perhaps the reward is worth more to me than your bikes.'

Kano steps up behind him. She looks at me for confirmation, and when I nod she wrestles him into a headlock. Kano isn't tall, but she's twice the size of the rest of us, a solid unit of muscle and fat. The man turns red in the face as his arms flail in vain. Bo-min steps before him and reveals her knuckle-duster.

'Stop struggling,' Su-young says. 'You'll only die quicker.'

The man spits but soon stops fighting Kano's vice grip.

'I told you we'd give you a good deal,' I say. 'And if we get a sniff of trouble, if a single person recognizes those bikes, you'll die with a fucking engine shoved halfway down your throat.'

Kano releases him and he falls face-first into a puddle, coughing and spluttering.

'One million,' he says, shooting evil glances all round.

'One point five,' I say.

Kano takes a step closer to him.

'Done,' he says.

We split the money between us and for a moment no one says anything. We're bike-less. It doesn't feel real. *I* don't feel real.

'You sure you're not coming with us?' Su-young asks.

Kano and Mia shake their heads. Kano has an ex in the Rivers who's agreed to put them up.

'If the dust clears,' she says, 'and our names aren't in neon when it does, we might stick around. If it turns out the police are after us too, we'll split.' She taps the pocket of her jacket, the cash from her bike stowed safely away.

'You shouldn't have been involved in this,' I say. 'It wasn't you who threatened Baek.'

'We *chose* to be involved,' Mia says. 'We chose everything together.'

'And we don't regret any of it,' Kano adds.

The five of us converge and join arms.

'This isn't the end,' I tell them. 'Just a break.'

We watch Kano and Mia join the gathering throng near the subway station. Regular faces in the crowd, lost in a sea of umbrellas. Bosozoku no more.

'We need to get the last of our stuff to Broken Hill,' Su-young says. 'Clean out the bar.'

'You two get on it,' I say.

'What are you gonna do?'

'Me? I need a word with that woman who's been watching us ever since we arrived.'

'I didn't realise I could be seen,' Sara Barnes says.

'The others didn't see you,' I say.

'I suppose that's why you're the leader. I like the new look, by the way. If it weren't for your bikes, I wouldn't have known you. I suppose that's why you sold them?'

'Suz-', I start, but her name catches in my throat. 'One of our girls, Suzie …'

Sara nods. 'I heard what happened. I didn't know Suzie, but when I heard what they did I died a little. It was barbaric.'

'She was a good person,' I say, remembering the smile beneath her wild mop of hair. 'She didn't deserve to die—she'd already sacrificed so much for us.' I feel the weight in my stomach as anger summons tears to my eyes. 'But she was murdered, butchered like an animal, and now *we're* the ones who are wanted.'

'You threatened Baek,' Sara says quietly. 'A pretty dangerous person to mess with. Did you really think she would accept your demands?'

I brush away tears and stand at the window. 'And that's why I won't be the leader anymore. That's why there's no gang anymore. We're finished, all because of my stupid decisions. Your little Nightshades will be pleased to hear it, I'm sure. The central Rivers are yours now.'

'They were mine already.'

I turn and see that Sara's smiling.

'Take a drink, Jiko. It's been a while since I had intelligent company.'

She pours out two glasses. I don't like whisky, but I've never admitted it. I accept the glass and try to conceal the grimace as the drink kicks down my throat.

'Please excuse the smell,' Sara says. 'The dear next door is an aggressive cook. Specialises in anything that can be violently fermented.'

'How do you do it?' I ask. 'Lead that group. The Nightshades. Make calls that can affect their lives forever.'

'The difference between me and you is that I don't give a shit what happens to my guys. It's purely business. They don't respect me, they don't love me. I've seen the way your girls look at you, Jiko. They believe in you.'

I take another slug of whisky. 'They shouldn't.'

'Everyone makes mistakes. Don't punish yourself for them. I've got my fair share of horror stories, things I wish I could take back. I shot Goichi Fujii two months ago—killed him. I made a snap call, and now I have to live with it. Just like you have to live with the death of the Rose you killed. Put it in your pocket, carry it with you, but don't let it drag you down.'

'It's been dragging me down for a while. The others don't understand.'

'They've got their own worries, their own troubles. I don't know your girls, but I know most of them were part of Fumiko's flock. I know they grew up on the streets. I know they've done things they probably regret. But unlike me, they didn't have a choice.'

'What do you mean?'

'I mean I'm no orphan of Sonaya,' Sara says shortly. 'I didn't have to come here, I didn't have to stay. I don't have to do the things I do. Sometimes I scare myself.'

'So follow your own advice. Don't let it drag you down.'

'I don't mean that. I don't regret killing Fujii, not really. But sometimes I snap. Lose control.'

She brings the glass to her mouth. Her movements are so smooth, so precise, she doesn't look capable of losing control of so much as a blink.

'I almost hurt Ganzo,' she says, so quietly I hold my breath. 'Almost beat him to a pulp. Can you imagine that? I almost became one of the people I despise. One of the people I came here to stop.'

'What did you do?'

'Nothing … in the end. Ganzo talked, told me what I needed to know. But if he hadn't … it scares me what I was about to do.'

I swallow, and I swear the sound of it echoes around the room.

Sara finishes her drink and refills her glass.

'You wouldn't have done it,' I say. 'You're not that person.'

'I used to think that too,' she says in barely more than a whisper. 'But it's this place. These men. These secrets. There's a set of rules here, and I don't follow them, even if I try.'

'Because you're a woman?'

'Because I'm a woman. Because I'm foreign. Because I'm Black. Because I'm the only fucking person trying to break through this goddamn shield of corruption. I tried getting through, Jiko. I tried doing it my way, but it didn't work. Kenya Oh was right—I have to do it *their* way. Even if it means losing myself.'

She downs her second glass and stares at a point on the floor.

'If it means anything,' I say, 'you have my respect, Sara. I tried it their way, too. I tried threats, I tried violence. None of it worked. Keep doing it your way—you'll get there in the end.'

'And you?' she asks. 'Are you still giving up the fight?'

I shake my head. 'I don't know. I'm tired of trying to be something I'm not.'

Sara Barnes smiles again; it's a smile that exudes confidence and cool.

'So don't,' she says. 'You've got fears and regrets, Jiko, the same as every other fucked up human in this city. It doesn't make you weak. Take those flaws and own them, and then no one can touch you.'

I nod and finish my drink, and this time I let the grimace show on my face.

'I fucking hate whisky,' I say.

The Dove.

A street kid in tattered clothes. I think back over our meetings, try to remember every look in her eyes, every motion, every word out of her mouth. Plucky, difficult, scathing. Now that I know, I can't believe I didn't see the similarities. My own blood. My kin. My little Dagette.

Suddenly the little pigeon isn't a pigeon; she's a beautiful creature with life and wit and a brain. She fooled everyone and made a life for herself, right under our noses. She must have escaped Fujii and slipped straight into a cocoon to transform. Sonaya is crawling with streetwise kids, but she's something else.

I wonder what she must think of me. If she knew Fujii wasn't her real father and that she shared blood with a criminal. The very person who killed her mother and ruined her life.

I don't waste any time. On my way back from the Fish Nets I stop by the aviary. It's almost midnight, but the goshitel is a hive of activity. Kids play tag on the stairwell, leaping gleefully over cockroach carcasses, while teens slumped against corridor walls share bottles of beer.

I avoid a maze of mouse droppings and knock on door 302. Hee-chan's mum peers out at me from the darkness until her eyes widen in recognition. She slips out into the corridor and closes the door carefully behind her.

'Mr. Kawasaki,' she whispers. 'We weren't expecting you at this hour. I'm afraid Hee-chan is asleep. He needs his rest, you see. It's a school night.'

'I've got some work for him. It's important. Remember I told you I'd pay extra for inconvenient hours.'

Worry lines etch themselves onto her forehead.

'He'll be a couple of hours at most,' I say. 'If I can be blunt, this kind of thing should be a pigeon's bread and butter. Your son is a sweet boy, but there are a lot of kids in this building looking to make easy money. If Hee-chan can't do night jobs, I'll find a pigeon that can.'

'Just give me a moment, please, Mr. Kawasaki.'

She re-enters the room, and through the paper-thin walls I hear the kid being woken, the mother's gentle assurances, the exchange of love-yous and I'll-miss-yous. I almost wish she'd slammed the door in my face and told me to find someone else. In this tower of poverty and ruin, I've stumbled across the only happy family in Sonaya. And I've burst in and ripped off their blanket of peace.

Hee-chan squints into the garish light of the corridor. Part of me expected him to come out wearing teddy bear pyjamas. His mother appears behind him and brushes his hair to one side like a choir boy. He beams as she plants a kiss on his lips.

'I'll be waiting up for him, Mr. Kawasaki,' she says, placing her hands on his shoulders and presenting him to me.

'I don't doubt it,' I say.

Her eyes trail us until we disappear down the stairs.

I buy Hee-chan a hot chocolate at a grubby all-night café, and he cradles the paper cup like he's terrified it might float away. He can barely take his eyes off the steaming liquid.

'You got a father, kid?'

Hee-chan shakes his head. 'It's just me and mum and Hee-kyung.'

'Your mum do anything for work?'

'She helps clean the goshitel.'

'And your sister?'

'She goes to school sometimes. Not very much anymore. Mum thinks she's wasting her talent.'

I watch the rain hit the window beside us. A bicycle skids through a puddle and soaks a skeletal street cat.

'And you? What do you think of these pigeon jobs so far? You enjoy it?'

He shrugs. 'I'm not sure yet.'

'Well you're about to get a lot busier. Make some money, help out your mum, right? Now, do you have a pencil and paper?' He whips a notebook and pencil from his pocket, holds them gleefully between us. 'Good lad. Now listen up.'

He scribbles down names and addresses with his tongue sticking out. He stops halfway through sentences to take sips of hot chocolate, and I wait for him to finish before continuing. It feels like I'm sending a pre-schooler out into a foreign country.

'Now repeat all of that to me,' I say.

'Find the woman called Jiko first,' Hee-chan recites, squinting at the scrap of paper in his hand. 'Check the wine bar Vino Isorimu.'

It's a risk, I know. If Nishi finds out I'm still drinking buddies with her prime target, I could lose it all. But until I get answers, I need to keep all my plates spinning.

Hee-chan continues reeling off my directions. Jiko, Shinji, Sara. Three messages—I wonder how many of them will get through.

Sometimes you hear a knock and you know the person behind it is trouble. I drag myself from my armchair and open the door to two strangers.

'You Kawasaki?'

'Who's asking?'

They push past me without invitation. The tiny man has a squirrelly face and bristly hair between monkey ears. His grey suit was made for someone twice his size and his steel cap boots could double as battering rams. He noses around the corners of my flat like a terrier sniffing out a bone, while the woman stands before me with her arms folded. She's broad and tall, her hair a short back and sides.

'Can I help you with something?' I ask, watching the terrier thumb through my clothes.

'You holding?' the woman asks.

'Yeah, and good thing I am,' I say. 'People keep bursting in here without invitation.'

She draws a baseball bat out of her suit jacket and weighs it in her hands. I'm about to recruit Trusty from my ankle when she speaks again.

'I let him carry the gun,' she says coolly, running her eyes up and down the bat. 'He enjoys it more than I do.'

The little man has a pistol in his hand and he bares his teeth when he points the barrel my way.

'Drop whatever you're holding, Kawasaki,' the woman says. 'We're just here to talk.'

The little man sneers at me. I slowly remove Old Trusty and kick it across the floor. The woman picks it up and examines it.

'What do you want?' I ask.

The little man laughs. 'Maybe my pistol can tell you what we want.'

I cross to the kitchen counter and rinse out two glasses. I pour a dram of whisky in each and hand one to the woman.

'Maybe you should talk to me nicely in my own house,' I say, drinking from the other glass.

The little man steps forward and shakes his gun like he's trying to get bubbles to come out the end.

'Calm it, Koo,' the woman says, sipping her drink. 'This guy's name is Koo. He's a good guy, but he's having a bad week. His wife left him, you see. Give him a drink and he calms down a bit.'

The little man glares at me with his corn-coloured teeth still bared. I set my glass down and pour another whisky.

'Were you out tonight, Kawasaki?' the woman asks.

'I go out a lot,' I say. 'You were lucky to catch me in.'

I hand the drink to Koo, who keeps his gun trained on me. 'We weren't lucky with anything. You were out in the Fish Nets tonight.'

I lean against the counter. 'Is that a question?'

Koo shakes his gun again. He could have fallen out of a comic book.

'Calm it, Koo,' the woman says. 'He's just playing with you.'

She places her glass on the coffee table and grips the baseball bat in both hands. She does a practice swing that could knock a head clean off its neck.

'Ask the man the question, Koo,' she says.

The sneer returns to the little man's face. 'Were you at the Fish Nets tonight, asshole?'

My mouth is drying out fast, and I sip whisky just to get some slip on my tongue. 'I might have been there. I enjoy the company. I get lonely up here on my own.'

'That's good,' the woman says. 'Look at us all, playing nicely.'

A wild look enters the little man's eyes. 'Playing nicely,' he says.

'You went to an establishment called Grade A, didn't you?' the woman says. 'You started asking questions to a girl who works there. Is that right?'

I nod and finish my drink. I return to the bottle and top up my glass. 'Is there a problem with that?'

Koo laughs. 'Fish Nets ain't the place to go for questions.'

The woman nods solemnly. 'They don't like smart guys sneaking around. It turns the customers off, do you understand?'

I smile into my glass.

'He don't seem to hear you well enough, Mo,' Koo says, putting his glass down.

She raises a hand. 'He hears us, don't you Kawasaki?'

I take a long drink. 'I hear.'

'You ended up with something from there, didn't you?' Mo asks. 'Fell right into your pocket, didn't it? As you were leaving.'

I reach into my pocket and extract the menu of street kids. Mo snatches it from my outstretched hand.

'Who sent you here?' I ask.

Koo snickers.

'No one,' Mo says. 'That's why we're here. No one is bad people, someone you don't want to piss off. Look how cooperative Kawasaki's been, Koo. He's given us everything we wanted. I told you we wouldn't have to shoot him.'

'I prefer it when we shoot them,' Koo says.

'I think Kawasaki's a smart man. He doesn't want any trouble, same as us. We could get along, the three of us. Have a drink somewhere. Somewhere quiet, where no one will hear us. But if he keeps his nose down, we might not have a chance to see each other again. That would be sad, wouldn't it?'

'Sad,' Koo says.

I roll the ice around my glass. 'Are you two finished or is this tired pulp spiel gonna go on all night?'

'You think he's got the message, Koo?'

Koo shrugs. He's starting to look put out again. Maybe now that the fun's over he's remembering his wife.

'I got the message,' I say. 'I've seen more subtle messages scrawled in blood across toilet cubicles.'

Mo smiles gold; the contents of her mouth are probably worth more than my entire apartment. She crosses to the kitchen, raises the bat above her head and brings it crashing down over my drink shelf. Glass shatters all over the counter and floor. I try not to wince with each crushing blow. When she's done, Mo regards the new collage she's made of my kitchen.

'Just making sure,' she says.

The little man snickers. 'That's why it's me that carries the gun. Old Mo, she can't control her emotions.'

Koo joins Mo in the kitchen. Broken glass crunches under his steel cap shoes.

'The whisky's good,' he says, picking up the only bottle that Mo didn't shatter. 'You don't mind, do you?'

I shake my head and swallow. Mo hands me my knife; I've never seen hands so calm after such an outburst. She flashes another gold smile and opens the door. They exit and leave me alone without a single shot left to take the bitter taste away.

20

I don't know why I've come. Hee-chan already told me the Bosozoku have left. He was lucky to catch one of the girls as she was leaving with sacks of clothes. I didn't recognise his description, but maybe that's a good thing—it means they've already been transformed in cocoons. Whoever it was, she promised to pass my message onto Jiko.

I stroll down the stairs, maybe for the last time. They didn't even bother to lock everything up; I guess there was no point. The lights are off, the tables empty, the air stuffy and sour. At the bottom of the stairs I glance around and remember the time I saw the Dove at the bar nursing a glass of white. Then I realise I'm not alone. There's a figure on a barstool with his back to me. His silver hair glows in the darkness like a steel scratch in a midnight sky.

I step quietly through the room and soak in the smells of wine-soaked carpet and unwashed leather.

'What are you drinking?' I ask as I take a stool.

He doesn't look up; he simply slides the bottle towards me. I pull down a glass from the rack above the bar and pour out.

'Riesling. One their worst Rieslings, by the taste of it. No wonder they didn't take it with them.'

I taste it and he's right; it's dour.

For a few moments we sit in silence. I glance sideways at Silver Beard. He has the same dishevelled look I saw in the

Cow Shed. The parting in his hair isn't as clean as it once was, the beard not as finely groomed, his eyes not quite as sharp. Still, his suit is pressed and his shoes shine, and his woody aftershave blasts me with nostalgia for a time I never lived through.

'What are you doing here, Kenya?'

'The same as you, I am sure.'

'I doubt that very much,' I say. 'I'm not here for the Bosozoku, nor for their wine or their business. You won't take this place so easily, old man. They've signed the deeds over to Sawa Nakata; if you want this place, you'll have to make an offer like everyone else.'

Silver Beard smiles, and his eyes twinkle through the dark. 'I told you, Kawasaki, I am here for the same reason as you.'

I stare into his eyes. We hold each other's gaze, one smiling, one frowning, until the frowning one cracks. 'You found out that she was staying here,' I say. 'Maaya.'

'Your daughter, yes. Perhaps I was a little off my game. It happens once in a while. You reminded me of my responsibilities towards Fujii, towards his daughter—*your* daughter. You were right: the Roses may be finished, but I am not. I had my people re-open the dig, and I eventually found a lead. I discovered that Maaya took on a new identity—shaved her head, disguised herself as a pigeon of the streets. Quite a little firecracker, no? And she was last known to be squatting here.'

'Who was your source?'

Silver Beard sips his wine and ignores me. 'I will find her.'

'And when you do?'

He pauses with the wine glass at his lips. 'I have my orders.' He turns and peers at me intently, then his face breaks and he chuckles. 'From the grave, as it were.'

'What did Fujii ask you to do?'

He studies my face and for a moment I'm sure he's gonna spill it all. Then he turns away and thinks better of it.

'I'm guessing he didn't see me as part of Maaya's future,' I say.

'He didn't see you as much of anything,' Silver Beard responds quietly, running a finger around the rim of his glass. 'You used to have a reputation for being a force of life, a symbol of Sonaya at her hedonistic peak. Look at you now: a mere hindrance to greater plans.'

I take a deep breath and sip my wine as I scan the room.

'None of your bodyguards with you today?'

Silver Beard's finger ceases its slow rotation, and the old man turns to face me.

'Confident,' I say. 'That you think you can beat up my friends and poison me, and then expect me to sit here and do nothing while you're unarmed and unprotected. You're a complacent fuck, aren't you?'

The beard stretches as he shows his teeth and another chuckle escapes him.

'Bravo,' he says, holding out his hands. 'What's it to be? The famous ankle knife? How about a broken glass, would that be more poetic?'

'You don't think I would?'

'No, Kawasaki, I don't. I don't believe you want to, and I don't believe you would even if you *did* want to. Because you're more intelligent than most people give you credit for, and you know killing me would do you no good. But mostly,' he says, standing up, 'because you know that when I find your daughter, I'm going to make sure she ends up in safer hands than yours. And, deep deep down, that is exactly what you want.'

He stands before me, challenging me to disagree.

'Last chance,' he says, opening his arms to give me a clear shot at his chest. 'No?'

I grasp the neck of the empty glass in my hand and close my eyes, feel the slow rise and fall of my chest as I control my breathing. I picture myself smashing the glass and shoving the broken shards into the silver forest at his neck.

I open my eyes and shake my head. He smiles and offers one final chuckle as he heads for the stairs.

'Kenya,' I say, and he turns with his hand on the banister.

'We're not fucking done yet. Not by a long way.'

'Whatever you say, Kawasaki,' he says, his eyes twinkling until they disappear.

○

There's a sign on the wall: *Don't complain about it being cramped. The man on the next table could be the one.*

I glance at the man on the next table but he doesn't look like the one. I stare at the girl opposite me. She could have been the one twenty years ago.

She's fresh out of a cocoon, a shady hole called Tatiana's. It used to be the go-to place for handsome tax victims before Fumiko monopolized the transformation game. It's behind the derelict department store, in the basement arcade beneath a piercing shop; elbow your way through the punk teens, down a piss-soaked staircase and you're in.

They did a good job on Jiko. Now's she got a buzz-cut that would look good with khaki and a machine gun. Caramel lenses transform her eyes, but everything else is black: lipstick, choker, fake eyelashes that create a draft when she blinks. Her eyebrows have been thinned, her skin bronzed two shades towards amber, and a great gold hoop swings like a pendulum from one ear.

'How about the tattoo?' I ask.

She pulls at the neckline of her top to reveal her collarbone. Some of the formerly red rays of her Rising Sun tattoo have turned black. Japan's imperial sun replaced by Sonaya's black one.

'A work in progress,' she says. 'It'll take a few sessions to cover it up completely.'

'And the bar?'

'We'll use the money to start afresh,' Jiko says. 'We sold our bikes, too, bought some less conspicuous replacements. Some of the girls are looking to leave the city altogether.'

'I can think of two who'll be staying.'

'Su-young and Bo-min are in for life, same as me.'

'I hope they didn't change their hair colour, it was the only way I could tell you three apart.'

Jiko smiles, but it doesn't last long.

'I never thought I'd sell my bike. I always told myself I'd die before I lost her. She was my world.'

I dig into the steaming stew of tofu, potato, and perilla leaves and chase a mouthful with beer.

'Your world's changed. Now your world is Su-young and Bo-min, or whatever their names are now they're out of Tatiana's. Your world is what you've started, and what you're going to finish.'

'How am I going to finish it, Dag?'

I haven't got an answer for her.

'I should have got out when you told me to. Weeks ago, before it all went to shit. I should've left Sonaya and tried to make something of my life.'

I shake my head. 'I was wrong to tell you to leave. I only said that because I cared about you. Back then I thought you were just a stupid girl in over her head.'

'And now?'

'You're a woman, and one of the strongest people I know.'

She looks down at the steaming vat before us and stirs the contents absent-mindedly.

'Ever since I got out of The Heights,' I say, 'everything I've done has been for myself. I'm a selfish bastard, and I've always known it. But you're different. You're making a change, and you're not doing it for yourself. I don't need to give you advice, Red. Follow your instincts. If that means going back on everything you vowed, so be it.'

Jiko refills our glasses with soju and we bring them together over the pot. We hold them there for a few seconds, looking into each other's eyes, our glasses clouding with steam. Two outlaws sharing a drink before the end of the world.

Jiko finally drinks and grimaces. 'What did you wanna see me for anyway?'

'It's the Dove.'

'What about her?'

'She's my daughter.'

If Jiko had any food in her mouth it would fall out. Her mouth hangs open and I see clear through to her tonsils. Her eyes remain fixed on mine as she refills her glass and shoots.

'Don't take the piss.'

'It's true. I saw a picture—she had hair and everything. She almost looked like a real person. I should've seen it before.'

Jiko chews on her chopstick and looks like she's trying to solve an algebra equation. 'Where is she? Does she know?'

'I've no idea. Your wine bar's closed up, that was the only place I knew to look for her. Any idea where she might have gone?'

Jiko bites her bottom lip. 'We hadn't seen her in a couple of days, and we had to take off from Vino in a hurry. Maybe Shinji?'

'Maybe. But he's not my biggest fan at the moment. I haven't seen him since …'

'Christ, you never make things easy, do you? Just swallow your pride already, can't you? Go and apologise, make it up to him.'

I sink another shot. 'Where are the rest of the Bosozoku?'

'Broken Hill. We're renting the room beneath the Tiger and Crane till we can get somewhere decent.'

'Another basement?'

'We like the darkness,' Jiko says with a smile, trickling soju into our glasses. Then she squints at me. 'You like the darkness, too, don't you, Dag? That's why you pushed everyone away when times got tough. You're scared.'

'Scared of what exactly?'

'Scared of showing that you care. Scared of being with someone again.'

My eyes do a lap of Jiko's new face. She doesn't look like Jiko anymore. She's still pretty, she's still cool... and she still looks like someone half my age.

'Maybe you're right,' I say. 'But I'm trying to think of someone other than myself for a change. I don't have many needs, and most of them can fit inside this glass.'

I raise the shot and sink it, aware of Jiko's unflinching eyes on mine.

'You're making me uncomfortable,' I say.

Jiko smiles. 'Good.'

I plunge my spoon into our vat and chew away on a mouthful of spicy, dripping mushroom. Jiko continues to watch me, as though seeing me for the first time.

'Don't tell me you've fallen for this ruinous creation before you?' I say.

Jiko scoffs. 'If you were my age …' she says.

'Yeah?'

'I'd steer well clear of you.' She fills our glasses once more and raises hers with a smirk. 'Promise me you'll never suggest that again,' she says. 'Next time I won't be able to hold back the vomit.'

Got it.

I try to match her smile with one of my own, then I kill my drink and stand.

'I'm gonna talk to your girls. Maybe they've seen the Dove.'

'No one's seen her, Dag-'

I drop money on the table. 'Take it easy, Red. And watch out for the man on the next table, he might be the one.'

The Tiger and Crane is a Broken Hill institution, a tin-roof bar that sets new standards for Sonayan squalor. In the shadow of a school with as many squatters as students, it's packed with bent-backed fogeys who stare over stale ales with sad, watery eyes. Mildew and mould colour the walls and flies swarm the bathrooms, the toilets backed up with weeks of shit.

I take a seat at the bar in front of Eun-joo, the squat owner who can barely see over the counter. She stands before me and we watch each other with straight faces. Eun-joo has a golden-blonde bob that frames hamster cheeks and eyes that could pierce a fortress wall. She's as wide as she is wily, and I guess that means she's a lot wilier than she was twelve years ago.

'You've got nerve coming back in here, Kawasaki.'

I stare blankly back at her. The last time I sat at this bar I was twenty-seven and Eun-joo greeted every customer with a smile. I guess a lot has changed.

'What did I do?' I ask, resigned to hearing more horror stories from my hellion past.

'I banned you for throwing up over the pool table.'

I look around the room. 'You don't have a pool table.'

'I couldn't get the smell out of the felt.' Her lips twitch at the corners. Maybe that smile isn't completely dead. 'What do you want?'

'Your best ale.'

She shuffles away and I grin at the back of her head before scanning the sorry state of the room. Two ancient women are hunched over a game of baduk in the centre, their claw-like hands sliding black and white counters across a board, while onlookers gaze transfixed over their shoulders. The wizened combatants show nothing in their faces, even when the surrounding crowd burst into cheers or torrents of abuse. The other tables are occupied by silent couples, groups of pot-bellied men slamming fists over politics, or stony-faced women comparing the crimes of husbands. I must be one of the youngest here.

Eun-joo slides a misty glass before me and takes my money.

This is the cheapest beer in Sonaya, and it tastes like it. The regulars call it tiger piss; I call that an insult to tigers.

'You look well,' I say.

Eun-joo doesn't blink. If she were tall enough, she'd reach over and cut my throat with her teeth.

'I've put on weight,' she says, deadpan. 'Business is good, and I've got no one to share it with. This is what success looks like, Kawasaki. Soak it in.'

'I'm trying. What happened to that guy you were seeing?'

'Handsome tax fucked him up, same as you. Got a nine, lost his job. He was too vain to slip into a cocoon, so he swallowed a bullet instead.'

'Sorry,' I say.

'It was ten years ago. I'm almost over it.' She smirks and pours out two clear shots from an unmarked bottle. 'Good to have you back, Dag.'

We clink glasses and a second later I'm gagging into my hand.

'You used to hold your booze better than that. What happened to Dag the Whale, swallower of ethanol oceans?'

'He got old,' I say, recovering from the burn. 'Or maybe his tastes in vodka matured.'

'I made it myself,' Eun-joo says, grinning from ear to ear. 'Now, you wanna tell me why you hiked up Broken Hill tonight? I'd like to think it was for me, but you've been out of The Heights for three months and this is your first visit. I'm starting to think I wasn't your priority.'

'The Bosozoku,' I say, chasing the shot with tiger piss. 'Jiko told me they've set up a den in your basement.'

'I don't know anything about Bosozoku. I don't like those bikers. Too noisy.'

'I'm looking for my daughter, Eun-joo. She was staying with the girls and now she's gone missing. I'm not a cop anymore, remember?'

Eun-joo stares at me hard. It's been a long twelve years, but it doesn't feel like it. She swipes our shot glasses away and drops them into the sink. 'I don't know any Bosozuku-'

'Eun-joo-'

'-But there are a couple of punk girls downstairs who look like they've just fallen into a dress-up box. Come through.'

She lets me slip behind the bar and opens the trap door in the floor. I put a hand on her shoulder. 'Thanks, Eun-joo.'

'Touch me again and I'll bite your hand off. Now hurry up, I've got customers waiting.'

○

The basement is a mess of boxes, barrels, and cups of instant noodles. I'm halfway down the stairs before I glimpse the girls on the battered sofa, and it's a few seconds before I realise they're Blonde and Purple. Except they're not blonde and purple anymore.

One side of Su-young's head has been shaved and the other half is a burgundy perm. Her face has been stripped of its garish makeup, and her eyes and lips look half their usual size. A fresh mugunghwa tattoo spirals up her neck and the pink petals blossom over one cheek. Bo-min sports a black Mohawk and new piercings in her chin and ears. She puts down her glass when she sees me and elbows Su-young.

'I'm disappointed,' I say, taking a seat on the sofa bed opposite. 'No nose jobs, no implants. Not even a missing ear.'

'Baby steps,' Su-young replies with a small smile. 'But at least one of us got surgery.'

I look dumbly between them until I notice a slight swelling in Bo-min's cheeks.

'I had a dimpleplasty,' she says.

I try to keep a straight face. Dimples on a girl who never smiles? About as useful as a nose job on a man without a head.

The girls are drinking beer from the bottle. Su-young folds away her newspaper and pulls another bottle from the crate beside her. She cracks the cap off with her teeth and hands the bottle over.

'Listen, I'm looking for the Dove. You seen her?'

Su-young shakes her head. 'We had to clear out of the wine bar pretty sharpish, and she wasn't there when we left. She'll realise soon enough that we won't be coming back.'

'What do you want with her?' Bo-min asks.

'She's my daughter.'

Bo-min stares vacantly at me, like I'm speaking another language and she's translating it one syllable at a time. Su-young smirks cynically.

'The Dove's your daughter?' she says.

I nod.

Su-young raises an eyebrow. 'Fuck off.'

I drink my beer and give them time.

'The Dove's a street kid,' Su-young says. 'But your daughter was brought up by that sergeant.'

'She was,' I say. 'And a few months ago she ran away. Got herself a makeover, made up a backstory and started working pigeon jobs to survive. Did you ever meet the Dove before summer?'

Su-young and Bo-min exchange a glance.

'But she's so pretty,' Bo-min says.

'Christ,' I say, 'when you open your mouth you really make it count, don't you? You're looking at a ten, don't forget.'

'No, Dag,' Su-young says. 'We're looking at a middle-aged man with a crooked nose, a missing ear, and a paunch. All that booze is catching up to you.'

I glug beer and try to pretend my feelings haven't been hurt. 'Did you get your personalities changed in that cocoon as well?' I spit.

Su-young suppresses a smile. 'The Dove. I never would have guessed.'

'Any idea where she might be?' I ask.

The girls look at each other and shake their heads. I kill my drink and stand.

'If she comes by, let me know.'

They nod.

'And don't tell her,' I say.

'Why?' Su-young says. 'Afraid she'll be disappointed?'

I walk up the stairs and look back as I push open the trap door.

'Your one-liners will go down well in The Heights,' I say, and the smirk soon slides off Su-young's face. 'Let's hope you don't get the chance to try them out.'

The trap door slams shut behind me, and I leave the transformed girls in silence.

21

'You know where she is, don't you?'

'Maaya?' Sara answers. 'I've no idea.'

She shoots sake and refills. We're in a dingy izakaya perfumed by hot candlewax and lacquered oak. A middle-aged woman across the bar nibbles skewers of grilled log like a rodent, while a pair of salarymen in a corner kill shot after shot, their conversation long dead. The owner hasn't stopped eyeballing me since I sat down.

'Why don't I believe you?'

'Because you've got trust issues. I've been busy, Dag, as you already know. Finding your daughter isn't my priority. In fact, it's pretty far down my list of things to do.'

I sigh and take a drink. The sake is hot and good, but so far the company's not as satisfying. With eyes like pools of melted bronze and a blink that slows down time, Sara Barnes must be used to getting what she wants. It's unfortunate that we never want the same thing.

'You still chasing my friends around for secrets they don't have?' I ask.

'If you're talking about Ganzo, he's told me everything he knows. And it was just as I thought: everything comes back to Ryoko Nishi.'

'Ganzo and the PM? They probably haven't seen each other in a decade.'

'The past and the present are all connected, Dag, like a

grand tapestry sewn through the decades. You can always find a loose thread. Pull it and the whole thing comes undone.'

'And where do I feature in this great connected tapestry? What was Ganzo hiding that he couldn't tell me?'

Sara glances at the owner, who's been staring so long his eyes are beginning to sweat.

'Well congratulations,' I say, when I see no answer forthcoming. 'You joined a biker gang and roamed the Rivers for weeks just to get a panda to talk—sounds like a lot of effort for no end product. Nishi's untouchable. You've reached a dead end.'

'Oh, she's not untouchable. Remember, the Nightshades aren't the only people I've been working with; they're simply my way into the Rivers and Sonaya's sordid underbelly. I've got contacts in high places, too.'

'Yeah? Who?'

'Bernd Schulte, for one.'

'The German?' I scoff. 'He knows how to lie in five languages, but he doesn't know the truth in any. Choose your allies better next time.'

Sara smiles. 'Liars are the easiest people to blackmail. All you need is their biggest secret.'

'I don't suppose you're going to tell me what Bernd's secret is.'

'Why don't you ask him yourself? You might find it interesting. As for me, I can't stay, Dag.' She kills another shot and stands. 'The threads are all coming loose at the same time —Sonaya's tapestry has fallen, and she's about to stand naked in the daylight. Someone has to be there to point a camera at it.'

'So what are you telling me? That you've got Nishi under your thumb? That she's gonna listen to what you have to say? Polling starts tomorrow, Sara. You haven't got a hope in hell.'

'We'll see, won't we?' She slips a couple of notes onto the

counter. 'Adios, Kawasaki. Maybe I'll see you once the smoke clears.'

○

The smell of Sara's perfume is still in my nostrils when the owner slouches over.

'Out,' he demands.

I glance at my sake. 'I'm not done.'

'I got the right to refuse tagged customers. Your girlfriend's a regular here; you're not. Out.'

I soon get tired of his unflinching glare. Without a word I down the sake and submit to my thirst for the twilight air.

I buy a box of greasy dumplings and feast on them as I steal through the city, chewing all the while on Sara's words. My conversations with the sorry cast of Sonaya all seem to go the same way: smug hints and condescending looks that tell me I've long since expired. The more time that passes, the more Fumiko's words seem to bury into my bones. While the great migration continues around me, I'm still wandering in my mist of pink feathers. But I'll keep moving; I'll push my way through and see the sky soon enough.

I'm right where I belong, intoxicated by the streets. Dusk is a sepia spell fermented with the promises of Sonaya's falling curtain, and the first wisps of night set my skin alight like an avalanche of burning coals.

A decrepit arcade materialises out of the big smoke. Two mangy mutts fight on the doorstep, and I have to tiptoe around their rabid dance just to get inside. I climb past two tea shops and a third-rate plastic surgery known as The Butcher and reach the pool hall on the fourth floor. Big-bellied men swig from hip flasks and stare at the tables, their eyes strangely beautiful with the reflections of green felt.

Shinji lines up a shot in the centre of the room. He doesn't even look up as I plant my hands on the table.

'Rack 'em,' I say.

'You came.' He hits the white and it ricochets off the cushion. We watch it bounce around until it returns to where it started. I scoff and make for the bar in the corner. One whisky and water for me; for the kid, one water with a drop of whisky.

'Wanna make this interesting?' Shinji asks as he drops the balls in the triangle.

The tip of my cue is blunt as hell. I blue it up.

'You're a family man now,' I say. 'Any money you got, better save it for that wrinkled mite you call a sibling.'

'Go to hell, Kawasaki.'

The kid's even starting to talk like me. He needs more friends his own age.

'Two thousand for the game,' I say.

Shinji nods and blues his cue. He wins the coin toss and breaks the triangle the way a light breeze breaks a brick wall. The balls hardly move, but it leaves me an easy first pot. I pocket the orange stripe and manage to spread some balls.

'Listen, kid,' I say, circling the table. 'I'm sorry for what happened. For what I did to you. I'm scum, and I know it.'

'Fuck your apologies.'

I pot the blue and sip my drink. The whisky's bad, but it feels like a night for bad whisky. I scratch more chalk onto my cue and stare at the boy.

'I see you found a new poor sap to deliver messages for you,' he says. 'Was he the best you could find? He was so green I wanted to hold his hand and walk him back to the aviary when he was done.'

'Well, you got the message, didn't you? You're here, I'm here —I'd say he did his job alright, and he did it without giving me any lip. It was a refreshing change.'

'Yeah, that's the world you dream of, isn't it? Everyone bowing down to King Dag, no one speaking back, no one shattering the illusion of greatness you built yourself twenty years ago.'

'Kid, I like you, but I could forget how. You've double-crossed me more times than I can count, and First Bands can count pretty high. I said I'm sorry, didn't I? Only a handful of people in the world have heard me utter that word, so understand that I mean it. I snapped because you told me the truth, and I didn't like it. I want my daughter, Shinji. She's all I've got.'

He drops his gaze to the table. He's got what my mum called alphabet eyes; even a kid can read them.

'It's Nishi, isn't it?' I say. 'The one giving you pocket money for your own flat. You know where she is, don't you? Maaya.'

Shinji removes his cap and scratches his scalp. His mouth hardly opens when he speaks. 'I was just following orders.'

'Nishi's orders?'

'I just had to help get her out of the city.'

I stare him down but his eyes are fixed on the motionless balls. 'When did you find out it was the Dove?'

Shinji sips his cocktail without blinking. 'A few days ago. I didn't have a choice. I've got Eiko to think about.'

'Did they threaten you?'

'They didn't have to. She's the prime minister, Dag. We made a deal: I get Maaya out of the city, Nishi pays me more than I can make in a year of pigeon jobs.'

I'm hanging onto his every word, but I try to keep it cool. I lean over my cue and pot another ball with feeling, then circle the table again. 'You don't need the money, kid. Eiko has a family now, one that can take care of her.'

Shinji laughs. It's the most unnatural sound I've ever heard. 'Am I supposed to sit back and watch another addict cradle my baby sister? If you thought I was going to let a wreck like Stones take care of Eiko, you're even dumber than I thought.'

I can't argue. Maybe this is what happens when a soulless ex-con tries to play family matchmaker.

'How did you get the Dove to leave?' I ask.

'Well, I told her that the PM was her aunt, but she knew

that already. I told her I could take her somewhere safe. Somewhere with her family.'

'What family? I'm her only damn family.'

Shinji looks up at me with a hint of belligerence. He places his glass on the table and swipes mine from under my nose. He takes a sip and grimaces as the whisky hits his throat.

'Where the hell is she, kid?'

'I don't know, Dag. But even if I did, I wouldn't tell you. My sister. I have to protect her.'

I try to breathe as the red mist starts to swirl like a twister inside my chest. Shinji's face is inches from mine, his neck crying out to be throttled. It takes everything I have to keep my hands to myself. In through the nose, out through the mouth. Gotta keep that twister buried.

'Listen,' he says. 'Think about *her*. Maaya. You don't know what she's been through. If you were her, would you really want someone like you as your guardian?'

I regard the boy in front of me, the slight curl of his upper lip, the disdain in his eyes. I draw my eyes away, take a shot on red and miss. I snatch my glass back. 'And *you* know what she's been through, do you?'

'Yeah, I know. I've known for a long time, even before I found out who she was. Of course you wouldn't know, 'cause you never even asked her. You look at people like us and think it's all our fault, don't you? That we've done something wrong, that we deserve it. Not everyone's like you, Dag. We're not all fucked up because of our own mistakes. We're fucked up because of people like *you*.'

He screws up his face and leans over his cue, takes a piss poor shot that simply moves the balls around.

'She's safe now,' he says, straightening up. 'She's safe and she's finally got someone to look after her. You don't know how bad she had it, growing up with Fujii. He was a drunk.'

'We knew that already,' I say, lining up a shot and trying to keep my hands steady. 'So am I. So are half the lemmings in this rat hole city.'

'He used to send her to the Homework Clubs after school sometimes. Let his friends talk to her. She hated it all. She had to sit there with all these old men.'

I abandon the shot and straighten up, let the cue lean against the table. 'Did anything else ever happen?'

Shinji shakes his head slowly. 'Some tried. Bought her gifts, she said. Brushed her hair behind her ears. Put a hand on her leg. There was one who asked for her all the time, tried to sit her on his lap, take photos of her. She heard from other girls the things he tried to do. But she escaped before he could do the same things to her.'

'Who was it?' I demand, the words scratching out of my throat.

'I don't know. There were loads like him, I think. Friends of her dad, all pervs. That's why I agreed to help her. I had to make sure she got away from all that.'

I stare at the balls on the table and they blur into nothing.

'Shinji, if you know where she is ...'

'I told you, I don't. I took her down to the old train station out east. There were people there, they took over.'

'What people?'

Shinji shrugs. 'Nishi's people, I guess. Suits. Never seen them before. They gave me my money and shooed me away. I hardly had chance to say goodbye.'

'If they took a train then they must have been headed for the port. So she really is off the island ...'

Shinji shrugs again.

I drop my cue on the table, destroying the game. I stand before Shinji and put my hands on his shoulders. My hands are shaking, my jaw clenched. The kid looks terrified, like I'm going to smack him back to the gutters. His squirrel eyes quiver and the rose tattoo seems to melt down his neck.

'I don't care what you do to me,' he says. 'I might not know much, but I know what's right. For me, for Eiko, and for Maaya. You don't figure in any of our lives, Dag. Not anymore.'

I stare at the acne on his cheeks, the white zits prime for popping. I've half a mind to squeeze his skull and watch puss fountain over the table.

But some part of me must realise that Shinji's speaking sense. I relax my grip and Shinji steps back. He stares at me but I can no longer meet his eyes.

'Thanks for looking out for my daughter,' I say.

Shinji swallows and shakes his head.

I pull the notes from my pocket, drop them on the table and make for the door.

'You win.'

22

SHINJI

I spit dregs of vomit against a wall and walk in a daze towards the harbour. The sounds and smells of the ward, and the image of Eiko shaking with her eyes alien white, will haunt me forever.

It must be past midnight. The nurses kicked me out once they got Eiko stable again, said I couldn't return 'til morning. I won't sleep. I'll walk these streets in braindead laps until they let me back in. A mindless marathon. Until I know Eiko's okay, I'll never sleep again.

The harbour looks fake, like a hologram dropped between me and the shitstorm of reality. Ryoko Nishi's giant profile smiles over the neon-lit streets, the pixels in her face flickering as she makes one final bullshit plea to the city. She explains how well the drug crackdown has worked, how crime and unemployment have dropped since she was elected. She's fulfilled all her promises. Tomorrow the polls open and she's asking Sonaya to vote for her again.

I stare at her projection and spit at the ground, the aftertaste of puke still coating my mouth. Those mannequins in suits are all the same. Where were the drug busts thirteen years ago, when my mum got pregnant for a payout that went straight into her veins? All these years later, nothing's changed. This time it was Eiko who was conceived for the price of a month of scag, and if I hadn't been there …

Now my mum's going cold turkey in a lowly cell in The

Heights. She's lucky she was arrested for child neglect and they didn't find her stash, or she'd be dead instead of locked up. Any which way, I'm head of the family. That's why I made the deal with Nishi and, fair play, she's kept her promises. I've got my money, and as soon as Eiko's well enough, we're out of here. The nurses don't understand; Eiko's stronger than she looks. She's going to get better. She's going to pull through.

I reach the jetties and see the Arkansas swaying gently on the water. I call Aimi's name and clamber aboard to find Stones splayed on deck with his mouth open and spittle down his unshaven jaw. An empty glass lies just beyond his outstretched hand.

'Stones,' I say, nudging him with my shoe. 'Wake up.'

He doesn't stir until I kick his shin, and then his eyes open and he blinks like it's his first day on earth. His rank breath almost makes me gag.

'Shinji,' he croaks, squinting around deck. 'What are you doing here?'

'Where's Aimi?'

He reaches for his glass and groans when he finds it empty.

'Be a good lad, refill this for me, would you? An artist's medicine, you see.'

I kick the glass out of his hand and watch it spin and drop overboard. Stones' bloodshot eyes widen in surprise and he tries to shake the pain from his fingers.

'What the hell was that for?'

'Eiko's been having seizures,' I say, as calmly as I can manage.

Stones scrunches his eyes shut and exhales, then rubs his face and pulls himself up onto his elbows. 'Is she … is she okay?'

'It's common for babies of addicts,' I say with spite. 'She's stable, but don't pretend you care. I came here for Aimi, not you.'

'Aimi's not here,' Stones says slowly, as though just realising it himself.

'Where is she?'

'I've no idea. No doubt chewing someone's ear off about yours truly.' He offers a weak smile that only makes me despise him even more. I think of Eiko in her tank with all those wires and menacing machines. I think of Aimi's dream of leaving the island and starting anew. *Our* dream.

A rush of blood surges through me, and a second later I see my foot flying towards Stones' face. He roars in pain and falls backwards holding his nose as blood streams through his fingers.

'What the hell are you doing, Shinji?'

I watch him roll pathetically across deck. I follow him and aim another kick into his stomach. He's winded and gasping for breath, peering up at me through watery red eyes.

'Stay the hell away from me and my family,' I say, and leave.

Shinji Okuhara, the bastard son of Sonaya. I never knew my real dad. Mum said he died before I was born, and only flashes of father figures remain. Boyfriends who beat me or sent me out to scavenge or steal, leaving me to live off scraps. All I learned from my parents was how to swear and straddle the line that separates the living from the dead.

I grew up on these streets. They're all I know. But who would notice if I'd never been born? How would Sonaya be any different? All I have is Eiko. She's the only thing that gives my life purpose.

I can't rely on Aimi's dream. It shattered before it even took shape. I imagine her now in a bar somewhere, crying into a glass of wine over her failed marriage. She wasn't there tonight; she wasn't there when Eiko needed her. When *I* needed her. And that means I can't rely on her. She's just another paper parent, a child's drawing come to life, only to be blown away by the first breeze.

I find myself back in the Rivers, barely aware of where my feet carry me. Jiko's girls have cleared out of the wine bar and the Dove is long gone. But I have money in my pocket, and money is the only thing you need in Sonaya. I could hit a liquor store and get drunk. Like Stones and Dag and all the other rotting fossils I know. That's how these shipwreck men disappear. How they cope. I'm a man now; I could do the same. I could disappear forever.

I pass a battlefield of fallen bodies. Wrecks of beings that were once human, now passed out in sorry heaps and decorated with their own vomit. Puppets slump in doorways clutching sake cartons, their eyes scarred by forks of red lightning. Some grasp at passersby like skeletons clutching passing orbs of life. I pass mangy cats with stumps for tails while rats scamper from restaurant kitchens and cockroaches scuttle across my path like armoured omens. Bent-backed women sort through piles of rubbish, collecting empty bottles to recycle into tomorrow's rice. Hopelessness, squalor, despair.

I want someone to blame. Politicians. Parents. Ghosts of people who came before. But I don't know shit, and that's the truth. I'm just one of the ignorant fleas hopping from alley to alley, dog to dog, a parasite sucking blood to survive. No future. Nothing. Only Eiko.

If she wakes … when she wakes, I have to be the one she sees. I have to be there. I can't disappear. I won't be the wreck Sonaya expects me to be, the kind of booze rat that Sonaya nights spawn in terrifying litters. I have to be stronger. I have to survive.

⟳

A fat man stews alone in a corner of the bar, staring bug-eyed at the uni students who chug beer like it's water. I pull my cap down over my eyes as I take a stool at the bar. I recognize the music churning on the record player because he used to be mum's favourite: Elvis Presley.

'Shinji,' Nakata says. 'Dag's not here.'

I scratch at the dry skin on the back of my hand and flakes flutter onto the bar. 'I'm not here for Dag.'

Nakata tilts her head to try and meet my eyes. I turn my head to keep them in shadow.

'I wanna drink,' I say.

'You're thirteen.'

'Fourteen,' I correct her. 'I'm fourteen. And I wanna drink.'

She doesn't move. 'How's Eiko?' she asks finally.

I shuffle on the stool. 'They won't let me back in 'til morning. I'm not gonna sleep. I'm gonna stay right here until they let me back in.' I remove my cap and try to relieve the itch on my scalp. 'They said she's stable now. But the sei—the seizures. They said the seizures might come again.'

I glance at Nakata, who in turn glances at the woman three stools down.

'I'll tell you what I'll do,' Nakata says. 'I'll make you a coffee. And you can sit here until visiting hours open. As long as you like. How's that?'

I don't say anything, and Nakata nods. She turns on the coffee machine while Elvis croons about a ghetto. What the fuck does he know about ghettos and angry young men and crying mamas? I get my head down and sniff and wipe my nose with the back of my hand. A steaming mug appears before me.

'Drink,' Nakata says. 'It'll keep you awake. Were Aimi and Stones at the hospital?'

'They don't care. I'm the only one who cares. Dag thought he was doing Eiko a favour by dumping her with them, but they're as fucked up as everyone else. There's no such thing as a happy family in this shithole.'

I sniff again and bow my head. Nakata passes me a tissue.

'Tell me about it.' She chooses a large bottle from the shelf and removes the cap. 'Irish coffee?' She pours a drop into my mug and then fills two shot glasses. The woman down the bar moves to the stool beside mine. She has pale skin and green eyes and long sandy hair.

'I'm Maria,' she says, extending a hand for me to shake.

'Shinji.'

They raise their glasses and I meet them with my steaming mug. We drink.

'Maria's my friend,' Nakata says.

I look between them. 'Girlfriend?'

'Like you said, Shinji,' Nakata says with the shadow of a smile, 'there's no such thing as a happy family in this shithole. You know the government does everything in its power to encourage Sonayans to have kids. People like us aren't exactly part of their plans.'

'They butcher addicts with bullets,' Maria says. 'They do the same to us with words. Propaganda.'

They fall silent and I feel their eyes on me. I catch myself scratching my hand.

'They shouldn't do that,' I say.

'We're glad you feel that way, Shinji,' Maria says.

Nakata tops up their whiskies. I hold out my mug but Nakata only smiles. 'One shot is enough. Excuse me, I've got a message to send.'

I watch her move along the bar and unclip the pager from her belt. Maria squeezes my arm and leaves to collect empty glasses. The next song begins: *Always on my Mind*. I sip my coffee. Something about this place always calms me. I guess that's why I always wind up here when I've got no place to go.

Maria returns to her seat and asks about my baseball cap. I take it off and show her.

'Yomiuri Giants,' I tell her. 'An old ball team from Japan.'

She examines the orange symbol and the frayed stitching.

'My mum brought a guy home one day. He was different to all the rest, didn't seem so messed up. He told me he'd take me to a game in Tokyo one day. This was his team.' I take the cap back and turn it over in my hands. 'I don't even know if they exist anymore, but—I dunno—I always thought I might be able to go one day.'

'And he gave you his cap?'

I shake my head. 'Mum kicked him out, he didn't last long. He tried to get her to quit, see, and she wasn't having it. He came back looking for it, it must have meant a lot to him, but I told him it was gone. I was angry at him. Well, angry at my mum. So I kept it.'

I replace it on my head.

'I'm glad you kept it,' Maria says. 'You might still go someday, Shinji. It's good to keep hold of dreams.'

Nakata returns and refills my mug with coffee, asks me about Eiko. I tell them. Everything. They listen, nodding. The students and the fat man leave, and they're soon replaced by a trio of ancient salarymen and a pair of dolled-up teens. Elvis continues to croon, and I continue to talk, and Maria and Nakata continue to listen until my eyelids become heavy.

Aimi appears at my side. I blink and sit up straight and wipe the drool from my chin. I don't know how long I was asleep. Aimi places a hand on my arm and looks deep into my eyes. I try to drag them away and ignore her but I can't.

'Nakata told me what happened,' she says. 'I'm sorry I wasn't there tonight, Shinji. You know how things have been between me and Peter. Maybe you don't know exactly, sometimes I forget that you're still a kid.'

'I'm not a kid.'

Aimi smiles. 'I know. I'm sorry. It's just that relationships are very complicated sometimes, and splitting with Peter hit me harder than I expected. But that doesn't change anything. Eiko is still my priority, do you understand?'

I nod.

'What do you say we get some breakfast? After that we can check in on Eiko, see how she's doing.'

I take my cap off, finger it absently, and put it on again. 'Okay.'

Aimi tries to pay my tab but Nakata shakes her head. I try to say thank you but something swells in my throat and suddenly I can barely swallow.

'He's had a big night,' Nakata says to Aimi as we make to leave. 'But he's a tough young man. He'll be all right.'

I nod to Nakata and follow Aimi up the stairs.

Once we're out in the open I take a deep breath and scan the sky. The clouds are yellowing at the edges with the promise of the coming sun.

23

I stroll the promenade that hugs the Pulse and crane my neck at the concrete high-rises that seem to hold up the sky. The revolving doors churn out workers like company action figures being spewed from the cogs of a morose machine. They march out onto the streets clutching briefcases and wearing expressions like limestone statues.

The polling station is in one of the banks the government bought out years back. It's the first of five voting days; I guess Sonaya's apathetic population needs all the time it can get. A woman with a bullet-proof vest runs a beeping stick over my body when I try to enter. She snatches Trusty from my ankle and drops it in a box in the foyer, then waves me through without opening her mouth.

I cruise in full of pulp. I'm a free citizen with a real vote— and not just one, a thousand. The lobby is a marble chasm of shining floors and unsettling echoes. Security guards watch the room behind dark glasses, their belts stuffed with guns and sticks. Glass-walled booths sit in formation like an exhibition of ancient telephone boxes, and people mill around in small groups, speaking in whispers like churchgoers in mass.

I'm about to do my civic duty for Sonaya when I notice the small hubbub in the far corner of the lobby. A squadron of police officers are holding court; two appear to be interviewing a frail-looking old woman. I make my way over and beckon to one of the officers.

'What's going on?'

The man looks me up and down before returning to his notepad. 'None of your business, Kawasaki.'

I get myself off the wanted list and suddenly every cop in the city knows my name. I try to peer over his shoulder at his notes. He looks up at me like an impatient parent.

'I might be able to help,' I say. 'I used to be a cop, you know.'

He looks pissed off, but all he does is huff in response. 'I don't suppose it matters. They're already broadcasting the story, surprised you haven't heard already.'

He pulls a clear plastic bag out of his vest pocket. Nestled inside is a human finger. I know what it means right away—the only ID you need to vote these days is a quick fingerprint scan.

'Whose is that?'

'It belonged to the Borrower Yoo-ri Baek. Her body was found at her home, one finger short.'

'She's dead?'

'They say she'll live, but she won't be happy when she wakes up. Whoever attacked her used her finger to place a scratch vote. A political statement, I suppose.'

I try to associate the finger with the shining plastic body it used to belong to.

'Any idea who it might have been, officer?' I ask with the innocence of a schoolboy.

He fixes me with eyes that look tired of being patronised.

'Place your votes, Kawasaki. And let us do our job.'

I leave the dogs to it, wondering how long it will be before the cops catch up with Jiko and her girls. But how did they get in here without being spotted? The cocoons spun them with slick enough silk, but with all this security around? Those girls are the ivory tusks of Sonaya's sordid safari, and it wouldn't take a genius to pick them out of a crowd.

I slip into the nearest booth and slide my index finger beneath the scanner. A green light flashes and a reassuring beep follows. The screen lights up and reminds me how many votes

I'm holding. *Please select which party you wish to vote for.* Ryoko Nishi, Conservative Party. *You have chosen to place 1,000 votes for the Conservative Party. Is this correct?* Confirm. *Thank you, your vote is complete.*

It's as easy as that. Hail the future of Sonaya.

I slip out of the booth and take another long look at the officers in the corner. Before I even reach the door two security guards converge on me. I'm about to protest my innocence but all they do is tell me to shut up and stay still. One reaches down to my ankle and rolls up my trouser leg. When he straightens back up he's holding my deactivated ankle tag.

'Wanna keep it as a souvenir?' he asks with a smirk.

'Why don't you put it round your neck and wear it as a dog collar?' I reply. 'You're the bitch on Nishi's lead, after all.'

I turn towards the exit but the guard grabs my arm and spins me back around.

'Your job's only half complete,' he says quietly. 'Don't think you're done yet.'

When he releases my arm I blow him a kiss and retrieve Old Trusty from the guard at the door.

Half of my homework is complete and my tag is finally gone, but the guard was right: I'm not done yet. The hardest part of Nishi's assignment is still to come, and someone might be about to complete it for me. My visit to the German's place will have to wait; I need to see Jiko—and fast.

Maybe if I can get her out of the city I can put an end to this. Nishi loses a threat to her votes, Jiko loses the heat, and I get my kid. Everyone wins.

I ride the Pipe to the base of Broken Hill. The station is busy with rushing commuters and voters gathering in excited groups. Students grasping badly written banners hand out flyers that get trampled straight into the gutters. I push through the throng and stare up at the moody mountain before me.

Broken Hill basks in the pink light of dusk, the shanty walls staring sullenly over the city. Climbing through the rising squalor, I follow paths that writhe and squirm between tin-roofed shacks, inviting the wrath of dogs with rabid eyes and schoolkids with potty mouths. A pack of girls chucks rocks from the roof of a charred building that might once have been someone's home; they watch suspiciously as I pass, turning stones over in their grubby hands. I guess the Sonayan homework load isn't what it used to be.

My forehead shines with perspiration when I reach the Tiger and Crane, and I slip inside to find it crammed with early evening drunks. I'm at the bar a good five minutes before I get a pint of tiger piss in my hand. Eun-joo watches me drink, her bayonet stare unwavering until I empty half the glass.

'No visits for twelve years, then two in two days,' she says. 'Is sparkling banter that hard to come by in the Rivers?'

'They attacked Baek. Red and her girls.' I look up to gauge her reaction. If she's surprised, it doesn't show in her face. 'I guess they had nothing to lose, but … I don't know.'

'What happened to you in The Heights? Did they give you a new heart in there? I didn't know you had an empathetic bone in your body, Dag. I'm hoping this is fatherly concern you're showing? You're more than twice their age, you know that, right?'

'Oh, I know it, all right. They remind me of it often enough. And it's not concern. I'm just …'

'Worried? Well maybe you're right to be. Anyway, if you're here for them and not for me, I can save you time. They're not here.'

'Do you know where they went?'

'Fumiko's.'

Hell. Baek and Fumiko in one day. It seems Jiko made her choice—the last stand it is. By dawn she'll either be dead or behind bars—unless I intervene. Shinji might have given up on me, but I'm not ready to lose it all. Not yet. I drain my glass and slam a note onto the bar. Eun-joo scoops it up and stabs me once more with a stare that could draw blood. I pause before leaving.

'What is it?'

'If you ever get tired of chasing punk teens with perky tits and lofty ideals, you might want to keep your backside on that stool one of these days.'

She smirks as I try to make sense of it.

'Hell, don't hurt yourself, Kawasaki. Go already.'

I turn on my heels and leave, glancing over my shoulder as Eun-joo busies herself with another customer. I march down the hill and try to clear my head. It's not easy. The slum is alive with the electric, loaded air that always precedes riot and revolution. Whispers and curious eyes seem trained on my descent, as though the slum dwellers know not only how many votes I have, but also that I've just sold them for my own selfish gains. I flinch at the sound of beer cans being crushed and the harsh barks of hounds, and hurry onwards with my head down and my eyes fixed firmly on my toes.

The Pipe stinks worse than ever. It's as if the impending eruption of discontent is struggling to contain itself; pus seeping from Sonaya's pores. I ride the green line south through the city and watch the passengers intently. Most of them are uni kids on their way back to campus. They probably all placed scratch votes, too, the woke little creatures, but at least they did it with all their fingers intact.

I emerge on the edge of the pleasure quarter and slip into the heart of the purple-tinged neighbourhood I've come to know so well. I don't know what I'm going to say or what I'm going to do; all I know is that I have to try one last time to get these girls to disappear. With Baek in a coma, their time is up. It's now or never.

Fumiko's usual spot at The Cross is empty—her wooden

chair sits unmanned. I charge down into her deranged den and find the place alive with activity. Girls and boys run wild, bags slung over shoulders, bursting in and out of rooms. The ant farm is flooded.

A girl crashes into me as I try to weave through the commotion, and I don't need to speak her language to translate her panicked apology. It's the Cambodian girl who had a knife to my throat just a few days back. I grab her by the shoulders and try to arrest the shaking of her small body.

'Where's Fumiko?'

She stares back at me, her large dark eyes pooled with fear.

'Fumiko!' I shout.

She points into the dark tunnel behind and I follow her finger, fighting against the stream. I push doors open wildly until I finally find what I'm looking for. A small studio swathed in black, and three girls poised around an old woman.

'Daganae,' Fumiko says as I slam the door closed behind me. 'The flamingo himself.' There's a sad inflection in her voice that I've never heard before. Maybe she knows this is the last night she'll wander the pulsing tunnels of her lair.

The girls turn to face me. They're almost unrecognisable here without their biker gear and signature hairdos. Bo-min and Su-young stand either side of Jiko like reluctant bodyguards.

'You did it, then,' I say. 'You attacked Baek, and now you'll be on the run forever. Why did you do it?'

I'm talking to all three of them, but it's Jiko I stare at. She returns my gaze with a faintly puzzled expression.

'Now now, Kawasaki,' Fumiko says. 'I won't let these girls take the credit for my success.'

I look between the four of them, momentarily dumbfounded. Fumiko's eyes close in a smile.

'*You*? You attacked Baek?'

'Of course it was me. Fumiko's last stand, they'll call it.' The smile slides off the old woman's face like a slug from a leaf. 'Better late than never, I suppose.'

Jiko crouches before her and takes the old woman's blue-veined hands in her own. They gaze into each other's eyes with a look I can't comprehend.

'I've done terrible things,' Fumiko says quietly. 'Unforgivable things. It was never my intention when I started, you know.'

Her voice is different. She no longer sounds like a wily crone with evil on her mind. She sounds like an old woman—suddenly vulnerable and decrepit. Mortal. The words quiver as they fall from her wrinkled lips. Her eyes glisten and lose focus.

'You'll never know how much I cared for you all. I have no right to be proud of you, I know, but I am. When I hear of the things you've done, seen what you've achieved, it breaks my heart. It breaks my heart because I know it wasn't due to me, it was *in spite* of me.'

She raises a shaking hand to her forehead and cradles it there.

Jiko remains on her knees, staring into the face of the woman she always swore to end. Su-young steps forward and runs a hand over Fumiko's lined face.

'None of us had mothers.'

I turn to see who has spoken. It's a moment before I realise it's Bo-min.

'Not really. We had no one. You saved us. We'll never forget that.'

Fumiko squints at the young woman and nods.

'You've made it right,' Su-young says.

I hear a commotion from the corridor outside. I ease the door open and see men in blue among the thronging crowd.

'As touching as this reunion is,' I say. 'It's time for it to end. They're here.'

Fumiko laughs, the familiar sound of slime pumping through an intestine.

'Fly, girls,' she says. 'Let me face them.'

205

Her cane stabs the stone floor and Su-young helps the old woman to her feet.

'It's been a damn fine life. I'm not going to tarnish it by spending my remaining years rotting away in The Heights. No, old Fumiko's going out with fireworks up her backside. Who has a gun?'

'Girls,' I say. 'Time to leave.'

'We're not going anywhere,' Su-young says. 'We've come too far to go out with a whimper. We're staying here.'

Fumiko runs a reptilian tongue over blue gums.

'Stay here and you die,' I say. 'Don't make it easy for them. Leave. Get out of Sonaya. Tonight.'

Jiko stares at her partners and they stare right back.

'We've done too much,' Su-young says. 'We can't abandon everything we've been working for.'

'You can't make any difference if you're dead,' I say.

'Dag's right,' Jiko says. 'We can't do any more here. It's over.'

Bo-min joins me at the door and peeks outside. 'They're coming.'

Su-young removes a gun from her belt. 'I'm not giving up everything we've done. If I'm made a martyr, so be it.'

I open my mouth to counter but Jiko beats me to it. 'Su-young. I can't do this anymore. I've led you here, and it's my fault, but I'm done. I'm out.'

Su-young's face falls as she stares at Jiko, a mixture of disbelief and disappointment etched into her features.

Fumiko edges towards the door and Bo-min stands aside as Su-young surrenders her gun. The old crone leans into the door and a smile forms on her lips as she watches the chaos of her underground lair.

'You might think this is me being weak,' Jiko says, more urgently now. 'But this is the hardest thing I've ever had to do. If there's a chance of making something of my life, I'm going to take it.' She pauses; the words catch in her throat. 'Even if that means leaving you two behind.'

Su-young and Bo-min look at Jiko as though her words were bullets. A gunshot explodes in the room and every one of us flinches. Fumiko stumbles as the recoil almost makes her fall on her backside. She croaks out a laugh. 'Got one of the fuckers,' she says gleefully. She looks reborn.

I join her at the door and glance outside to see four cops. Two are advancing down the tunnel; one is on the floor behind them, the fourth crouching over him. Fumiko shoves her gun arm past me and fires a blind shot down the corridor.

'Hell,' I say, snapping the door shut. 'You must have been a handful when you were younger.'

Fumiko bares her gums. 'Your father seemed to like it.'

'Just when I was starting to like you,' I say.

She grabs my shirt and pulls me into her neck. Her breath smells of liquor and other things, but the liquor is the highlight. 'See that they're okay,' she whispers.

We both glance at the biker girls. Their leathers are gone, along with their bikes and anime hairdos. They're in the centre of the room, holding each other in a way I haven't been held in fifteen years. Watching them whisper into each other's ears feels like an invasion of privacy. I turn back to Fumiko and nod.

Fumiko locks the door and cocks the gun, the smile returning to her wizened face. A fist pounds on the door, followed by a command to come out with hands up.

'Hands up,' Fumiko says quietly. 'I'd fall flat on my face. I have the cane for a reason. The mirror,' she barks over her shoulder. 'There's a lock on the lower right.'

Bo-min advances to the mirror in the corner and runs her fingers around the lower frame. Something clicks and she pulls the mirror open to reveal a tunnel carved into the wall.

More warnings sound from the other side of the door.

Fumiko stands with cane in one hand and gun in the other.

Su-young moves to her side, drawing a knife from her belt. Bo-min hovers between her and Jiko.

'So long, Dag,' Su-young calls over her shoulder. 'It's been a wild ride.' She flashes one last smile.

Gunshots pummel the door. The police are shooting at the lock and the door is slowly splintering apart.

'Go,' I command Jiko, pushing her towards the secret tunnel. She pauses for one last look at Su-young, while Bo-min looks between her partners like a kid trying to choose between parents. I take the choice out of her hands. I advance on Su-young and whip Trusty's handle over her crown. She tumbles into a heap on the floor, her knife falling away.

Fumiko laughs again. The door is seconds from opening.

'Help me with her,' I command Bo-min.

Bo-min lifts Su-young by the arms while I take her legs. We drag her through the tunnel and Jiko rushes to help. I force the mirror-door closed and we sit breathless in the dark. We hear the door on the other side being broken through, the tirade of bullets, and the last stand of Fumiko the Redeemed.

24

'Fumiko dead? No way.'

Disbelief doesn't suit Shinji. He sags against the doorframe as if a bullet's shot the bones out of his body. I guess to kids his age Fumiko was a permanent fixture of the city, but Sonaya doesn't do sentiment.

'Even cockroaches die eventually,' I say. 'At least Jiko will be off the hook for Baek's murder.'

'If they can prove Fumiko did it.'

'Yeah, *if*. I don't like ifs.'

Shinji looks a shell of his cocksure self, but at least he seems to have put our quarrel behind us. He talks for over an hour, and I let him. While I was watching Fumiko's last stand, Shinji was glued to Eiko's bedside. Poor sap. He tells me about his scuffle with Stones and his night at Nakata's, blissfully unaware that I'm nursing a hangover for the ages. I was up late helping Jiko's girls heal up in the Tiger and Crane. We drank to Fumiko and Suzie and all the ones we've lost. We drank till the sun rose clear over the rooftops.

I could do with a few more hours kip, but I can't kick Shinji out after what we've just been through.

'Fancy heading out?' I ask.

If I can't complete my nap, I might as well crack on. Back to the chase. Back to my daughter. And—whisper it—back with my favourite sidekick.

We head out side by side into the early evening light. The sky's the colour of burning coals and the wind is a warm caress that might be summer's farewell kiss. I sense Shinji's presence at my side like a weight in my pocket—something in him has changed. I can see it in his movements and hear it in his breath. It's as if his organs have been drained and then refilled with an entirely new substance, his skin stitched together with a harsh new thread that's at once painful and relieving.

When we reach Bernd's building he follows me up the stairs instead of bounding on ahead like he used to. He even hangs back when I poke my nose into the whisky bar and see no one but an old dame cackling into an empty glass. We carry on climbing and Shinji watches me rap my knuckles on Bernd's door. There's no answer.

'Maybe he's stuck at work,' Shinji suggests. I bang my fists again and hear Hildegard's bark. 'What's the big rush to see him anyway? Get your new pigeon to set up a meeting, come back another time.'

'Yesterday Sara told me Bernd had a secret,' I say. 'And I didn't like the look on her face when she said it.'

'You think it's something to do with Maaya?'

'I don't have a clue. Could be. But Sara knows something she's not telling me, and I'm tired of knocking politely when I need answers.'

I hammer on the door and resort to a shoulder barge. At the third attempt the lock breaks and the door swings wide open. A dust cloud sweeps over the floor. Damn Europeans are a dirty bunch.

Hildegard hobbles across the room and pushes her nose into my palm as I scan the place. Everything looks just as it did the last time I came. Shinji strokes Hildegard while I peruse the notebook left open on the armchair. Poetry; I toss it aside. Why use fancy words when a quick heavy one will do the damage? A half-empty bottle of scotch sits on the coffee table. I pour myself a glass and take it down.

All I see is paper. Envelopes with cherry seals are bundled and tied up with string, while parchments blotched with whisky are stuffed in drawers and crammed into bookshelves. I leaf through the loose sheets on the desk: correspondence with officials, letters from Europe. Nothing of interest. Bernd is a glorified propaganda filter; whichever side of Sonaya you feed him, it's only rainbows that come out of his backside.

'What exactly are we looking for?' Shinji asks. He collapses on the armchair and scratches behind Hildegard's ears.

'*Something*,' I say. 'Something secret. I'm not even sure if there's anything here. But there's something that old Bernd doesn't want people to see, and ...'

I glance at the windowsill and drop the letters in my hand.

'What is it?' Shinji asks.

I stare at the old cigar box, its rusted tin emblazoned with German in fairground font.

'He snapped at me when I touched this,' I say. 'The last time I was here. I wonder if the old badger's smuggled something illegal from the motherland.'

I open the box and peer inside. Notes, bills, receipts. I'm about to toss it aside when I see a photo peeking out behind scraps of paper. A teenage girl in school uniform. Underneath is another, and another. The girls are all different, but the forced smiles are identical. Some men can't tell the difference between a smile and a grimace, and that's where all this trouble comes from.

My heart plummets when I see her. I hold the photo right up to my nose and take in the Dove's sombre eyes and pout. Her hair is long past her shoulders, her fringe swept to one side. She looks so much like her mother it makes my stomach churn. There's not even a hint of a smile on her lips. She's just a girl in the wrong place, like all the others.

I glance down at Hildegard. She returns my gaze sadly, as if she knows. 'What are you going to do to him?' her eyes ask me.

'Maaya,' Shinji says, staring at the photo. 'Why does he have a photo of Maaya?'

'You said it yourself,' I say, trying to keep my cool. 'She was in the Homework Clubs. The men there …'

I close my eyes and try to breathe, but my imagination gets the better of me. The thought of my daughter in one of those places …

I launch my glass across the room and the glass explodes over the filthy floorboards.

'Dag …' Shinji says, his eyes wide in shock. Hildegard regards the damage and then observes me, unshaken. I pocket the Dove's photo and let the others fall to the floor.

'Sorry girl,' I say to the dog. 'You won't get a chance to say goodbye.'

I scratch her one final time and exit with blood pounding in my ears.

I feel winded and sick. I finger the photo in my pocket, and suddenly all the words and rumours sharpen into something tangible. I can see her there, the Dove—Maaya—in one of those sickening rooms, cowering before a hairy, leering figure. And now that figure has a face.

I need a wrecking ball to take to the heart of the city. Destruction Dag, flaming torch in hand. With one final look up at Bernd's window, I let my boots carry me into the shadows.

Shinji's voice is an echo I hardly hear. I see nothing; only a peripheral blur of shape and movement and colour. The Rivers are sucked away into a dark and distant abyss. I'm alone in another dimension, trudging through Sonaya's spinning gullet, even as it melts around me. I sense my body shutting down, the cells extinguishing one by one, all thought and reason slipping away into the void. I'm stripped to the core: wild and raw. A mindless carnivore thirsty for blood.

We're on the platform of the Pipe when Shinji's words start

filtering through. The train is approaching, the ground shaking, the rotten draft caressing our faces, and Shinji stands before me.

'Where are we going, Dag?'

'The Fish Nets,' I answer. I didn't even realise it myself until I said it. Some primal instinct has led me to this platform, something dismal and chaotic drawing me back to those horrible alleys.

'If you find him …' Shinji says. He hesitates, maybe because he knows the answer even before he asks the question. 'What are you going to do?'

The train rattles to a stop in front of us, and when the doors creak open the smell of piss hits us in the face.

'I'll know when I see him,' I say, taking a seat next to a passed-out drunk. Shinji grabs a swinging hand strap as the train shudders back to life and rumbles down the tracks.

'You remember what happened in the ramen place,' he says. 'Remember what you did to me.'

I don't answer. I don't need reminding.

'Before you do anything …' he says.

'What?'

'I dunno … breathe. Think.' Even Shinji seems to realise how stupid he sounds. 'Listen, you wanna find Maaya, right? You won't be any good to her if you're locked up again. Just don't do anything stupid, okay? I mean, just control yourself.'

'I can't promise that.'

He stares at me. I'm sure I'm headed for another lecture. Either that or a reprimand. But his face softens as the train stops.

'I don't want you to disappear again,' he says.

I stand and put a hand on his shoulder as I make for the opening doors.

'Me and you, eh? Just like old times.'

The pleasure quarter looks dire in the Sonayan twilight; like a smoky dusk in no man's land, before the corpses have been cleared away. A pair of prostitutes watch our approach through an alley drenched in blood-red light.

'What are you into?' one of them asks. His pectorals are bigger than Shinji's head.

'Revenge,' I answer.

They laugh as we charge past. The other one calls after us: 'And what's for dessert?'

Some of the neon has started blinking, but it looks weak and out of place at this time. We pass a pair of liquor lockers, their glass fronts smashed and the bottles of booze long since looted. A salaryman falls out of an unmarked door, his face a cherry bomb and his eyes shrouded by bloodied spider webs. He leans against the wall and wheezes as his gaze falls on Shinji.

'Put your eyes back in or I'll pop them like balloons,' I growl at him.

He smiles absently and slides down the wall in apparent ecstasy, his eyes rolling back inside their sockets.

We follow the blinking neon veins. They shrink as we get closer, the lights diminishing, the sounds seeping away through some hole into hell.

The Fish Nets.

It's darker here, the ragtag rows of shacks leaning into each other. The clouded roof of the city is reduced to a narrow strip of charcoal high above. A faceless child runs across the passage before us, giggling like a possessed doll in a budget horror.

Shinji curls his lip. 'What the fuck is this place?'

'Sonaya's rectum,' I say. 'Kids go free.'

The shacks are quiet. We stop outside doors and the sounds filter out like sad symphonies. Shinji's face loses so much colour his acne turns blue.

I don't feel like waiting around anymore. I push doors open at will and to hell with the consequences. The first place I try has five kids sitting along the bar. They look up at me without interest and only one gets off his stool.

'We're not open,' he says, looking over my shoulder at Shinji.

I produce a crisp note from my pocket. 'I'm looking for Bernd Schulte, a German with a badger beard.'

The four kids at the bar stare at my hand longingly, but the boy shakes his head.

'Not our customer.'

'Whose customer is he?' I ask.

The kid only shakes his head again, so I leer at him and leave. The second shack is shrouded in so much smoke I can barely see inside. For a moment I think the place is burning down, but then a fruity scent fills my nostrils and I realise I've stumbled into a vaping den.

Vapers are a rare breed in Sonaya these days; the e-cigs are as illegal as the real things. When people around the world started dropping dead like malfunctioning bots, Sonaya swiftly banned them altogether.

As the smoke starts to dissipate through the open door, the three figures at the table come into focus. They're in various states of inebriation, and that's the only positive I can garner when I recognise their faces.

'Why, look who it is,' Mo says slowly. She stands up, all six feet of her, her shoulders swallowing the room. 'Mr. Kawasaki.'

Her eyes are bloodshot but she seems far more lucid than the two men glued to their chairs. Koo the terrier grins stupidly, the metal pipe hanging limply between his teeth. Beside him, the pompadoured owner of Grade A chuckles quietly. I'm guessing the fruity smoke wasn't the only thing swallowed in here today.

'Sorry to interrupt takings time,' I say, motioning to the piles of cash on the table.

'You've brought someone with you,' Mo says, craning her tree trunk neck to see past me. 'Looking for work, boy?' she asks Shinji. 'We've plenty of customers who'd pay big for you. Lose this one-eared wanker and come in.'

'No one touches the boy,' I say.

All three chuckle this time. If they were any slower they'd be in reverse.

'Get out of here, Kawasaki,' Mo says, her gold teeth glinting.

'I'm not going anywhere until I find Bernd Schulte.'

Koo laughs and pulls out his pistol while Pompadour smiles sleepily. I'm not gonna get any answers, but I've had enough of answers tonight. This is a night for ending things. Drawing lines. And the best way to draw a line is with a knife.

My old cop instincts return, muscle memory, hands and fingers working like a production line. The handle of my knife cracks across Mo's crown and she drops like a mountain. Koo points his pistol as I dart around Mo's falling body, but the little man is too slow. I kick the gun from his hand and knock him out with a blow to the head. Pompadour is last, the smirk sliding off his handsome face as Old Trusty drives into his arm. He clutches the bleeding wound before my punch sends him into the world of the unconscious with his comrades.

I stare at their bodies, slumped over the tables and floor. Shinji lets a deep breath escape through pursed lips.

'Fuck me,' he says.

I nudge the next door open. Dust spills into the alley along with the smell of sour sweat and damp. The shack is a mirror image of Grade A: a tiny bar, shoddy furniture and curtains, and a mezzanine crammed in under a tin roof. A girl of fourteen quivers on the threshold, her eyes puffy with black bags. A large figure is slumped over one of the tables on the second floor.

'Get out, kid,' I say to the girl.

Shinji glowers at me and steps forward. 'You okay?' he asks her.

She looks between us, terrified. Shinji swallows. 'Please, you don't want to be here for what's next.'

She stares up at me. I try to arrange my face into an expression that might not terrify a little girl. The muscles in my cheeks stiffen unnaturally, and she scurries outside like a mouse through a hole.

Shinji frowns at me. 'How the fuck do you expect to be a father?'

'Take this.' I hand him Koo's gun. 'Anyone comes in through that door, you point that gun at them. Got it?'

'Just point it?'

'Just point it.'

'What if they come at me? Shall I shoot them?'

'You don't wanna be a killer, boy,' I say.

He nods slowly and stares at the gun in his hands. It looks too big for him.

'You okay?'

His breathing is shaky. I put a hand on his shoulder.

'You've got my back, haven't you, Shinji?' I think it's the first time I've ever called the kid by his name. 'That's why I wanted you to come with me. You know that? Because I trust you more than anyone else.'

Shinji doesn't look at me, but he manages another nod.

'Right.' I run a hand over his bristled scalp and push him towards the door.

I take the stairs slowly. The ceiling is low; I'm almost bent double once I reach the second floor. The lone figure is asleep, his balding crown the only part of his head visible. The smell of whiskey and body odour is sickening.

'Bernd,' I say.

The figure doesn't stir. For a moment I think he might be dead already, but his heavy breathing gives him away. I pick up the glass from the table and toss what's left of the whisky over his head. He comes to, slowly. Bleary eyed, he blinks at me.

'Dag,' he croaks, scanning the room. 'What are you doing here?'

I don't answer. I simply stare at his blotched cheeks and the spittle in his beard. Crimson veins spread from his pupils like cracks in parched earth.

He clears his throat and runs the back of his hand over his beard.

'I must have fallen asleep. One drink too many.'

'I was just at your place.'

Bernd nods. 'Get me a glass of water, won't you? My mouth tastes foul.'

'I don't work here.'

He closes his eyes in apparent discomfort. I can almost see the hangover pounding through his temples.

'What are you doing here, Dag?'

'I should've known the real reason you were working with Sara Barnes.'

'Barnes? She's out to save the city, Dag, and I'm on her side.'

'That's it, is it? You've spent half your life translating corruption into puff, and now all of a sudden you're Sonaya's moral lighthouse? I knew Sara had something on you, but I never imagined how much of a lowlife you were.'

Bernd swallows. A golf ball, by the look of it.

'I found some photos in your attic,' I say. 'Photos of girls. Pretty young, some of them.'

'Now, Dag,' Bernd says, and there's a bit of bluster to his voice now. 'I've as much right to visit Homework Clubs as anyone else. You want to bully every man who's ever talked to a fifteen year-old girl? It'd take a lifetime.'

'Why the hell do you have their pictures?'

'I need a drink.' Bernd moves to stand but I shake my head and he slumps back in his chair.

'My daughter was one of them. Did you know that?'

All of Bernd's languages seem to have deserted him.

'Her name is Maaya, but you might remember her as Echo. You knew she was my daughter, didn't you?'

Bernd wets his lips. 'I knew she was *Fujii's* daughter. He was the one who let her come to these places. He was a sick man, Dag. The booze had taken him, he wasn't in his right-'

'*He* was a sick man?'

'I assure you, Dag, nothing untoward happened with her. If I'd known that she was your daughter-'

'You've known for weeks.'

'Barnes wouldn't let me tell anyone, Dag. She threatened to expose me. I could have lost everything.'

'Bernd,' I say. I look him right in the eyes so he can understand me clearly. 'Maaya's twelve years old.'

Bernd's brow is more wrinkled than ever. I bring Maaya's photo out of my pocket.

'Look at her.'

He does, but he makes it look difficult.

'What exactly were you doing with those other girls?'

He keeps his eyes fixed on Maaya's photo, and they shine with regret.

'I'm sorry, Dag,' he says, his chin quivering.

'What did you do to those other girls?' I ask again.

It's a pathetic creature I see before me now. Tears stream down Bernd's face, dribble spilling over his lips. He tries to speak, but convulsive breaths are all he manages.

The sight makes me feel sick to my stomach. Not because I'm seeing the emotional collapse of a man I once respected, but because I'm finally seeing everything it represents. I picture all the kids in Sonaya living through a shitstorm created by my generation. All the girls and boys without voices; the oppressed, the ignored, the abused. I thought I could live with it because I never really looked. I told myself it was all okay; that the kids are streetwise and tough; that the old pervs who make the city cogs spin would never truly cross the line.

But as Bernd raises his eyes to meet mine I see the guilt

emitted by his soul. He might not have laid a finger on Maaya, but how long until he did? How long until the next poor street urchin felt his hand on their leg?

'Sorry,' he whispers again, but he isn't speaking to me.

I squeeze past the table, slip behind his chair and put my hands on his shoulders as he blubbers into his palms. I put my hands on his shoulders nice and tight. Slide them around his neck. He doesn't put up a fight.

The crack echoes through the room.

25

My heart hammers against my ribs as we escape the seedy shack, and Shinji's eyes burn with fear. He told me he didn't want me to disappear again, but you can't kill someone and carry on as if nothing happened. I wonder how long until drones descend and make me an outlaw. How long before I'm back in a cell, meditating on my myriad of sins?

We're barely out of the hovel's sleazy clutches when a bike skids across our path. I breathe a sigh of relief as Sara Barnes removes her helmet.

'Just a happy coincidence that you're here, I suppose?' I ask.

Instead of answering, she gestures to the back of her bike.

'I'm in no mood for a cruise. The kid and I have some hiding to do.'

'I know where she is,' Sara says. 'Maaya.'

'What? How could you know?'

'Just climb on.'

I look at Sara and Shinji and the Fish Nets over my shoulder, as though expecting Bernd's ghost to emerge from the depths of the squalid shanty. But he won't. He's dead, and suddenly I have another person's blood on my hands. Another victim of Dag's flamingo mist.

Time to get clear of it. Time to remember what this is all about. Maaya.

'Shinji,' I say, mounting behind Sara. 'Hole up, hang tight. Keep your head down, you hear me?'

His face has drained of colour and his tongue searches for moisture on dry lips.

'Listen,' I say. 'I know a dog that's just lost an owner. Get Hildegard somewhere safe before the cops show up and put her down.'

'Dag …' he says, but the rest of the sentence evades him.

'Don't worry, kid,' I say. 'This night's still young. Find Aimi and make sure your sister's safe. Don't worry about the rest.'

He nods absently as Sara revs and I manage a last command before Shinji disappears from view.

'And get the hell clear of this shithole.'

We're off, and the Fish Nets dissolve behind us.

'Where is she?' I shout in Sara's ear.

'Just do as I say, okay?'

'Sara, I'm going to find my daughter. And if you get in the way of that …'

'You won't get to your daughter without me. So shut up and let me ride.'

Snapshots of Sonaya slip past in a shimmering blur as we navigate the Rivers. I can't focus on anything or absorb a single image. The gravity of the last hour's events begin to sink in, stacking a slow concrete wall from my stomach to the base of my throat. I've just killed a man. A friend. And a government official.

I try to convince myself he deserved it. I told him last week that I was Death, and I guess I was right. Deathbringer Dag, scythe in hand, standing at the gates of hell dealing judgment for every miserable sinner who dares come near.

'We're here,' Sara says.

I hadn't even noticed we'd stopped. Sara dismounts and I follow suit, looking up to see the blinking sign for Solo, the underground honsool.

'Why the hell are we back here?'

Sara heads silently to the stairs. We pass Solo and keep descending. Maybe she's taking me directly to hell. She pushes through an unmarked door and I prepare myself for flames.

We're met instead by a flashing mess of ancient arcade

games and noise. The place is heaving with rebel hipsters drowning in leather; it looks like a roll-call of Bosozoku rejects. Sara cuts a path through drinkers, dancers, and button bashers. The boys comb their quiffs and dab at their eyeliner with painted nails, while the girls pull their collars up and pose with hair like clouds of candy floss.

Sara pushes through a door marked *Staff Only* and we enter a shabby office empty save for the woman on the weathered sofa.

'Dag, you made it.'

Ryoko Nishi nurses a glass of wine. She's back in her usual getup—a smart black suit that looks as out of place as she does. Her hair looks freshly straightened, her nails and lipstick violent red. Even the birthmark on her left cheek looks like it was designed with painstaking attention to detail.

'Sara said she'd know how to find you,' she says.

'What is this place?' I ask, taking in the dusty floor and tatty furniture. 'Secret investment?'

'Just a place to get away,' Nishi replies with a wry smile. 'Everyone needs somewhere to de-stress.'

I can't help but picture the rebel Ryoko of thirteen years ago. It seems the girl I knew isn't completely gone after all.

'You're not interested in a quiet life, are you Dag?'

'The German,' I say. 'He had her photo. Maaya's.'

'Big news, Dag,' Nishi says. 'A middle aged suit is a pervert. What did you do to him?'

I answer by looking at my shaking hands.

'Outstanding judgement, as always,' Nishi says drily. 'Tell me, are you going to kill every poor sod who ever looked at your daughter?'

'I don't think that's all. With some of the girls ... he ... I think he would ...'

I can't finish the sentence. Maybe I'm still too much of a coward to say it out loud, to make it real.

'Well, congratulations,' Nishi says. 'You've finally pierced

Sonaya's neon skin and seen what lies underneath. Welcome to the real world, Dag. What an entrance you've made; now you'll be locked up before dawn.'

Sara takes a seat on the opposite sofa and gestures for me to join her. I'm too annoyed to accept, and it's my own dumb self I'm annoyed with.

'I'll stand, thanks. Just tell me what the hell this is about.'

'We're short of time, Dag,' Nishi says. 'So let's jump straight in, shall we?'

'Please,' I say, pacing before them. 'What is it? You pissed that I haven't taken care of Jiko yet? Well I'm not going to, do you hear me? I've given you your votes, but you can forget about the rest.'

Nishi only smiles.

'None of that matters anymore,' she says. 'The election's gone to shit; your votes are meaningless. It turns out it was hardly worth all the trouble, making you a First Band.'

I stop my pacing and stare her down. 'What the hell does that mean?'

'Oh, Dag, get over yourself,' Nishi says, raising her wine glass to her lips. She smirks over the rim. 'Like I said, it doesn't matter anymore.'

She glances at Sara.

'As usual, Dag,' Sara says, 'you've been chipping flakes off the tip of the iceberg while the rest of us have been under the water, carving a universe out of the bulk.'

'And?'

Sara and Nishi exchange another meaningful look. A few seconds pass before Nishi speaks again.

'I knew it was a set up,' she says simply.

'*What* was a set up?'

I'm distracted; the ruckus of the club, the idea that I'm not truly the First Band genius I thought I was, the impending countdown to I-don't-know-what.

'Thirteen years ago,' Nishi says, placing her glass down. 'When you shot Hana-'

'You know that was a mistake,' I say, the blood rushing to my face. 'That bullet was meant for Fujii.'

'The day after it happened,' Nishi continues, ignoring me, 'I was with Fujii in the hospital. Maaya was on life support, they still didn't know if she would pull through. And I heard a conversation. Fujii, crying on the phone, saying it was done.'

I struggle to conceal the sigh of frustration. I've taken responsibility for Hana's death; I've done everything I can to bury that night in the ground. But everyone else seems intent on digging it back up.

'Dag, he was on the phone with Zenzo Goto.'

'The Deputy PM?' I ask. 'So it was him? He was behind it all?'

'He assures me he was against Hana's hit, but I don't know who that leaves. I was with Fujii when Hana died—I know for sure it wasn't what *he* wanted. He was a wreck of a man, Dag. When he coaxed you to the lighthouse that night, he was only following orders. And he promised me he tried to stop it.'

'He *did* try to stop it,' I say. 'But that didn't save Hana, did it?'

I watch Nishi sip her wine. Her eyes are somewhere else entirely; they're probably back in the past, where we all should've stayed.

'So you're telling me you've known it was a setup all these years,' I say, almost to myself. 'You sat silent while I rotted in The Heights. You watched your sister die, and then you fell in with the very people who arranged it.'

'Do you think I didn't care, Dag? Really? You think I didn't dig deeper after you got locked up? I didn't leave it alone, I promise you. Fujii fell apart and cut ties with me; I couldn't get a word out of him. But even while I mourned, even in my lowest moments, I didn't give up. I worked hard and I greased palms and put myself at risk. And finally I got answers.'

'What answers?'

'Hana had information,' Sara says. 'That's why someone tried to have her killed.'

'What information?'

'About an individual in government who was bribing higher-ups to advance themselves.'

'Zenzo Goto,' I say.

'That's what I thought, too,' Nishi says. 'I confronted him. It wasn't easy. I was just a kid, with no links to anyone. But I cornered him and threatened to expose him. And he made me an offer.'

'Ah, now it all makes sense,' I say bitterly. 'So that's how the rebellious little sister got into politics. Blackmail.'

'I couldn't change what happened to Hana, Dag. She was gone. But in my digging I found a lot of names. A lot of suits who'd accepted bribes. The corruption ran deep, and there were more people involved than I ever could have guessed.'

'And you did nothing about it.'

'Where would it have got me? Into the grave, the same as Hana. My sister was dead, my mother passed away shortly after. My father abandoned me. I was alone, with no prospects. So I made my own prospects.'

'And you used what you knew to climb all this way?'

Nishi smirks, and her birthmark creases. 'Oh, after a time I found that I had a talent for politics. And the party liked me, too. I was a pretty face for an ugly cabinet. They made me the head of the snake, and I let them.'

I rub my face. I'm tired. I'm tired of talking, of hearing about things I've no control over. I'm so damn tired of the past.

'You said we're short of time,' I say.

'While you've been chasing shadows, Dag, Ms. Barnes has been churning up the Sonayan graveyard. Bernd Schulte gave her proof of illegal acts within government—decades of stuff—and all she needed was one name, one domino to push and start the tower tumbling. Ganzo gave her that name. *Me.* In other words, Sara dusted off the bones and she's put together quite a skeleton; there's nothing for me to hide behind anymore. My time's done, Dag.'

'So what?' I ask, looking between them. 'What are you telling me?'

'Tokyo are on the way as we speak,' Sara says. 'The dam is about to break, and Ryoko is the one opening the gates.'

I look to Nishi. 'So you're blowing the whistle on yourself. You'll be joining me in a cell, it seems.'

'Very likely,' Nishi says. 'But like I said, I've got a lot of names to give.'

I manage a laugh. 'The pirate captain going down with her ship. You're going to try and broker a deal.'

'I don't mind throwing a traitorous crew to the sharks if I can shave a few years off my sentence.'

'Tokyo, eh? Hell, you did fuck things up, didn't you? And what's Tokyo gonna do about it all?'

'Wrap Sonaya up in red tape and take away our toys, I expect. They'll probably give us back our training wheels until all the corruption's been wormed out.'

'That could take some time.'

'Then so be it. It's been going on for far too long.'

I smile despite myself. Our Sonaya. We well and truly fucked her up.

'So what's this, then?' I say. 'A last drink before they take us away?'

'I've already given names, Dag,' Nishi says. 'And the names aren't happy about it. Zenzo Goto, especially. Even if he wasn't the one to put the hit on Hana, he was there at the heart of Sonaya's descent. Dodgy deals, bullshit policies, and backhanders galore. Goto's about to become Sonaya's most wanted, and he wants revenge before they catch him.'

I shrug. 'So you better hope Tokyo reach you before he does.'

Nishi looks down at her perfectly manicured hands.

Sara stands. 'He knows about Maaya, Dag. You need to get to her before Goto's people do.'

I rub the back of my burning neck, trying to make sense of it all.

'Surely Goto's got more pressing matters to deal with,' I say. 'Why would he waste his time with revenge when he could be arranging his escape?'

'Escape?' Nishi laughs. 'There's no escape. Not for any of us.'

I look to Sara.

'We're running out of time, Dag,' she says. 'He knows where Maaya is, and I'm afraid he's going to go after her.'

'For the hundredth fucking time then,' I say. '*Where is she?*'

'She's with family,' Nishi says quietly.

'You and me are the only family she has left.'

Nishi shakes her head. 'You never got on well with my father, I know. But he's a good man. He's the only one I trusted Maaya with.'

Of course. Hana's father.

Sara grabs her helmet. 'Ready for one last ride?'

26

JIKO

Su-young paces around the lookout point on Broken Hill as night spreads across the city like a silent spell. Bo-min watches the lights flicker to life with her elbows on the rusted railings while I sit on a bench and listen to the screeching chorus of singing cicadas.

'Something's not right,' Su-young says. 'He was supposed to be back by now. Where did you find that kid anyway? How do you know he won't sell us out?'

'He's Dag's new go-to pigeon,' I say. 'He's a little wet behind the ears, but maybe that's a good thing. He's no schemer, believe me. He'll be back with the tickets soon, and we'll be gone by morning.'

I catch the other two exchange the briefest of glances.

'We've caused our fair share of havoc,' I say. 'But we can't go on like this forever. Getting out is our only choice. Dag's right.'

Su-young shakes her head but the pacing doesn't cease. 'Lions will always say that antelope have no need to revolt. Dag doesn't know what we've been through. He doesn't know what women like us will *continue* to go through, unless something changes. Yoo-ri Baek knew, and she let it slide because there was nothing in it for her. It doesn't matter if we don't win, Jiko. What matters is that we fight. That people take notice. And if we don't win, if we die, someone will take over and continue our fight until... until it changes.'

'Japan are on the way, Su-young,' I say. '*Everything* is about to change.'

Su-young stops dead and stares at me. 'Japan are on the way,' she repeats humourlessly. 'Have you forgotten why you're covering up that Rising Sun with Sonaya's black rays? Look at that mess on your chest and tell me again that Japan will change everything.'

I don't look down. I look right back at Su-young. 'History is history. What do you want?'

'The reason Sonayans wanted independence in the first place was because of Japan, because they treated the people of this island like lab rats. Rolling out shitty social experiments to solve their own problems. Well, big news: the experiments didn't work. Independence failed, too, and do you know why? Because in the end our politicians were no different from theirs. Corruption doesn't have a flag, Jiko, so I don't give a shit if the whole of Honshu comes to *tidy up*. Corruption is rich smug men in ironed suits. That's all corruption has ever been.'

She drops onto the bench beside me. Her face softens as she places a hand on my shoulder.

'Jiko, we could take that boat tomorrow. We could hide in some big Japanese city, reinvent ourselves all over again. But that's all we'd be doing: hiding. Japan isn't the promised land, no more than Korea is. Think about the Borrowings. We've been plucking green policies from Europe for years, but what about the rest? What about the gender gap? Equality? Something isn't *right*, Jiko. Think about Ume, think about Suzie. Fuck. Women like us are nothing to those pigs in office; we're disposable, nothing but cuts of meat.'

I know she's right. But it still hurts to hear the truth; to know we're so far from what we want.

'The Borrowings are a gimmick, Jiko, the same as all the other crackpot policies. Sonaya still has all the same problems as our sisters across the water, and it's not gonna change unless someone takes action. And that someone has to be us.'

Bo-min approaches. We both look up at her. She nods.

I look between them. I know they're right; we were right the whole time. Ume started something, and I liked following. I liked being angry, and I liked burning rubber and swearing to put an end to suits in faraway offices. But for me it was only ever words. Words and an outlet for teenage angst. I'd never truly understood. I'd never truly believed.

But now I get it. No one is going to swoop in and click their fingers and change everything we want. No one is going to do anything. Not unless we do.

'Before anything happens,' I say. 'There's something you should know. I'm not the person you think I am.'

'And who do we think you are?' Su-young smirks.

I can't get the words out. I can say anything to these girls. *Anything.* But the words won't come.

'I'm not a leader,' I say eventually. 'I'm not brave. I don't wanna hold a gun again—ever. That night—Earth Hour—I killed someone. A human. I took his life.'

Su-young takes my hand. Bo-min sits on my other side and links her arm in mine.

'We won't do anything you don't wanna do,' Su-young says. 'And it's okay to be fucked up. It's okay to be haunted. All three of us are. But don't torture yourself for something you had to do.'

I try to hold back the tears.

'And you don't have to hold those in,' Bo-min says.

We head back to the bar and push through the customers. It seems like half of Broken Hill has converged in the Tiger and Crane. The population of the slums are delighting in the promise of chaos. They're saying the government has fallen, that the PM is headed for The Heights. For these people, any change is good change.

Eun-joo motions me over to the bar.

'I'm hearing rumours that the city is about to be flipped upside down like a pancake,' she says. 'They're saying the whole pyramid might fall, top to bottom. Even Yoo-ri Baek was involved. If you girls keep your heads down a few days you might just get a clean slate handed to you.'

'A clean slate?' I say. 'I doubt it.'

'Just don't do anything rash, not until the dust settles. Get down in the basement and stay under the radar for the night.'

We slip behind the bar and take the stairs.

Bo-min pours out drinks. Three glasses full to the brim clink together.

'To Fumiko,' Su-young says.

'To Suzie,' Bo-min says.

'To Ume,' I say.

We drain our glasses and refill.

'No more playing,' Bo-min says.

Su-young and I look at her. She stares at the table, her eyes dancing over the glasses as she searches for the right words.

'We can't keep burning places down and sneaking around, threatening people in back alleys. It hasn't got us anywhere and it never will.'

Su-young smiles. 'And do you have an alternative?'

Bo-min looks at us sheepishly. 'We need people to understand. We need *people*. Numbers.'

'And how do we get them?'

'Fumiko's cocoon has burst, and that means there's a whole network open. Cocoon weavers, sex workers, pigeons. Mercenaries suddenly out of work. A real racket, not just a backstreet gang. That's a start.'

'Someone will claim Fumiko's business before she's even in the ground.'

'And who better to claim it than us?' Bo-min challenges us

with a stare that surprises me. 'If what they're saying is true, the PM has thrown a grenade at the heart of the city. All the shit is about to fountain out from the sewers. And Eun-joo's right, if we can make it through these next few days, we might get a clean shot at things. We can do it.'

Su-young and I exchange a look.

'Let's say it works,' Su-young says. 'Let's say we take over Fumiko's cocoon, tether her followers to us, what are we gonna do next?'

Bo-min kills her drink and grins. 'Start a movement.'

I move quietly up the steps and ease the trapdoor open. Eun-joo's still standing behind the bar, but the music and chatter have died. A man's voice bellows across the bar.

'Are you deaf? We're after the Bosozoku, and we know they're here. No one else needs to get hurt, so if you're not one of them, get the fuck out right now.'

I duck back down the stairs and close the trapdoor behind me.

'Well it looks like the grand plans are going to have to wait,' I say. 'The Nightshades have arrived, and they want Bosozoku blood.'

Bo-min stands and clenches her jaw. Su-young downs her drink.

'You been harbouring any more secret plans in that head of yours?' Su-young asks.

Bo-min shakes her head. 'This one's on you.'

'Good, I've been itching for this.' It's been a while since I've seen Su-young smile so genuinely. 'Fumiko made her last stand. But this isn't going to be *our* last.'

They join me on the stairs and I push the trapdoor open. We file out one by one behind the bar and observe the scene.

The customers are streaming out, and some are being

pushed through the door by Shades. As Eun-joo vaults the bar and tries to wrestle her invaders away, I tally up four black helmets. Once all the customers have cleared out, the bikers surround Eun-joo and back her into a corner. She pulls a knife out of nowhere.

'You fuckers, I told you they're not here,' she says. 'You can turn this place upside down if you like, but I promise you I'll make you bleed as you do.'

One of the Shades laughs as he closes in on her.

'Actually, you're in the right place,' I say.

The four helmets turn our way. We're lined up behind the bar like an underworked staff.

'You boys looking for something?' Su-young asks.

The Shades take a step towards us, drawing weapons from their belts.

'Only a little money,' one answers.

'Then you're in the wrong place after all, flower boys,' I say. 'This is Broken Hill.'

'We've come to collect a bounty. The three of you have mighty fine rewards on your heads, and it just so happens that someone was happy to point us in your direction.'

'Who?'

'The little duckling you sent to fix your ferry tickets to Honshu. Cute little kid, waddled into the agency clutching a piece of paper in his chubby hand. Course, security's tighter than ever this evening, they won't let any street kid with cash just roll up and buy a ferry ticket, not with Japan on the way and a government full of guilty cats scrambling to get off the island. I watched him myself, saw them turn him away. Hell, you had to feel sorry for the kid. Never seen anyone look so disappointed.'

'You better not have laid a finger on that boy,' I say.

'I didn't have to. I told him I could help him, said I had some spare tickets and was interested in selling them. He couldn't hand the money over fast enough. I even offered to make the delivery myself. He seemed mighty happy about that, said his mum would be waiting for him at home.' He laughs. 'She's probably still waiting for him now.'

'I thought you said you didn't hurt him.'

'I said I didn't *have to* hurt him. He pointed us right here, to the Tiger and Crane. And I'm sorry to tell you, girls, there are no ferry seats available.'

I glance at the girls by my side. Both respond with stoic nods as Eun-joo watches from the corner.

'That's okay,' I say. 'We're not in such a rush to leave anymore.'

I'm not the leader; I know that now. This isn't about me. We're a team, and we do everything together. But that doesn't mean I can't be the first to make a move. I climb up onto the bar, pull out my knife and grasp a vodka bottle in my free hand. Su-young and Bo-min reach for bottles from the shelves behind them.

'Take off your helmets,' I command.

The leader shakes his head. 'This isn't going to end how you want it to.'

He reaches for his belt and holds a sphere in his palm. Eun-joo charges at him from behind, but he tosses the device before she reaches him. It smashes against the back wall of the bar and explodes in a cloud of violet gas.

For a moment I'm blinded and breathless as the gas catches in my throat and makes me gag. I hear coughs and shouts from my girls as their bottles catapult through the air and disappear into the smoke. Then the first helmet emerges out of the toxic cloud with a knuckle duster raised and poised to punch.

27

When we reach the edge of the city I hop from Sara's bike and gaze at a graveyard of rusted trains—the ghosts of Japan's heavy industry push. Many of them are toppled and burned and decaying under dust and debris, a home for rats.

'Sorry I can't take you any further,' Sara says. 'Nishi's organized your ride to the farms; it'll be here soon.'

'Yeah, I guess you've got places to be,' I say. 'Time to reveal yourself as the saviour of Sonaya.'

Nothing on Sara's face moves, and it takes longer than it should for the cogs to fall into place.

'So you knew how to find me, huh? You knew I'd be paying Bernd a visit because you told me to.'

Sara's eyelids close in cool instalments like a lioness at rest.

'You knew the whole time,' I say. 'You knew exactly what Bernd was; you knew what he'd done to those girls, you knew he'd met my daughter, and you used it to blackmail him. To get what you needed.'

'This is bigger than you, Dag. I knew how you'd react if you found out. I couldn't let you interfere, not again.'

I feel the mist returning, and even when I close my eyes the haze doesn't disappear. It swirls before my vision as I listen to the hammering of my heart and try to suppress the fire that threatens to erupt from within.

'Sara.'

I think about everything that could happen after opening my eyes. I could tackle her to the ground and bloody my fists on her face; I could fall to my knees and watch her leave; I could open my eyes to find her gone, an apparition who doesn't even care enough to see what becomes of me.

I breathe. In. Out. Slow.

Finally I open my eyes, and I discover two things. First, Sara's still there. Second, there's a tear on my lashes as they part. Is it there because of her lies? Or is it for the red tornado that has grown within me, the parasite that seems to swell with each passing day? Maybe it's for the lives I ended, for all my mistakes. For the daughter who lived the way she did. For the lives I've ruined along the way.

Sara watches the tear slide down my cheek. Slowly she dismounts and steps forward. Her index finger slides up my jaw and collects the salty bead. She draws her finger close to her face and observes the moisture there, living proof that Daganae Kawasaki is a human being with a beating heart.

She smirks as I blink again and a second tear trails from the other eye. 'Who would have thought it?' she says.

'Me least of all,' I manage.

She leans in close and draws her arms around my back. She brings her lips close to the earless hole at the side of my head, just as she did once before, and whispers so softly I hear nothing.

'What?'

'You'll always be a fool, Kawasaki,' she says, and buries her face in my neck.

I don't know how much time passes before she brings her face before mine, her lips inches from my own. I feel her breath and see the hypnotic flicker of her eyelashes, her pupils like pools of liquid space.

'I'm not sure what that tear was for,' she says quietly. 'But if it was for me, I'm sorry. It's nothing personal. I weaken for no one. Not anymore.'

We stare at each other for hours before she releases me and returns to her bike.

'Go get Maaya. She needs you.'

I nod and swallow. I've been swallowing a lot tonight.

'We might not see each other for some time, Dag.'

'Don't count on that,' I manage. 'I've got a few lives left yet. Go on, get out of here.'

Sara revs up her bike and disappears, leaving me with no one for company but rats and the skeletons of Sonaya's past.

I soon discover what's become of my ride. Between the wrecks of steel I glimpse of three figures across the graveyard. Two are padded in police blue and the third is handcuffed to a trashed ticket booth. I'm guessing the Sonayan cops are already under Japanese orders, and that means I've lost my wheels to the countryside.

Looks like I'm on my own from here.

Just as I'm plotting my next move, a spotlight sways over the train corpses nearby. A drone. I take cover behind an abandoned carriage, and as the spotlight passes I dive through the open door. I crawl in the dark past overturned chairs and smashed furniture, watching the windows for the drone's progress. I move into the next carriage and stumble across a bearded man in blankets.

'Evening,' I whisper.

He chews his lips and nods with a nervous light in his eyes. I survey his belongings: a pile of clothes beside boxes of junk and a bottle of soju. I resist the urge to ask for a swig and edge towards the door.

I peek outside and wait for my moment. The drone is thirty feet away, flashing its spotlight through the windows of an overturned freight train. I scramble out of the old man's hideout and hop across the tracks into a carriage littered with needles. A second drone drops out of the sky from nowhere and hovers like a metallic beetle before moving up and down the train.

Shuffling on my elbows through the dark carriage, I slowly make my way towards the only set of tracks still in use. Trains still shuttle from the city to the port, but not at night. All I need from the tracks are directions.

I scan my surroundings. Fifty yards away I glimpse the cops in wait, while above them the drones play hide and seek, drifting back and forth over the abandoned trains. I wait until they're both heading away then burst from the carriage.

Time to run.

I race alongside the tracks that lead away from the city, my boots tossing up dirt. Head down, I don't dare look back. Up ahead is nothing but darkness to swallow me.

A few minutes pass before I risk a breather. I glance back and take in the neon-spangled silhouette of the city. Sonaya looks stunning framed by the night sky. I haven't been this far from the lights since I was a young man. From here the city looks so big and full of possibility. I guess sometimes it's good to step back and view your world from afar.

It takes a moment too long to realise that one of the city lights has detached itself from the picture. It glides into the air like a giant firefly, and it grows with each passing second. One of the drones is on the way.

The race continues. I run through a barren, night-washed desert of empty fields, but I can't outrun a drone forever. A couple of miles out I'll reach one of the industrial bases, now a ghost land of rusting cranes and giant containers that scar the landscape with empty metal. But I'll never reach them; I'm already slowing and I feel the drone gaining.

The sound of bullets destroys whatever illusion of peace the night granted me. I glance over my shoulder and catch a glimpse of my pursuers. The drone isn't alone. It's flanked by three black motorbikes, and I recognise them even from the briefest look. The Nightshades.

The bikes are gaining and bullets rain as the distance between us dissolves. I expect each desperate step to be my last, certain that any minute a red fountain will sprout from my chest and I'll bleed to death alone in the dirt, so far from my beloved city.

But the hit doesn't come, and soon the bikes are so close I can feel the heat and purr of the motors as though they're inside my own chest, the vibrations of the wheels through the earth below my feet. Surely the Nightshades can't be such poor shots.

'Is that as fast as you can go?'

One of the bikes skids and showers me in a storm of dust. It's a Nightshade bike all right, but the rider doesn't have a helmet. Instead she's wearing a windswept perm and a smile that almost makes me laugh with relief. Su-young.

Behind her are Jiko and Bo-min, who ride one-handed while firing shots at the sky. The drone above them strafes and spears them with swaying white light, and then clouds of dirt explode between the bikes as the drone fires back from the air. It's like a scene from an old Western flick, only the horses have wing mirrors and the bandits are chunks of flying metal.

Su-young and I add our guns to the attack. Now it's four on one, a rhombus raid on a metal mosquito. We land a few spark-lit hits and pretty soon the drone drops from the sky, smoking like a burned steak. Once it hits the dust, we converge. We might as well spin our guns and spit like cowboys.

'You came,' I say, looking at each of them. 'On your way to the port?'

Jiko shakes her head. 'We don't leave one of our own behind.' She looks out to the country with eyes that seem to find solace in the darkness.

'You came back for the Dove,' I say.

'Those Shades aren't as tough as they look,' Su-young says.

'Shades?'

'Four of them cornered us in the Tiger and Crane,' Jiko explains. 'One sight of blood and broken glass and two of them scarpered like frightened kids. Eun-joo knocked another out from behind, and the last one … well, with a knife to his throat he was pretty cooperative.'

'How did they find you?'

'They got a hold of your new pigeon. Hee-chan.'

'He okay?'

Jiko raises an eyebrow. 'Let's fucking hope so.'

Before we have chance to group hug, Bo-min points to the sky above the city.

'Another one on the way.'

Su-young re-mounts her bike. 'Damn, being wanted is a lot of work. What do you say we lead her a merry dance, Bo-min?'

Bo-min mounts and tightens the velcro straps of her gloves. They rev their engines and in a flash they're speeding back towards the lights and the oncoming drone.

'I guess that means you're with me,' Jiko says.

There's no red hair in my face, but otherwise the ride feels familiar. I hold Jiko's waist and she leans over the handlebars and gobbles up the country. Over the roar of the engine I hear the occasional gunshot, but I don't turn back. The gunfight's behind us, and my future awaits.

A sickness grows in my stomach with each passing mile. I don't feel nerves; I've never cared about my life enough. But I associate this feeling with a certain time in the past. It was when I first met Hana. I fell hard, and in a way I never thought possible. My stomach used to shrink and squirm every time I saw her, and my chest became a glass case with a hammer thumping it into shattered pieces. And that's exactly how I'm feeling now.

Jiko pulls up and glances over her shoulder. 'We won't have

much time. But I figure you'll want to say something to her first. Before we all burst in there, I mean.'

I dismount and see the cabin ahead. My mouth is dry; swallowing is an art I seem to have forgotten. I begin the walk. It might be the longest walk of my life.

'Dag,' Jiko calls. I turn to look at her. 'You're a good man. You have it in you to be a good dad.'

Staring at her, half-silhouetted against the black country, I'm almost overcome. I've never felt so weak or exposed. And there she sits, a vision of youth and power and goodness, sitting astride a stolen motorbike. Her head shaved, an earring dangling from one ear, she looks entirely different from the hot-head redhead I first met in The Heights. Now she's a woman. And I can't even summon a word of thanks for her.

I turn back to the cabin and feel a breeze on my neck as mozzies swarm. It smells like the end of summer, of tilled earth and corn and forests. I could run and leave it all behind, start a fresh life in the pines like the hermits who gave up on the world. I could build myself a little house and hunt for rabbits and catch fish from the stream. I could live in peace.

The cabin lights are lit. It's a handsome little plot with lots of space to run; not a bad place for a kid to grow up. I steal around to one of the windows and take a deep breath before peeking between the grey rag curtains. The old man is sat at a great oak table cradling a steaming mug. On the floor is the girl.

28

I can't believe I didn't recognise it before. Her nose, her mouth, her frown of concentration—they all belong to her mother. Her father is somewhere in there, too, but it doesn't ruin the picture. She's staring at the pages of a book as if trying to will the contents into her brain. Looking at this child through the window makes my hands feel dirty. Dirty and bloody and nowhere near good enough.

I study the old man; it's been twelve years and it shows. Less hair, more wrinkles, less of his chest and shoulders. Less of that look of me not being good enough for his daughter. He turns slowly and sees my face at his window, like he's been expecting me this whole time. I don't move. The old man stares at me and shakes his head minutely.

He stands up, makes an excuse to the Dove and picks up his shotgun. He exits the cabin and makes for the path towards the train tracks. Doesn't say a word or turn his head. I follow him, twenty yards off in the shadows. He doesn't stop until we're well out of earshot.

'That you, Kawasaki?' Okimoto Nishi asks. It's a voice that sounds tired and stretched with age.

I step out of the dark and let him see the tattoos and missing ear and broken nose.

'You look like shit,' he says, raising the shotgun to his shoulder and pointing it at me.

Tall and wiry, his aged body still looks tough and capable;

it's a body used to long days of manual labour, and the gun looks like a natural extension.

'You were always behind the times,' I reply. 'Fashions change.'

He's bald on top, with thin wisps of grey around large ears. His long face is brought to life by large, dark eyes that belong to someone thirty years younger. They fix me with a calculating stare, just as they did all those years ago when Hana first introduced me.

'A murderer always looks like shit. It's in the eyes. Is that your friend over there with the bike?'

I glance at Jiko in the distance. I wonder if the others have taken down the drone. In any case, it won't be long until more arrive.

'Why are you here, Kawasaki?'

Good question. What exactly am I offering?

'My girl,' I say finally. 'Maaya. She's not safe here. Right now Ryoko is spilling every one of her sins to the world, and her accomplices aren't happy about it. They know Maaya's here, and they're going to take their anger out on her. So I've come to take her away.'

Okimoto keeps the barrel of the gun pointed at my crooked nose. One of his eyes is closed while the other stays fixed on the sight. He's absolutely still.

'Maaya might be your daughter, Kawasaki,' he says slowly, 'but she needs a man to take care of her. Not a murdering pig. Not a coward. Not a worm like you.'

It's everything I expected to hear. The words might be different, but the tone is the same as it was all those years ago. Okimoto Nishi always saw me for what I really was. He saw what Hana didn't.

'So pull the trigger already,' I say. 'I killed your daughter. I'm the reason your life fell apart. Kill me.'

The old man bites his bottom lip. His eyes sharpen and his bushy eyebrows twitch. His whole face contorts with the tension of the moment. It's a moment I'm sure he's been thirsting after for a decade.

I stare into the barrel and wonder if these are my last breaths. Part of me thinks it would be easier for everyone if the bullet came. The night would sing with the crack of the rifle, and the sad cast of Sonaya would be free of this poor excuse of a lead man.

But then I think of Maaya: now she comes first. And right now, despite what everyone else seems to think, I can actually be of use to her. I would lay my life on the line for her, I realise as I stare down the barrel.

Just as I'm about to plead my case, Okimoto's hands begin to shake. He lowers the gun.

'I'm not like you,' is all he can say. 'I'm no killer.'

Soft old man.

'Stay away from her, Kawasaki. She doesn't need you. Never has.'

I remember the Dove running messages in the Rivers and evading cops in the pachinko hall. Maybe Okimoto is right. He drops his rifle to the earth and watches me, and I stare right back at him.

'And when they come?' I say. 'You'll need more than a shotgun and a cantankerous stare to protect her.'

One corner of his mouth twitches in a sardonic sneer. 'I know this island pretty well, Kawasaki. I'll take her away and hide her for as long as it takes.'

His scornful eyes bore into mine, challenging me.

Maybe he's right; maybe there's time. If they're fast enough, they can disappear into the depths of the countryside before Zenzo Goto's people get here. The old man will keep Maaya safe until Goto's locked up and this is all over.

'Fine,' I say. 'Then get your things together and move fast.'

Maybe I can hold off the drones a little longer; maybe that's all I'm good for. I head for Jiko and feel Okimoto's eyes on the back of my head. I turn back for one last question. I can hardly bring myself to say it; men like me can't afford to look weak. But I suppose I've got to start somewhere.

'Is she happy?'

Okimoto's face is lost in the darkness now. What kind of question am I asking? I killed her mother. I helped kill the man who brought her up, too. She lived alone on the streets like a stray, and neither I nor anyone else did anything to help her. Of course she isn't happy.

'She's a strong one,' the old man says. 'She gets it from her mother.'

We stand and swallow our swollen Adam's apples like pubescent boys.

Suddenly the lights of drones swarm like locusts over the fields.

'Looks like our time's up,' I say.

'You've been here five minutes and already you've brought the first of the plagues.'

Indeed. The seven plagues of Dag the Absent Father.

The rhythm of helicopter blades chops up the dandelion night and stirs up the pool of blood in my stomach. I realise I'm not quite ready to throw in the towel just yet. This trip's about to become a family affair.

'Go get the girl,' I say. 'We're all getting out of here.'

I have a way of letting people know when I mean something. Reluctance hardens the old man's jaw, and I know exactly what he's thinking. He doesn't want her to see me. He doesn't want to shake up her life again or put her in danger. But now there's no choice; the drones have arrived with a chopper in tow, and now we're ducks trailing across a hunter's sky.

Jiko's bike skids across the earth between us.

'Reunion time's over, boys,' she says. 'Let's move.'

The old man grimaces and makes for the cabin.

'Bring an extra gun,' I call after him. 'And all the ammo you can carry.'

The drones are swiftly followed by Su-young and Bo-min, who arrive shrouded in clouds of dust. I hop behind Jiko and the three bikes rip up Okimoto's rice paddies while we fire stray bullets towards the stars. We head for the forest line and try to draw them away from the cabin. The drones might be master filmmakers but they're lousy shots. All they do is bury bullets in the ground while we churn up the earth before the trees.

Then the helicopter arrives. It hovers above the cabin, a spotlight focused on the little house. Maaya's home. Maybe her first *real* home, and it barely lasted a week.

Jiko doesn't waste any time. She accelerates back towards the cabin with Su-young and Bo-min in tow, and we unleash another tirade of bullets at the hulking machine. Sparks fly off its body as the bullets find their mark, and it soon pulls back and rises until it's almost out of range.

'We need to act fast,' Jiko says.

'Three bikes, six people,' I say. 'Jiko, I want you to take Maaya.'

She stares at me like I've just asked her to cradle the future of the planet in her hands. A resolute nod quickly follows.

'Where are we going?'

'For now, back to the city,' I say. 'Better the playground we know. If we get separated, we meet at Kosuke's.'

I jump off the bike and run for the cabin just as two figures emerge from the front door. Okimoto has a bundle over his shoulder and Maaya at his side. The three bikes converge on us as the chopper watches from above and two drones flash by its side like faceless bodyguards. Okimoto tosses another pistol to the bikers and Bo-min fires above to keep the flying machines at bay.

I look at my daughter. White fear explodes from her eyes but there's something else in them, too. It's a strong cocktail of stubbornness, anger, and acceptance.

'Hey, Dove,' I say.

'Hey, Dad.'

'This isn't the time for talk,' Okimoto barks. 'What's your blasted plan?'

'Ma—Dove, you're with Jiko. Okimoto, why don't you ride with Bo-min? Your conversations will be thrilling.'

The old man snarls but doesn't argue. He climbs behind Bo-min while Maaya mounts behind Jiko.

'Let's get the hell out of here,' Jiko commands.

I jump behind Su-young and seconds later all three bikes soar through the country night.

The drones fire at us. Whoever's aboard the chopper fires at us, too. The Nightshades' bikes are fast but our hunters are gaining. Earth explodes around us as the bullets close in.

'We're not gonna make it,' Su-young says.

'Just keep going,' I tell her, but I know she's right. Our pursuers weren't sent with intentions of justice or morality. They're here to get revenge, and none of us are immune.

I glance over my shoulder to see Jiko behind us and the Dove's skinny arms wrapped around her waist. The third bike is fifty yards behind us, and it's no longer cutting a track through the dirt. Bo-min is still astride it with her pistol in the air, firing shot after shot at the helicopter above her. Okimoto is standing by her side, his shotgun pointed the same way.

'Everything okay?' Su-young asks.

'Bo-min,' I say.

The name is enough for Su-young to slam the brakes. We skid to a stop and watch as Bo-min and Okimoto exchange bullets with the chopper. Jiko pulls up next to us.

'What are they doing?' the Dove asks, breathless.

'They're making a stand that would make Fumiko proud,' I say.

'We have to go back,' Jiko says.

Su-young and I exchange a glance. 'They don't want us to come back,' I say.

'How do you know?' Jiko asks.

'Because we were about to do the same thing. Come on. They won't be able to hold them forever.'

Su-young takes one last look at her friend, then revs up her bike. As we charge towards the city lights, I catch a glimpse of Bo-min's bike falling to the earth, and two distant silhouettes falling with it.

29

Chaos reigns.

People spill out onto the streets with their necks craned to watch the news streaming on government building walls. Ryoko Nishi's face is everywhere, and it's not alone. Zenzo Goto and other cabinet members are there too, while suits from Tokyo try to assure everyone that order will soon be resumed. So much for the elections and my precious thousand votes. After all that fuss, it looks like the pacifiers are set to be shoved back into our dumb mouths.

We don't stop until we reach Kosuke's. No sooner am I off Su-young's bike than she revs her engine and takes off without a word. None of us need to ask where she's going. Bo-min.

The penguin suits in front of Kosuke's giant apartment block are frazzled. One comes trotting down the front steps with sweat glazed on his forehead.

'Where's the old man?' I demand.

'Kosuke's been rushed to hospital, Mr. Kawasaki. I'm afraid he's been attacked.'

'Attacked? By who?'

'I wouldn't know, sir, but it appears to be quite serious. I'm told he's in a stable condition, but he'll be required to spend the night in hospital. The police are inside,' he motions over his shoulder, 'and they've instructed us not to allow anyone to enter.'

I glance up at the windows as if expecting to see officers peeking out from behind curtains. I re-join Jiko and Maaya.

'What's going on?' Jiko asks.

'I don't know,' I admit. 'But Kosuke's been attacked, and if he isn't safe then none of us are. We need to hole up somewhere, and fast.'

'Nakata's,' Jiko says.

'Good. You take Maaya, I'll meet you there.'

'I can go by myself,' Maaya says. 'I don't need you all to protect me. I've survived well enough on my own, haven't I?'

I resist the temptation to roll out a proud father smile. It's too soon.

'None of us are safe, Maaya,' Jiko says. 'We need to get our heads down, do you understand?'

'You don't need to patronise me. I understand. If we have to go, let's go already.'

'Dag,' Jiko says.

I follow her gaze to the line of scrapers behind the harbour.

'Oh, damn.'

One of the buildings is projecting my mugshot. I don't know what they're saying, but I don't imagine it's any good.

'Where are you going?' Jiko asks.

'Checking that Kosuke's the only one.'

I'm about to take off towards the harbour, but I hesitate and glance at my daughter. She paws nervously at the ground, as if she knows what's coming.

'Red, would you give us a moment?'

Jiko looks between us and then strolls towards her bike.

Maaya stands awkwardly before me, looking for the first time like she doesn't know what to do with herself. She crosses and uncrosses her arms and shoves her hands inside her pockets, making a point of staring at Jiko's slow withdrawal. I've had a lot of time to prepare for this, but the script I'd written inside my head is being ripped to shreds where I stand.

'Dove,' I swallow. 'Maaya.'

She can't meet my eyes. I get down to my haunches to get closer to her level, but she only glowers at me. I might not know much about my daughter, but I know she's not one to be patronised. I straighten up again.

'Listen. I'm sorry I wasn't there for you.'

Every word seems to drain a gallon of liquid from my body. By the time the first sentence is done it's feels like I've been chewing cotton wool. I try to moisten my lips but my tongue turns to sand. Maaya continues to glare at Jiko, who's pretending to adjust something on her bike.

'I didn't know,' I say. 'I didn't know you existed. If I had …'

What? What would I have done? I was trapped in a cell anyway.

'I know I'm not the ideal image of a father.'

She studies me with her keen eyes, as if to make that appraisal herself. There's no repulsion in her face but there's nothing like fondness either.

'But I swear I'll do my best by you. I'll give it all up, the booze and all. I'll take care of you … if you want.'

Maaya's eyes begin to glisten. Shit.

'How the hell are you gonna take care of me from a prison cell? In case you hadn't noticed, your face is forty feet high. So before you go stringing together promises, work out which ones you can keep.'

With that she strides purposefully to Jiko and mounts the bike. Jiko shrugs at me. I shrug back. Jiko revs up and a moment later I'm alone again, stinging from my latest parental failure.

○

Sirens blare from police bikes while drones record the mayhem from the sky, and I spot at least two helicopters on the harbour road. I'm guessing the first batch of suits from Tokyo has arrived, and the red tape is well and truly being rolled out. The harbour is usually little more than a showcase for the yacht collections of the elite—half of the vessels have never been out to sea—but I suppose these are special circumstances. It looks like Sonaya's doors have been bolted shut.

The harbour master's office is a small concrete building on the road to the jetties. Among the crowds outside I pick out Stones carrying a bundle of papers. It's a risk me calling his name, but the crowds are so thick that a marauding elephant could get by unnoticed right now. Stones catches sight of me and detaches himself from the throng before ushering me off the main strip and into an alleyway that leads into the Rivers.

'What the hell are you doing here?' he asks. 'I just saw your face flash up on the wanted boards. Word is you killed Bernd Schulte.'

I let my face confirm the story.

'Hell, boy. You've really messed it up this time.'

'Thanks for the analysis,' I say. 'What's the commotion about?'

Stones glances over his shoulder. From our nook between two giant slabs of concrete we can see it all: crowds swarming the harbour road and cops barking orders beneath the bright lights of Sonaya's most polished corner.

'The whole place is going crazy. Local cops are taking orders from the Japanese now. The port across the island's being watched and now they're making sure no one tries to sneak away from this side.'

'And the papers?' I ask, looking at the bundle in his hand.

'Permission to leave.'

'You? On the Arkansas? Do you even know how to sail?'

'Enough to take me to Honshu, maybe. Seems they're happy for the expats to get clear of all this. They're checking the Arkansas as we speak. Making sure there are no stowaways, I guess.' His laugh is a poor imitation.

'What about Aimi?'

He shakes his head. 'She was right all along, Dag, but I never listened.' He sighs as he admires the glistening lights across the harbour. 'Damn, I had some good times here. Thought I'd stay here forever.'

'Then why don't you?'

'It's all coming to an end, Dag. The drug busts, the corruption. This isn't a place for a writer.'

'It sounds like the perfect place for a writer.'

Stones forces a smile. 'Maybe it is. But it's not the right place for me. I've been sinking for years. Haven't written anything good in months. Can't seem to get my head straight, know what I mean?'

I nod.

'I'm going to clean up, Dag. Get some help, and maybe one day I'll have what it takes to be a family man. But I'm not now. Not now.'

He stares absently at his papers and I watch him for a moment, wondering if I'm witnessing cowardice or bravery. I don't come to a conclusion, but I decide it's a step in the right direction. For Aimi and for Eiko.

'I'm glad you're not dead, Stones,' I say and make for the depths of the Rivers. I've got other friends to check on.

'You sure you don't fancy it?' Stones calls. 'I could smuggle you aboard; it could be one hell of an adventure. An expat and an ex-con, taking to the high-seas. There's a buddy movie right there.'

There's a pleading look in his eyes, and I almost pity it. He doesn't wanna do this alone. But maybe he has to.

'Sounds more like a snuff movie to me. This is one journey you'll have to make alone.'

Stones smiles that hollow smile again. He raises a hand in farewell and I leave.

○

I've half a mind to check Shinji's apartment to make sure the kid's alright, but I realise there's little chance he's there. He's probably at the hospital with Eiko, or else with Aimi, or even at Nakata's with the others. I figure I better head for the bar; at least Nakata has a pager and we might be able to gather everyone in one place.

I'm barely out of earshot of the harbour madness when I notice something off. Ex-cop instinct maybe, or perhaps I've been stalked so much in these past few weeks it's simply become second nature to look over my shoulder.

As I turn I see a large figure back off into the shadows, disappearing in the narrow opening between two apartment blocks. I could make a run for it, but I recognise the square line of the shoulders and the big barrel chest, and I'm not ready to let the events of this evening slide by without consequence.

On an impulse I decide to charge for him, and he takes off down the alley like an overfed rat shuffling down a sewer. I gain quickly, and in a flash I've got the big bull around the waist. I tackle him into a wall and when his head cracks against stone he drops to the ground in a heavy heap.

'Zenzo Goto,' I say, standing over him.

Goto blinks away the pain and wipes a dribble of blood from his forehead. His suit is dirty and bloodied, his hair a greasy mess of sweat.

'Got your daughter away, did you?' he says, managing a grimace.

'She's safe now,' I say, still catching my breath. 'Your threat to Nishi didn't work. She's spilled it all and you're headed for The Heights with the rest of your rotten cabinet. I'm guessing that's why you were lurking round here. Trying to find an escape route at the harbour, were you?'

'I have a little vessel of my own, yes,' Goto says with a bitter smile. 'Damn Japanese have put an end to that plan, though. It looks like I'll have to bide my time after all. No quick fix.'

'Bide your time?' I scoff. 'You'll have a lot of it once you're locked up in a cell of sorry stone.'

'Don't be so naïve, Kawasaki. I've got lawyers, and plenty of friends across the East Sea. Barnes and Nishi are trying to make me the fall guy, but it won't be as simple as they expect. Nishi will make her deals, and so will I. This has a long way to go.'

'We'll see,' I say. 'Normally I wouldn't give a shit, but you tried to get at my daughter, and then you attacked Kosuke for good measure.'

'Kosuke?'

'Don't deny it.'

Goto examines me and a smirk spreads across his lips. 'You're quite the character, you know. Really, one of a kind. You're as bad as any of us, Kawasaki, but you're determined to look down at us from some self-forged throne of morality.'

'Maybe you're right,' I say. 'I don't care. But no one messes with my family. You had a hand in Hana's death too, didn't you?'

Goto blinks slowly and turns gingerly onto his side, propping himself up on an elbow. He looks bruised and beaten, but I'm aware that he could pounce at any second and tackle me to the ground with his huge bulk.

'Listen Kawasaki,' he says slowly. 'I had nothing to do with Hana's death. She was a bright woman. She would have been a great leader, too, and I genuinely mean that. But she stumbled upon the inevitable skeletons of Sonaya, and she wouldn't let it go. The truth is, if you want to be in politics, you have to accept that it's a poisoned chalice. There's no room for sentimentality. There's no room for the moral high ground if it means the whole tower could crumble.

'Hana was killed because she dug too deep. She uncovered a slice of corruption and chose not to ignore it. Do you know why she didn't squeal her secrets as soon as she found out something was wrong?'

'Knowing Hana,' I say, 'she probably wanted to give the guilty party a chance to come clean. She always looked for the best in people.'

'That's right. Partly. But there's more to it than that. The main reason she didn't blow the whistle was because there was a conflict of interest.'

'What conflict of interest?'

'You still don't know who was at the head of the snake all those years ago, do you? The one calling the shots.' He smirks and stares at me with apparent relish. 'When was the last time you spoke to your mother, Daganae?'

I almost laugh out loud. 'My mother? What the hell does my mother have to do with all this?'

'Homura Kawasaki was once the most dangerous woman in Sonaya. It can't have been easy for Hana to find out that her lover's mother was behind all the corruption. She wanted to give her a chance, I believe. But your mother makes you look like a romantic, Daganae. She was a heartless bitch, all right. *She* was the one who ordered Hana's murder. A murder that you unwittingly carried out for her.'

I shake my head. 'I don't believe you.'

'Believe what you want, Kawasaki. I'm not going to labour myself. The truths are about to spill out once and for all, and then there will be nowhere for any of us to hide. My people and I are ready to tell Tokyo everything: the way your mother blackmailed us, forced us into illegality; that she was at the heart of the rot that destroyed Sonaya. Probably better that you hear it now, before it becomes common knowledge.'

I look down at him.

'Now then. Are you going to deal with me the same way you dealt with Bernd?' he asks, sneering.

I take a breath and think of what Maaya said. I'm no good to her locked up.

'I'll let Japan deal with you,' I say. 'I've got friends to see.'

As Goto's bleeding face breaks into another smile, I aim a fierce boot at his neat moustache. I leave him unconscious on the ground and sipping his own blood.

30

The dog is the first to raise her head when I descend the basement stairs. She sniffs the air and her ears twitch, and her little whimper alerts everyone to my presence. I drop onto the empty chair next to Jiko and wait for someone to speak, but Hildegard's whine is my only welcome.

Nakata pours a stout and Shinji drops it in front of me. I take a sip and glance at my companions. Su-young is wrapping a red-soaked bandage around Bo-min's arm. The sullen expression on Bo-min's face tells me she'll live.

'Okimoto?' I ask.

Bo-min shakes her head and everyone else averts their eyes. Maaya looks for a moment like she might cry. Grandpa. The latest of the Nishi clan to disappear from my daughter's life. I never got on with the old man, but I'd give my other ear to have him sitting at the table now. Hildegard nuzzles at my daughter's feet.

'Did you find Stones?' Shinji asks.

'He's gone. The Arkansas is sailing across the East Sea as we speak. Aimi?'

'At the hospital, with Eiko. They can't move her. Do you think … do you think they'll go after her, too? Like they did with Kosuke?'

I shake my head. 'I think Zenzo Goto and his band are out of time. By morning they'll be rounded up and rooming with Nishi in The Heights. This is gonna be some shake-up.'

'And what about you?' Ganzo asks from a barstool. 'Are you headed back to your old cell?'

The biker girls stare at me.

'I killed someone last night,' I say. 'He might have been rotten, but I killed him. The coat hangers from Tokyo can't overlook something like that. But you girls,' I nod to the Bosozoku, 'who knows? Yoo-ri Baek was part of the ring, and once she's out of hospital she'll be tossed into The Heights with the rest of them. Maybe your warrants will get ripped up.'

Bo-min returns to her drink but Jiko maintains her stare. Su-young smirks like she doesn't believe it. I'm not sure I believe it either, but this is a room in need of hope.

I down half my drink and stand and put my hand on Bo-min's shoulder. The expression that greets me is one of such complexity it almost makes me feel something. And I thought all this girl could do was glare and glower.

'I wanna thank you, Bo-min. For what you did out there. It should have been me. Maybe I was too much of a coward, as usual.'

'We didn't do it for you,' Bo-min says.

She looks at Maaya and her lips twitch in a way that looks both unnatural and disarming. Dimples appear on her cheeks; it's almost a smile. Next thing you know she'll be forming compound sentences.

'I'm glad you're not seriously hurt,' I say.

She glances at her arm. It looks serious enough, but it won't kill her. I get the feeling a battering ram wouldn't kill her.

Nakata turns the radio up. 'It's Sara Barnes,' she announces.

We all fall silent and the American's rich voice fills the basement.

'This is just the tip of the iceberg. Ryoko Nishi's confessions have lifted the lid on a box that's been nailed shut for a long time. The names she's provided will lead to more. The corruption that's

259

been rotting Sonaya for years isn't the work of a small number of people. We expect dozens, perhaps hundreds to be implicated, and investigations will be ongoing. All we can promise is that we won't quit until everyone responsible is found and punished accordingly.

'The elections have been suspended indefinitely. It remains to be seen to what extent the government in Tokyo will need to intervene with the political situation in Sonaya, but it seems unlikely that the city will be able to function independently for some time.'

'Are you suggesting that Sonaya might lose its independence from Japan?' the reporter asks.

'It's too soon to speculate,' Sara replies. 'But I will say it's a possibility. The corruption in Sonaya has seeped like a poison through the veins of the city. It's not just in the elections. It's everywhere. The Borrowings, the sex trade, taxes, even international trade. The rich have been filling their pockets at the expense of the poor, and it's time for that to end.'

At the mention of the rich, I can't help but think of Kosuke. The old man's no saint, but it looks like there's only so far one man's money can go, even in Sonaya.

'We advise citizens to remain calm and be patient at this time,' Sara continues. 'There's a long way to go, but there's no reason Sonaya can't soon be restored to her former glory.'

The interview is winding down. Nakata turns the radio off.

'So what's next?' Shinji asks to no one in particular.

Why everyone looks to me for an answer I've no idea. Jiko stands and relieves me of the weight of six pairs of eyes. 'That's obvious, isn't it? We make the Rivers ours. We take the city back for ourselves. The wine bar, Ganzo's place, all the old haunts. Tokyo's about to toss the pieces of Sonaya up in the air, and we're gonna catch them before anyone else does.'

Everyone looks at everyone else. Steely expressions and slow nods.

'I've said it before,' Jiko continues, 'and I never really meant it. But I mean it now. The Rivers are ours. Sonaya's ours. Let's take it.'

○

'Sorry to leave you at the scene of the crime,' I say to Shinji.

'Used to be you didn't know the meaning of sorry,' Shinji replies with a smile. 'Now you slip it into every sentence. Forget it. I know how to take care of myself.'

'I know.'

'Besides, someone had to get the dog.'

We both look to Hildegard. She's sitting at Shinji's feet, looking between us as if waiting for an explanation.

'She knows, doesn't she?' Shinji says.

'That Bernd's not coming back? I wouldn't be surprised. We gonna take care of her then, are we?'

Shinji peers at me. 'We?'

'To tell you the truth, Shinji, I don't know how this is all gonna turn out. I expect they'll try to lock me up again, but I'm not planning on letting them. If you want … if you wanna make our little partnership more permanent … well, you don't have to keep living on your own, you know. Think about it.'

Shinji lays a hand on my arm. I'm too taken aback to say anything. 'Dag, you find a decent place to live—one that isn't coated in dust and doesn't have cops knocking on the door every hour—then I'll think about it.'

He moves to Maaya's table and the dog trails him, glancing back at me with a look I swear is pure contempt.

'She'll be okay, you know,' Ganzo says, taking Shinji's vacated chair. 'Maaya.'

'I know. She's like her mother.' I peer into his benevolent eyes. 'We've been friends for a long time, Ganzo. You wanna tell me what happened?'

'I'm guessing you know most of it by now. Ryoko Nishi was just a kid. Her sister had died and her family were falling apart.

She had no one to talk to. So she talked to me. Told me everything.'

'That she found out Hana's death was a set-up,' I say. 'That she used that information to start a career in politics.'

'It didn't make any difference, Dag. You were locked up. I thought if you found out then you'd do something stupid as soon as you got out.'

'Maybe I would have. But it wasn't worth losing your bar over. And I went and did something stupid anyway. It was all for nothing.'

'You've always been a wild card, Dag, but you're my friend.'

'I'll make sure you get your bar back, Ganzo.'

He waves a hand. 'All you need to focus on is that one.' He flicks his eyes in Maaya's direction.

I raise my glass and he meets it with his own.

'Just promise me one thing,' I say. 'Don't ever try to protect me again.'

Ganzo's smile has barely formed when we hear the door opening. All of us stare at the stairs and the polished shoes that make their way down.

'Quite a cosy little gathering you have here,' Silver Beard announces, scanning the room.

Ganzo stands, Jiko stands, Bo-min and Su-young stand. Pretty soon we're all at it; a whole basement full of standing idiots. Hildegard growls, the only one of us to make a sound.

'My, my,' Silver Beard says. 'I am touched. But really the ovation isn't necessary. I have merely come to settle matters.'

'To settle what?' Ganzo says. As he steps forward, his chair slams to the ground behind him.

'Ms. Barnes informed me that you were close to finding the girl. And now I see you've found her,' Silver Beard says, nodding at Maaya.

Jiko steps in front of her. 'And what does that have to do with you?'

'I was the one tasked with finding her, don't forget. Goichi

Fujii may have been a sorry case of a man by the end, but at least he settled his affairs before he died.'

He steps towards the bar but Su-young and Bo-min make a wall in front of him.

'Not another step,' Bo-min growls.

Silver Beard chuckles. 'Really, what a charming bunch. Then who might I give this to?'

He holds an envelope before him. I step forward and snatch it from his grasp.

'This is what's left of Fujii's estate,' he says as I unfold the paper inside. It's a cheque, and the number at the bottom isn't small.

I automatically look to Maaya, who peers at me from behind Jiko.

'Now I can wash my hands of the matter,' Silver Beard says. 'The last of the Roses' business finished.'

'And now only the Nightshades to tidy up,' Jiko says bitterly, as I slip the cheque inside my pocket.

'It sounds like you got the better of my boys again,' Silver Beard says, turning to face her. 'Three against four, wasn't it? And still you humbled them. I believe we can draw a line under all of that now, can't we?'

Su-young and Bo-min advance slowly towards the old man. Silver Beard grins at me with his hand poised inside his jacket pocket. I know that his fingers must be millimetres from his silver gun.

'Another truce, Kawasaki? With Sonaya in this state, we don't want any more trouble, do we?'

I scan the faces of my friends. Every set of jaws is clenched.

'A truce,' Ganzo says, advancing on Silver Beard and extending a hand.

The old man is about to take it when Ganzo throws a lightning-fast right hook into his face. Silver Beard clatters backwards onto the stairs with his face bloodied.

'That's for my bar,' Ganzo says, inspecting his knuckles. No doubt he's worrying about tomorrow's sushi.

'You get blood on my stairs, you pay for them to be cleaned,' Nakata says, throwing a towel into Silver Beard's chest. He dabs at the blood on his face and blinks blearily. Dragging himself up with the aid of the banister, he takes one last look around the room. He manages a rueful smile as he trudges up the stairs.

'Until next time,' he says, his eyes still alive with a hint of their old sparkle.

'You better hope there isn't one,' Su-young says darkly as he disappears. For a moment we remain in silence, slowly returning to our seats. Then Nakata sighs audibly.

'For fuck's sake, someone lock that door.'

Kosuke's eyes are surrounded by huge purple pouches, his lips are bloodied and swollen, and his nose is stuffed with red tissue. The rest of him is tucked under hospital blankets.

'As if your handsome tax score wasn't low enough,' I say. 'I didn't know you were due for another assessment.'

It looks like it pains him to smile. 'Kiki made the same joke. You're getting predictable.'

'Where is she now?'

'Oh I sent her off to get some sleep. The doctors said I'll be fine. A couple of minor fractures, bruising, nothing a month of R&R won't fix.'

I take a seat beside the bed, and he observes me carefully.

'Is everyone all right?'

'Mostly,' I say, glancing around the room. 'But I lost the man who almost became the most hostile father-in-law in history.'

Kosuke frowns and grimaces. 'Not Okimoto?'

'Okimoto. Ryoko Nishi had Maaya shipped out to her

father. He has a plot of land out west, a cute little cabin. At least, he *did* have—I went to rescue her, but I wasn't the only one after her.'

'I didn't know that old crank was still alive.'

'Well, he's not now. What happened, Kosuke?'

'Goto's people,' he says, shaking his head. 'He wanted off the island, tried to threaten me into sneaking him away. Helicopter, yacht, whatever. I refused.'

There are tears in the old man's eyes. I don't like seeing him like this. Without the fine clothes and the jewellery and beautiful women on his arm, he looks so much older; so much more frail. He turns his head away.

'I'm sorry, Kosuke. I know you trusted him.'

'A fool,' he says eventually. 'That's all I am. A fat pony posing in the stables with the stallions. And as soon as the race begins they trample me beneath their hooves. Showing me for what I really am. A joke.'

'A rich joke,' I say.

It almost buys me a smile.

'I saw him, you know,' I say. 'Goto, down by the harbour. He told me something.'

'What did he tell you?'

There's trepidation in the old man's voice, and I can barely bring myself to answer.

'It's stupid,' I say. 'He was just bullshitting.'

'What did he say, Dag?'

I sigh. 'He said my mum was the one behind it all. The one calling the shots when the corruption started, when Hana was killed.'

I can't help but look at him, wanting him so badly to laugh the idea away. Instead I see confusion and concern creep across his features.

'Crazy, no?' I say, knowing full well how pitiful I sound.

Kosuke stares at the ceiling for a while, and when his eyes

finally return to mine there's something like resolve in his expression.

'Listen, Dag. You know very well how I felt about your mother. She was a bulldozer. One of the most incredible people I've ever known. I won't claim that I knew her inside out, but I know one thing about her for certain: she loved you. She wouldn't have done that to you.'

It's everything I want to hear, but the look on Kosuke's face brings me no comfort whatsoever.

'A man with his head on the chopping block will say anything,' he says. 'Forget it.'

I nod and chew my lips.

'Well, he'll be behind bars soon, I guess,' I say. 'And everyone in that viper's nest with him. It looks like it's over, old man. You've still got your riches, and I've got my daughter. I'd say we could have come out of it worse.'

Kosuke blinks but says nothing. For a moment we suck in the silence.

'I heard about Bernd Schulte,' he says eventually. 'Are you that desperate to get back to The Heights?'

I shrug. 'Don't worry, I'm not going back in there. Not yet. Not until everyone's paid for what they've done.'

'Dag,' he says, and there's a pleading note to his voice now. 'I beg you, put this all to bed. Let the authorities deal with the fallout. You got your daughter, now step away and leave it all alone. For your sake and for everyone you know. I don't want to see anyone else get hurt.'

I tap his hand. 'Don't worry, old man. From now on, I'm the one who chooses who gets hurt.'

I leave the room and head for the stairs. I've got one more check to make tonight. Twelve floors down from Kosuke's private room, I find Hee-chan in a ward bed with his mother by his side. Mother bear isn't too pleased to see me. Once all the expletives are over and I manage to calm her down, she lets me close enough to Hee-chan to ask him how he's doing. He's got a black eye and a split lip.

'I'm sorry, Dag. Your friends.'

'Don't worry about them. From the sounds of it, the boys who did this to you took a good beating.'

'I was stupid to believe them.'

'You're a good kid with a good heart. You did nothing wrong, Hee-chan. Okay?'

He nods sheepishly.

'That was your last pigeon job, you hear me? You were a star, but I want you to focus on your studies from now on. You listen to your mother, got it?'

His mother beams at me as I stand to leave. Before I go, Hee-chan beckons me towards him. He cups a hand around my ear and whispers, his eyes alight with mischief.

'But I'm starting to really enjoy it.'

31

Very few Sonayans will sleep tonight. It's the night I've been working towards ever since leaving Manhattan. I knew it would only take one cloud to break for the heavens to open and the old Sonaya to be washed away. Ryoko Nishi broke, and the downpour has begun.

I gather what I can from the squat—I don't expect to come back. The old dear next door is boiling kimchi stew, and the sour stench coats the walls. I'll miss it here. I shovel handfuls of clothes into a sack and head downstairs. The mechanic is watching a grainy news stream on a battered TV, and I pause in the doorway to watch it over his shoulder. I see stills of Nishi surrounded by reporters and police, followed by interviews with Japanese politicians. They're already here.

'What can you give me for the bike?' I ask.

The mechanic turns and gapes through bloodshot eyes. 'You selling her?'

'I don't need it anymore. What can you give me?'

He looks at it, blinking dumbly through his calculations. 'A hundred thousand.'

It's half what the bike is worth, but it doesn't matter. I take the wad of cash and turn to leave.

'The helmet,' he says, nodding to it. It's tied to the bag on my shoulder. 'I want the helmet with it.'

I consider it for a moment. This is the end of one chapter, a new start.

I grasp the helmet and smash it into the wall with all the might I can muster. It drops to the floor with a crash, cracked and deformed.

'Take it,' I say.

○

While half of Sonaya spirals into panic, the other turns to the bottle. The youngsters have seen it all before. The government has failed them and their city spills open like a stuffed toy with split seams. They take to the streets to drown their sorrows and bid farewell to the world they knew; a new era is upon them, and it's being ushered in by Tokyo suits.

The Cow Shed is bustling. The bouncers wave me through the front doors and watch me with lecherous smiles as I pass between them. The dancefloor is packed, and I have to push my way through to the staircase. Kenya is at his usual table overlooking the dancefloor, looking more dishevelled than ever. His nose and cheek are swollen, and an ice pack sits beside his glass.

'You finished up with Dag and his friends, then?' I ask, inwardly smirking.

'Quite a little party they were having,' he replies. 'This is your final visit, I take it?'

'I got everything I needed. Here, this should settle everything.'

I pull the mechanic's wad of notes from my jacket pocket and drop it next to his rum glass. He stares at it for a moment before reaching for the rum.

'Your employer has already settled everything,' he says. 'She's waiting for you. Here,' he grabs the money. 'Buy yourself a ticket off this island before she sinks.'

'Are you going down with her?'

He looks over the balcony at the dancers. Strobe lights illuminate the faces below in stuttering red flashes. They look unreal, like mannequins with painted expressions of ecstasy, lust, and dumb acceptance. 'Until she sits at the bottom of the ocean.'

I take the money and leave him to his drink and despair. I push open the door at the far end of the mezzanine. The room within is dimly lit, with a leather sofa that curls around a large polished oak table. Homura Kawasaki stands when she sees me.

'Ms. Barnes. It's been a long time.'

She bows to ninety degrees. It's eighty degrees lower than any bow I've seen in Sonaya. Japanese through and through. She gestures to the sofa and I sit opposite her.

'I'm drinking champagne, does that suit you?'

I nod and watch as she fills a second flute.

She looks much the same as the last time I saw her in person, two years ago on my way to Sonaya. Her long black hair is streaked with natural grey and pinned to one side with an enamel butterfly hairclip. She has an elegant beauty, with sharp features and slight wrinkles at her forehead and mouth, rectangular glasses with thick black frames.

'Congratulations, Ms. Barnes, it appears your job is complete.' She raises her glass and I meet it with mine. 'Just when I was starting to consider giving up, you came through. I'm sure I'll be eternally indebted to you. I hope you came through everything unscathed?'

I think back over the last two years. Posing as a journalist, killing a man, riding with the Nightshades. The long lonely nights in my old basement and the squat above the repair shop. The bars, drinking sake by lantern light. The neon-lit streets unrolling under the wheels of my bike. The nights I spent hiding beneath my helmet.

'Nothing I won't get over,' I answer.

'I just heard your interview. You'll be busy over the next few days, I take it?'

'There are still a lot of things to be cleared up. But once all the mopping is done, I suppose that's it.'

'And what will you do next? Do you have plans to return to America?'

I sip my champagne. It's amazing how the most expensive drinks are usually the least satisfying. I'd trade the flute in my hand for a cheap box of sake any day.

'I haven't thought that far ahead. I suppose I won't be able to stay.'

It's almost a question. Homura takes it as one.

'You're here illegally, of course, but that doesn't have to be the case now that Tokyo have stepped in. If you wish it, I'm sure a visa could be arranged.'

'I'll think about it.'

'Do that.' She sips her champagne and places the glass on the table with long, slender fingers. 'I suppose you haven't seen much of my son?'

'More than I'd expected. Less than I'd have liked.'

Homura opens her mouth to reply but then simply smiles. I take a guess at the question she might have swallowed.

'He's not a bad guy,' I say. 'He lost a good portion of his life in The Heights, that's all, and he's about twelve years behind where he should be. He still thinks of himself as a hotshot twenty-something with a reputation for ladies and the life of a lush. But the only thing he's reclaimed from his past life is a drinking problem.'

Homura smiles again.

'Don't worry,' I say. 'I haven't fallen for him. I'm not that stupid.'

'Sometimes we don't choose who we fall for. I wish *I* could have chosen.'

'I once told Dag that I'd only had one serious relationship, and that I ended it because he wasn't exciting enough for me. But that's not what happened. I was dumped. He said I was too cold, cared too much about my work.'

'I hope you didn't take that to heart.'

'I did, for a while. I was heartbroken. Then I took this job, came to Sonaya and started afresh. It changed my life. In some ways Sonaya is half a century behind the rest of the world. But I also see a lot of good. A lot of women here put their careers before men, won't let anyone stand in their way. Are they cold? Hell no. They're sculpting their lives the way they want. It's inspiring. And I'm not saying I've sworn off men. But I'm not going to change just to appease them.'

Homura scrutinises me over the rims of her glasses. 'It sounds like you know what you want.'

'I don't. Not yet. But I'm finding my way, day by day. Dag isn't the kind of man to pin your life to, I know that. He's the personification of everything I love about Sonaya: unpredictable, endearing and disappointing in equal measures. That's why I was drawn to him. But I'm in love with the city, not him.'

Homura refills our glasses. 'As his mother, it's a shame. You would have been good for him. But as a woman, as a professional, I'm pleased for you.'

I nod. For a few moments we drink in silence.

'And what about you?' I ask. 'What's next?'

Homura sinks her champagne in one gulp. Like mother, like son.

'Oh, I've only just begun,' she says.

EPILOGUE

I don't know how we ended up like this. A man with one ear, a dog with three legs, and a little girl with a flaming beacon for a heart.

I watch her for what feels like hours. She stands at the railing with her elbows pointed to the Rivers. From the strip to the Rivers to Broken Hill, it's been a hell of a slide for the little dove, but you wouldn't know it from looking at her. Hildegard sits at her feet, scanning the rooftops of Broken Hill with practiced diligence.

There's no way for me to stay in Sonaya, not with another murder to my name. But I don't see how I can leave, either. The port and harbour are being watched and the Arkansas is long gone. Maybe Kosuke could smuggle me away in an empty mutton box aboard the boat that bears my mother's name. But what about Maaya?

Eun-joo emerges from the Tiger and Crane. She's kicked out the last customers, who retreat to the Rivers or their rooftops to drink and watch the city crackle like a sizzling fire.

'First it was three hot-headed Bosozoku, now a mass-murderer and his tag-alongs,' Eun-joo says. 'My bar's become a boarding house for Sonaya's most wanted. And if you don't mind me saying, you're not making a great deal of effort to keep yourself hidden. Out in the open like this where everyone can see ...'

'One last night of fresh Sonayan air,' I say. 'Just give me that, won't you?'

Eun-joo takes a seat beside me and joins me in watching the back of Maaya's head. 'You're a big boy, Dag, and I'll leave you to make your own decisions-'

'Very generous of you.'

'But if you fuck things up for that girl-'

'I won't,' I promise. 'It's the only thing I'm damn sure of right now. And I'm sorry to laden you with more trouble, but my hiding places are starting to run dry.'

'Stay as long as you need. My life's been far too dull the past few years. I could do with a little shake-up.' She stands and places a hand on my arm. 'I'm turning in for the night. Lock up, won't you?'

I nod and watch her leave. Hildegard hobbles over and pushes her wet nose into my hand. Maaya turns and gazes at me blankly.

I join her at the lookout and we watch the sun rise slowly over Sonaya. The horizon is aflame, the thunderheads rolling in from the west touched with an ethereal glow. It's as if Sonaya itself is burning, its neon veins charged and ready blitz open the sky.

Maaya takes my hand and looks at me with eyes that are so painfully familiar. Then she does something that almost floors me. She smiles. A genuine smile of white teeth that transforms her face. She looks more like her mother than ever, and I know in that moment that something has changed.

I swallow the daggers in my throat and try to compose myself.

'This ain't gonna be an easy ride, kid. You know that, don't you?'

'We're Kawasakis,' Maaya replies. 'We don't do easy rides. We do fucking rollercoasters.'

I can't help myself. I beam at her, and she beams right back. Hildegard nuzzles between us and together we turn our eyes to the electric dawn.

THE END

TOMAS MARCANTONIO

Tomas Marcantonio is a novelist and short story writer from Brighton, England. He graduated from the University of Sussex with a degree in English Language and Film, and his fiction has appeared in numerous books and journals, both online and in print. Tomas is currently based in Busan, South Korea, where he teaches English and writes whenever he can escape the classroom. You can follow him on Twitter @TJMarcantonio.

Author photo by Seung-Jin Yeo

ACKNOWLEDGEMENTS

UNTITLED

UNTITLED

UNTITLED

UNTITLED